CW00501780

Let Me Die In My Footsteps

Published by Long Midnight Publishing, 2022

copyright © 2022 Douglas Lindsay

ISBN: 979-8801968773

www.douglaslindsay.com

Podcast: Cold September, on Apple, Spotify and Amazon

LET ME DIE IN MY FOOTSTEPS

DOUGLAS LINDSAY

LMP

1

We all make mistakes. Even me.

Weirdly, the one that led me to take a month off work and disappear to the Highlands was made during a rare, but brief, period of sobriety. I guess that's when you discover just how much of a giant, colossal fuck-up you are. Even when you're sober, you still can't go five minutes without doing something monumentally stupid.

It was October school half-term. DI Kallas had gone to Estonia with her family for ten days, leaving me as the senior detective in town. No one wants that, but that's what Police Scotland has come to. Job cuts all over the place, no one to fill anyone's boots. Thankfully I wasn't actually in charge of the whole station. If that ever happened, the place would probably end up like *Animal House.*

As it was, DI Kallas's leave coincided with me attending AA meetings, and sticking to the rules of those meetings. The day Kallas walked out of the office, saying goodbye to her sergeant with the kind of formal nod I've come to expect, I hadn't had a drink in seventeen days.

I didn't know what I was doing really. Seventeen days? Whatever. Seventeen months, seventeen years, it was never going to last. It was respite, that was all. Giving my liver a little breathing room. Letting him recover for the next onslaught of debauchery. Every day a struggle, every day one day nearer taking a running jump off the wagon.

There was an afternoon the chief stopped by the desk. Three days in. She'd barely spoken to me the previous two days, just as she barely speaks to me when Kallas is here. There'd been no need. She had her work, I had mine.

DC Ritter was out on a small insurance fraud case somewhere on Main Street, and Chief Inspector Hawkins came and stood by her desk. She held my gaze for a few moments, nodding to herself as she did so, obviously debating whether she ought to say what was on her mind. Usually, this would've meant she was formulating how she was going to lecture, censure or suspend me, but this was different. If nothing else, I hadn't done anything wrong for at least a fortnight.

'You've got much on, Tom?' she finally asked.

Tom?

'Things are pretty quiet,' I said. I looked at my monitor, considering if any of my small cases were worth mentioning, and then I realised she didn't actually want to know, and said, 'Very quiet. What's up?'

'I've got a favour to ask.'

She looked around the open-plan as she said it. The place was pretty deserted. When we moved in, downsizing as we were, we had fifteen desks for seventeen staff. Now it's fifteen desks for ten staff. These are the days.

'Sure.'

'It's a little delicate.'

I nodded in the direction of her office.

'Maybe we should…' and left it at that, and she nodded, and off we went, and that was how I found out she had a cousin in Rutherglen who ran a shop, and who was being troubled by a very small-time case of extortion and how the local feds were waiting for it to escalate before they did anything, and how she didn't have a very good relationship with the chief there, and she wondered if I wouldn't mind just going and putting a bit of pressure on the extortionist. Off my patch, a quiet, unofficial word.

I'm not really *that* kind of officer, as she knows, but I wasn't going to say no. And you know, the low-key extortion people, they are fucking awful. Maybe it's not that big a deal, but someone starts up a business, they just want to get ahead and do their thing and make a success of it and earn some money, and you get some fuckwit sticking his nose in saying, sure you're going to be a success, but only if I'm part of it, and only if I get some (most) of the profits.

I said yes. I did what she asked. I saw the guy, I had a word, I got him to back off. In reality, what I likely did, was make him transfer his business, and take out his anger on someone else. But that wasn't my problem. I did what the boss wanted. And, far as I know, it worked. That wasn't the mistake.

The mistake began with me going round to the boss's house to give her an update. It wasn't the stupidest thing on earth, since she lived in the vicinity, and she was obviously happier talking about it away from the office. And she didn't want any texts or phone calls. But when she asked me in, she was likely just being polite, so I should have said no. But I went in, compounding the error of having gone in the first place.

She was drinking wine, dinner was on. She offered me wine. I said no. We sat and chatted. She was very grateful. She had another glass of wine. She offered me food. I found myself accepting. She didn't offer the wine again at least.

There's always been a barrier between us, based on any number of things. Mostly her air of competence and authority, and my air of rebellious diffidence. Yeah, we'll call it that. *Rebellious diffidence*. But I'd done her a favour, and she was grateful, (and she was drinking wine), and we were talking, and some of the barriers got lowered.

I didn't leave after dinner.

The barriers continued to get lowered.

* * *

So, sure, I didn't have to take a month off, but you know, it was just shit around the office, and I felt bad for her, and I hadn't taken any leave in a year, and then DI Kallas came back to work, and her spider sense let her know something was up, but I didn't tell her, and I'm damned sure Chief Hawkins didn't tell her, and so here I am, in a small cottage in the Highlands, and then there's a knock at the door at eleven o'clock in the evening.

2

I can't find the switch for the outside light, so when I open up, the late night visitor is lit from the small lamp in the hallway. I wasn't really expecting it to be a hairy, mad-eyed guy with an axe, and sure enough it's not.

'Hey,' I say, managing a smile. My heart sinks at the same time.

She's thirty-five maybe, hair tied up, wearing a warm winter jacket. She's in plain clothes, but I recognise the look. She's one of my people.

'Detective Sergeant Hutton?'

I nod.

In her tone, I see confirmation of the worst case scenario.

Wait, that's an exaggeration. A zombie horde would probably have been worse that a fellow officer turning up at my door. Significantly worse. Unlikely to have knocked, to be fair.

'Look, I'm sorry to trouble you, but could I have a quick word?'

I take a moment, then step back and indicate for her to come in.

Hang on. Vampires. Don't vampires traditionally need an invitation into the house? Isn't that a thing? She could be faking the air of police authority in order to get an invite, she seduces me, and then, boom, just as we're in the throes of passion, we get the neck biting. Or, you know, she bites some other part of the body.

Maybe she's an actual vampire police officer. There's all sorts of weird shit in the Highlands, right?

She's staring at me, and I realise I'm standing in the hall, drifting off in some fantasy world. At least she doesn't snap her fingers in front of my face like the chief would've done.

'Sorry,' I say, and start to walk through to the kitchen. 'You want a cup of tea or something? There's wine,' I throw into the mix.

Yep, the wagon was abandoned after the sex. And now I'm

on holiday. What exactly would be the point of coming on holiday and not drinking? Two days ago, I was sitting on the top of a Munro, the name of which was lost on me. Indeed, was it even a Munro? But the sun was shining, the air was crisp and clear and perfect, and I drank a half bottle of Vouvray. And it was the finest Vouvray any bastard ever drank.

'Cup of tea would be nice,' she says, then, as I'm reaching for the kettle, she adds, 'Hell with it. Been a long day. Wine, if you've got it. Just a small glass.'

I smile, lift the wine from the fridge, which, of course, is an unopened bottle, because who leaves a bottle unfinished when they're on holiday, and I pour a couple of glasses and take a seat at the table.

And here we are. That happened quickly. Two minutes ago I was sitting here with a cup of tea, and I was about to head to bed. And now I've got a glass of wine, a woman opposite, she's taking her jacket off and draping it over her chair.

She lifts the glass, makes a cheers gesture, closes her eyes while she savours the first sip, and then places the glass back on the table.

'Nice,' she says.

My sip didn't taste so nice. End of the evening, a bottle already drunk, my mouth anticipating toothpaste.

'So, you just invite anyone into your house at eleven o'clock in the evening?' she asks, with a curious smile.

'I'm making some assumptions,' I say, and she raises her eyebrows. 'You're police. I'm going to say…' and I pause while I consider whether or not I might offend her, 'I'll say you're the constable from the village. And here you are, at the home of the visiting police sergeant. So… I didn't book the accommodation using my rank, and I obviously haven't broadcast my arrival, which means you must have a problem, you contacted the centre looking for help, they said they couldn't afford anyone, you said, I really could use some help here, and word somehow found its way out into the world that DS Hutton from Cambuslang was in the vicinity, because my line of command knows where I am, and now you're turning up at eleven in the evening to ask for help. And I'm guessing you meant to come earlier, but the day got away from you.'

She's taken another couple of drinks of wine while I talked, nodding the whole way through.

'You passed your detective's audition,' she says.

—

5

'Thanks.'

And I'd love just to be the guy who says, *and no, I can't help you*. But that's not who I am. At least, it's not who I am when an attractive woman pitches up at the front door, late at night.

Is she attractive?

Yep. And I'm a good judge. I have, after all, pretty much judged every woman I've ever met based on their looks, and while that might make me a bit of an asshole, it does mean I've got plenty of experience.

Her hair's tied pretty severely back, so she'll likely go up a notch or two on the attractiveness scale when she lets it down.

'Have you got a name,' I ask, 'or are you to be known on the cast of characters as Police Officer One, or something? Though that probably means you're going to get killed in the first five minutes.'

She laughs, extends her hand.

'Constable Mara,' she says. 'Elaine. Thank you for asking me in.'

Shake her hand, and then nod, enough of the jokey, might-be-flirtatious bullshit, time to get down to business.

'What's up?'

'Missing girl. Woman. Missing young woman, twenty-two, hasn't been seen in a couple of days. Lives with her mum and stepdad in the village, has a boyfriend who stays over sometimes. He's the same age, also lives with his parents. She works part-time at the Post Office, no history of running away, no history of just disappearing. I gave it a day, a day and a half, but really, it's just kind of weird. It's not like her. I need to do something.' She pauses, then says, 'You heard about the movie?'

'The movie?'

'There's a film production in town.'

'That's what it is?'

I haven't spoken to anyone since I got here, bar a nod and a thank you to the kid who was working check-out in the small supermarket. But on the far side of the village there are a few mobile caravans, a couple of large trucks, set up in a field. There was obviously something going on, but I hadn't asked, and I hadn't been out that way.

'Yeah, low budget vampire movie. Kind of trash, but you know... There's a little bit of that movie glamour around town, although if Hollywood is ten-out-of-ten movie glamour, this is about a one. Maybe one and a half, since the lead actor was in *Vigil*, so some people have heard of him.'

'How does this involve the girl?'

'Potentially, not at all. But they'd been looking for extras, she'd volunteered, and done a couple of days filming. That was last week. Might be of no significance, but it's the only thing that's really disturbing the peace of our sleepy little village at the moment.'

'The boyfriend?'

'Sandy. Nice kid. Everyone knows him. I mean, it's tough for me to judge. Just one of those kids that's been no trouble to anyone. A boyfriend's always going to be an obvious suspect, of course, but there's nothing there.'

She leaves it at that for the moment, then gets to it.

'So, look, I know you're on holiday, but if you could lend a hand for a day or two, I'd appreciate it. Maybe you can see something I'm missing.'

I take another drink of wine, even though I don't want it. Stare off to the side. There isn't really a decision to be made of course.

'So, missing girl, no suspects, some strangers in town, but nothing obvious standing out about any of them?'

'There we have it.'

'You asked Fort William for help, and…?'

'They don't want to know. Well, look, I'm not going to go biting anyone on the ass, here. Everyone's stretched, everyone's chasing their own tail.'

'And there are a thousand missing persons reports every day, and how many of them…' and we're nodding along together long before I get anywhere near the end of the sentence, and so I don't bother finishing it.

We take a drink in unison, setting the glasses back on the table with the kind of precision that wins Olympic synchronised chugging medals.

'OK, you've got me for a couple of days, then let's see where we are.'

She looks relieved, which has to be something of a first. Let's be honest, there aren't many people who are relieved to find me working a case with them. My reputation obviously hasn't preceded me quite this far.

'Thanks, Sergeant. You're sure?'

—

'I've got a month to walk in the hills. A couple of days won't make too much difference. Where've you got to so far?'

'Thank you.' Another drink. I think she's getting through the wine quickly to get out of my hair, rather than to crack on with the bottle. 'I've had a word with all the principal characters in the village, but no time for the in-depth interview.'

'And no one's leaping off the page?'

'Nope.'

'How about the film people?'

'I've spoken to the producer, and there's someone in charge of,' and she pauses to find the word, 'casting, I guess. In charge of extras, and whatever. So, I've had those conversations, but that's it for now.'

'How many people involved in the movie?'

'Twenty-seven here for the duration, a yet-to-be-determined number coming and going.'

'OK, we've got a lot of talking to do.'

She puffs out her cheeks, lets out a long breath.

'I appreciate it, Sergeant.'

'And, you know, I'm just the hired hand here,' I say. 'There'll be no rank crap from me. It's your show.'

'Thank you, but…,' and she finishes the thought with a dismissive hand, lifts the glass, drains the drink and places it back on the table.

'We can work together,' she says. 'Hopefully, we'll get to the office in the morning to the message that Miss Schäfer has arrived home from a forty-eight hour bender in the sleazy strip joints of Fort William.'

'Fort William has sleazy strip joints?'

She gets to her feet, starts pulling on her jacket. That particular line was out of my mouth before I could do anything about it.

She smiles, doesn't answer, heads for the door.

'Thanks, Sergeant, I'll see you in the morning.'

'I'll be there at eight,' I say boldly, and then she's opening the door, a small wave, and then she's gone, closing the door behind her.

And I'm standing there in the silence of a small cottage in the middle of the Highlands, and suddenly I'm investigating the disappearance of a young woman and from nowhere I get a familiar ill feeling in my gut.

Sure, most missing persons cases are cleared up in a few

hours, and when the dust has settled, no one's been hurt. But every now and again you end up with the photograph of a young woman on the news, and there are worried parents, and then there are grieving parents, and then there's a murder investigation.

Walk back into the kitchen. The half-finished glass of wine, and the unfinished bottle stare back at me.

'Fuck,' I mutter to the room, and then I lift the bottle and stick it back in the fridge and lift the glass and pour the contents into my mouth, and then I'm walking through to the bathroom and the tiredness that had been catching up with me comes flooding back.

3

I arrive at the small station at five minutes to eight. One office, a couple of doors off. A bathroom, an interview room. Maybe there's a short corridor, with a holding cell. There won't be much, whatever's back there.

Mara is at her desk, there's the comforting aroma of coffee in the air, and the station has an unexpected position of prime real estate, beside the loch, looking along the length of it, to the distant shore away to the west. Hills on all sides.

We nod, and I can't help myself turning and looking out at the view. What a spot. That's a never-get-any-work-done kind of a view.

'You're thinking, how come this place hasn't been sold off, and the station moved to a crappy little building at the back of the village facing the septic tank?'

I nod in reply. Today, and I don't suppose this happens often, the loch is an absolute flat calm. The sky is bright, the sun yet to appear from behind the hills.

'I don't have an answer,' she says. 'Just hasn't happened yet. Maybe we've just been too far off the radar.'

I turn and look at her now, and she's watching me, kind of smiling.

'I think what we need here,' I say, 'is some kind of cinnamon confection. I don't know, like a Danish, or a slice of pumpkin pie.'

She laughs, then indicates the coffee.

'I'll try to do better tomorrow. You can help yourself.'

I've already had a cup, but I may as well. There's no such thing as too much coffee in the morning.

There's a small desk against the other wall, which seems largely used for the printer and to stack paperwork, and I pour myself the coffee, then pull the chair out at the desk and sit down. Behind Mara on the wall is a large whiteboard, with two photographs of the missing woman, lists of names, some of which have ticks against them. A few lines drawn between names, a couple of printed-off pages stuck to the board, another couple of pieces of information written in neat red marker.

'OK,' I say. 'What's on the cards?'

'I see the people we have to question as being in two distinct groups. We have the townsfolk, and we have the incomers. Since I already know most, if not all, of the townsfolk, I thought I should concentrate on them. As the outsider, people can lie to you more easily. So, if it's OK, I'd like you to spend the day with the movie people.'

'And you've only spoken to two of them so far.'

'Yep.'

'The producer and the casting director.'

'Yep.'

'There's only one producer?' I ask. 'Some movie credits you see have got producers coming out their backside.'

'Just the one, far as I know. You know, she has an air about her. Perhaps there are others, but she's definitely the authority figure.'

'What's the movie called?'

'*Endless Crazy Love*.'

'*Endless Crazy Love*?'

'*Endless Crazy Love*.'

'Sounds like a terrible romcom with Jennifer Anniston and Adam Sandler.'

'Doesn't it?' she says, nodding. 'Ours is not to reason why. It's about vampires. Everybody wants vampires these days. That's what the producer said.'

'Which likely means a lot of make-up, and fake blood and the like.'

'Oh, yes,' she says. A pause, and then, 'What are you thinking?'

'At some point maybe the fake blood and real blood got mixed up. The fake slaying of a victim, became the actual slaying.'

She looks concerned, and kind of shrugs.

'Not usually around here, I have to say.'

'You never had a murder?'

'Nope. You?'

I take a drink of coffee. I have something to say about that, but decide not to bother. Let's not talk of the murders that have taken place down our way. The murders that have played out, right in front of me. The glint of light on the flashing knife, the splay of blood.

Enough.

'I'm afraid so.'

I get up from the desk, walk to the board, take a quick read through the names and the information while the coffee cup moves automatically to my lips.

'You IMDb'd any of these people?' I ask.

'All of them. Doesn't really tell us much'

'And our producer here, Petra Hunt, she's been around?'

'Nope, this is her first film.'

'Really? Isn't producer the kind of thing you get promoted into or something?'

'I'm no expert, but Petra – and by the way, she's Finnish, and her name is pronounced *Hoont*, although every single person she meets in the UK must pronounce it wrong, so she's likely used to it by now – anyway, Petra was in the City. Some generic finance gig. She was involved in finding finance for film, she knew how the system worked, she decided to give it a go herself.'

'So, just anyone can make a movie?'

'I guess. That'll be why so many of them are terrible.'

I share her smile, though I don't look at her.

A look through the names of the film people, noting the job title ascribed to each, and then I turn to the two pictures of Alice Schäfer. An ordinary looking twenty-two year-old, smiling in one photo, the other taken from her driving licence or her passport.

'You've got a bad feeling about this?' I say.

I turn away from the board, once again finding myself drawn to the window. There's someone in a rowing boat out on the loch, a distance away. Nice morning for it.

'Yep,' she says, and I feel her coming round her desk, then she's standing beside me, and we're drinking coffee, looking at the view.

'Who's in the boat?'

'Mr Ellis. He lives on the other side of the loch. Likes to row his boat across to the town when there's a flat calm.'

There's a pause, and then I say, 'Me too,' and she knows I'm referring to her having a bad feeling about the disappearance of Alice Schäfer, rather than anything to do with the guy in the boat.

'Based on anything other than instinct?'

12

'Nope. You?'

'Hmm.' She takes a drink. 'I know Alice, and she can be a little wild, but just disappearing into the ether? Definitely not like her. Seems kind of weird, that's all. Hard not to fear the worst.'

I take another long drink.

'OK, Elaine, thanks for the coffee. I expect the movie people will give me some bullshit about having a tight schedule, so I should crack on with it.'

'Thanks, Sergeant.'

She reaches behind her to the desk, then hands me a card.

'You can call if you make any progress. Either way, maybe we could reconnect at lunchtime, compare notes?'

She says it like she's not sure I'm going to agree to it, so I nod, slip the card into my pocket, and down the coffee.

'Let's do this,' I say, although to be honest, I don't really have the enthusiasm the phrase suggests.

4

You kind of imagine movie sets being hives of activity from the early morning. The set-up for the day, people spending six hours in make-up getting turned into vampires, people getting stressed and shouting at each other because of art.

I park on the road leading to the field where they have their base, get out of the car and stand in the silence of the morning. The air is cold and clear, the light is perfect. To my right, the loch stretches away, still the same flat calm.

Silence.

There's one guy sitting in a deck chair, steam rising from the mug in his hand, looking out on the view. He's wearing a large red puffer jacket. Hills on the other side of the loch, the town back to his right, and on behind that, to the stretch of road leading to the glen and the mountains topped with a fresh fall of snow.

I approach, hands in my pockets. Kind of cold, and I didn't entirely dress properly, a familiar lifestyle choice.

'Hey,' I say.

'Morning.'

'Seems pretty quiet.'

'We had a late night.'

I turn away, looking around the other caravans and trucks. No sign of any other life.

'Partying or working?'

'Ha! It was a night shoot. I mean, sure, it's dark from about five, and we were aiming to be done by, like, midnight or something, but we didn't finally wrap until almost four this morning.'

'When are you getting going again?'

'Another night shoot, so people aren't coming back until two this afternoon.'

We hold the look for a moment, and then I turn away again, taking another look around the surrounding area.

This was a good idea. Coming here on holiday. The escape.

That's how it's been anyway. Not sure getting involved in a missing persons is really the way forward to a relaxing break.

'Where are you filming?'

He indicates a large building down by the lochside, a couple of hundred yards along from the last house in the village.

'The old Loch Eribour Hotel. It never managed to reopen after the pandemic. Perfect for a film shoot. I mean, it's still in decent nick, and they just shut down with, like everything still inside. Apparently the bankruptcy proceedings were a bit of a shitshow, no one quite sure what's going on. Ms Hunt did a deal with the liquidators.'

'Ms Hunt still in bed?'

'She's having breakfast at her hotel. I just spoke to her.'

'Where's that?'

'Fort William.'

I turn and look curiously at him.

'That's an hour away.'

'Forty-five minutes. You don't really get traffic jams. Who are you? You looking for work as an extra? I mean, I think they've stopped hiring.'

I take my ID from my pocket, take a step closer, and let him have a proper look at it.

'Oh, right. Investigating the missing woman.'

'Yep. When will Ms Hunt be here?'

'A couple of hours, maybe.'

'And how many others are staying in Fort William?'

'Just Mr Bancroft, Karen and Carol.'

'The star, the director and the cinematographer?'

'That's correct.'

'Where's everyone else staying?'

'Kind of dotted around here. Air bnb's, traditional b&b's, the small hotel at the other end of town.'

'And you?'

'Me and Randall stay on site, make sure nothing happens to the stuff.'

'You're security?'

'Not exactly. I'm props, Randall's the odd-job man kind of a thing. We're all joking that by the end of filming, he's going to have done every job on the set.' He laughed. 'He was a vampire's apprentice two nights ago. Nailed it, 'n all.'

'Good to know. Randall's sleeping?'

'Yeah.'

'What's your name?'

'DeShaun.'

'DeShaun?'

'Sure.'

'What's that? Like, D-apostro –'

'D-E capital-S H-A-U-N.'

He shrugs. Guess he's had to have this conversation a few times in his life. If this is his actual name.

'That's your first or second name?'

'I've only got one name.'

I leave that there for a moment, but he owns it. Fine, he can have it. If I ever have to arrest him for abduction or murder, I can make the effort to find out what he's actually called.

I let out a long breath, turning away again. This promises a slow start to the day. Dammit. I got out of bed this morning, and fancied sweeping through the investigation like the Visigoths across a barely-armed border, before presenting Constable Mara with my findings shortly after lunch, identifying the location of the missing woman and bringing her home safe by dinnertime, and then letting Mara make me dinner and take me to bed to show her appreciation.

'What about Abigail Connolly?'

Head of casting. That's her title, though there doesn't appear to be anyone else in casting. It's probably unionised and the position has to be given that name.

This is how it goes sometimes, early on in any investigation: a succession of names without faces, with the investigating officer completely clueless as to where their focus ought to be.

'She's got a place to herself, back of the town. No view of the loch.' He smiles, then adds, 'We've all heard about that.'

'You know the woman we're looking for?'

'Me?'

'Yes, genius,' I say, acerbity appearing from nowhere in face of an interviewee's familiar curiosity at being asked a question.

'Why are you asking me?'

'I'm the police. I'm going to speak to everyone on the crew. More than likely, I'll ask everyone the same questions. That's what happens. So, do you know Alice?'

'I mean, we had a bit of a bash the evening after we filmed the big climactic scene. You know, the big vampire battle scene.

———

Lots of vampires, lots of vampire hunters, lots of virgins.' He laughs.

'You already filmed the climax?'

'Sure, but you know, it was just related to light levels and getting people on board, that kind of thing. We're not done filming.'

'You don't film the end last?'

'Not necessarily. I mean, think about it, there's no need. There are way more important factors in filming than doing it in the right order.'

'So, tell me about the bash. What night was it?'

'Friday. We'd spent a couple of days doing the thing, and there were about fifty extras involved, you know. So pretty much everyone who wanted to do it got a part. We were having a day off the next day, so we just had a bit of a thing here that night. Went on pretty late.' A pause, then he adds, 'It was fun. A bit drunken, but what the hey, right?'

'And Alice was at this thing?'

'Yeah.'

'You remember her? Out of fifty extras?'

'Well, not really.'

I give him the appropriate look.

'I mean, it was pretty mental, and me and Randall... well, we were kind of making sure nothing bad happened to any of the kit. We were like tasked by Ms Hunt, so you know, we weren't going to dick around. But after the police showed yesterday asking about her, you know, everyone was talking, and people were saying she was here, so you know...'

'Who was saying?'

'People.'

He smiles, lifts the mug to his face.

'Look, kid, I'm not about to arrest anyone for abduction here. You're not implicating anyone in anything.'

'It's not that. The people who said it to me likely just heard it from other people. It wasn't like, I mean, this woman, this Alice woman, she wasn't dancing on tables, or going round the back to get, you know, gangbanged, or anything. It wasn't that kind of thing. Just folk having a good time, and she was just someone who was here... You should speak to Ms Connolly.'

'You got any ideas of what might have happened?'

'Me?' he says again.

'Yeah, kid, you. What d'you think?'

He looks a little offended to be asked the question, then he makes a sweeping gesture with the mug, indicating the wide, wide world.

'I just don't see this as having anything to do with the movie. I understand completely why you're asking. We're the strangers in town. We're the, whatever. We're the gypsies. We're the travelling folk. Or we're the immigrants. We're the people townsfolk are suspicious of.' Jesus, he'll be comparing the film crew to Jews in Nazi Germany next. 'Something bad happens, they point their finger. But that's not us. We're just a bunch of folk doing a job. There's literally nothing untoward going on. I don't even know that I've heard about anyone shagging, it's been that boring around here. So, you know,' and he makes another sweep with the mug, 'spread your wings. Fly, you fool. Go and look out there, it's a big old world. She's probably just nipped down to Glasgow, or if something bad *has* happened, chances are it's a villager, or one of her family.' A beat, then he adds, 'It's usually the family. Don't they teach you that in detective school?'

'You haven't had the press snooping around?'

'What for?'

'Asking about the missing woman.'

'Really? I mean, the press might show up because the movies are in town, but I don't even know what the local paper in Fort William's called, and it's hard to imagine the central belt papers coming all the way up here. Those people couldn't give a stuff about the likes of us.'

'Is there PR on the movie? I didn't see a name on the list.'

'Think it's all going through Ms Hunt for the moment. We're too small to have PR at this stage. The PR'll kick in once they start trying to sell the film.'

'D'you think it's possible the whole thing, Alice's disappearance, is a set-up to try to attract attention?'

He gives me a comedic double take, like he's in some shitty sitcom.

'Really? I mean, why would anyone do that?'

'No such thing as bad publicity.'

'Sure. That was what I said to Randall last night when we were watching the new Gary Glitter and Rolf Harris variety show.'

'Nice. So, you haven't heard about that kind of thing?'

'No! I mean, really? Just no, man.'

He looks annoyed, holds my gaze for a moment, then re-positions himself on the seat, and looks back out over the loch.

'Are we done now?' he asks.

'Since no one else is awake,' I say, 'I think we're only just getting started.'

'Jesus.'

5

Being stuck on the periphery of an investigation can feel a little like going through the motions. Collecting data to hand over to someone else, not always sure you're asking the right question, because you can't be inside the head of the lead officer. Finding yourself trying to think like *they* think.

Sure, when you're the detective sergeant working with and for a detective inspector, it's really their case, but you develop the connection at least. You know what they're after. Me and DI Taylor, we nailed it early on. Me and DI Kallas, same effect, but a whole different kettle of fish. There's that thing where she's gorgeous, funny and literally the most perfect woman on earth, while I'm intriguingly attractive to women for reasons that transcend fiction, so inevitably sex and the kind of awkward, inconvenient romance that fuelled a million movies came to the party. Nevertheless, we work well together. Play to each other's strengths, cover for each other's weaknesses. That's Sun Tzu level shit right there.

Well, she covers my weaknesses.

Now, however, I find myself working with a constable I don't know. Her patch, her case, and I'm detailed to do the donkey work. Hard to get excited about it. And for all that the movie folk are the strangers in town, and who knows what kind of baggage they could have brought with them, if there is anyone behind the disappearance of Alice Schäfer, chances are it's someone close. The boyfriend, the stepfather, the weird guy who lives in the village who everyone has always regarded with a little bit of suspicion.

And so it makes sense that those are the people Mara's interviewing, and it makes sense that I'm talking to the incomers who are just here making a movie, and who will be gone in a week.

I'm standing down by the shore of the loch, tossing stones in the water, waiting for the arrival of Abigail Connolly. Head of casting. We arranged to meet here. 'Better than sitting in this lousy, so-called cottage,' she said over the phone.

Tossing stones in the water appears to be a reasonable metaphor for the state of my contribution to proceedings so far. Have exchanged a couple of texts with Mara, feeling a little embarrassed by my lack of progress. I suggested I go to Fort William, she insisted that wasn't necessary.

Ellis, the guy in the rowing boat that I saw earlier, has been slowly making his way across the loch towards me. Wouldn't have taken him all this time; he must have been fishing, or exercising, or something. Although there's a small jetty a little further along, I assume he's aiming to beach the boat, and walk into town. Errands to run, rather than an eagerness to speak to me.

I stop throwing stones as he approaches, in case I let go of a stray one and whack him on the head. That, by the way, would not be a first. I don't have the best aim, even when there's an entire loch before me.

I missed Loch Fyne once. Hit a toddler. There was a scene.

The waves on the shore are silent, the air is still, and the only sound is the gentle splash of the oars in the water. I stick my hands in my pockets and watch his approach, as he pulls the oars inside the small boat, and lets it glide to a stop on the beach. If I picked up some other vibe, I might help him pull the boat up onto the stones, but this guy doesn't want anything from me.

He steps onto the shore, then quickly pulls the boat up out of the water, dragging it up to the top of the small beach, so that the bow is dumped in the long grass. He sorts the oars out, straightening them up, and then starts to walk up the short path towards the road. Throughout his brief arrival on land, there's been nothing to indicate that he's even noticed I'm here. I'm like an unseen ghost, or a woman at a meeting of senior executives.

'Hey,' I say quietly to his back.

He doesn't immediately stop, but there's a hesitation, and then finally, when he's about ten yards away, he gives in to the moment, and turns. He doesn't speak. I get the look, with which we police are very familiar.

'Detective Sergeant Hutton,' I say, not bothering with my ID. He won't care. 'Can I have a word?'

'Detective Sergeant?'

He doesn't bother approaching. I don't answer.

'Weren't you just throwing stones in the water?'

I don't answer that either.

———

21

'Can I have a quick word about Alice Schäfer, Mr Ellis?'

His gaze is unwavering, but he's doing that thing. The staring at the police officer thing. The look that asks, *really?* And, *is that all you've got?* And, *you're so predictable.*

'I barely know the girl,' he says.

'But you know her?'

'Of course I know her. I know everyone between Inverness and Fort William, same as every other bastard.'

'You know I'm in the police, right?' I say. 'I mean, that was how we started the conversation, with me revealing that to you.'

'What does that mean?'

'It means you shouldn't talk shit.' We all have our own styles. Don't judge. 'There are over six hundred people in this town. I don't believe you know everyone. Over five thousand in Fort William, fuck knows how many in Inverness, with a bunch of towns and villages in between. You do not know them all. So, you know Alice Schäfer?'

'No, I don't.'

'You just said you did.'

'And you just observed I was talking shit, so I bow to your superior knowledge.'

He turns and walks quickly away. Doesn't look back. A longer, quicker stride than when he walked up the beach, meaning I would have to run if I was going to catch up with him.

I'm still watching him go when a woman, holding two coffee mugs, comes in to view, heading for the shore. Soon enough she's standing beside me, holding forward one of the mugs.

'Sergeant Hutton,' she says, as I take the drink.

'Ms Connolly?'

'Abigail. I felt bad about not inviting you to the house, so…' and she indicates the drink.

She's open, smiling, relaxed. Somehow I'd got a different idea of her from DeShaun.

'What's up with the house?'

'Spiders. I hate spiders. Can't get out of that place quickly enough after I wake up.'

I don't really have anything to say about spiders.

'I mean, I carry spider repellent spray everywhere, obviously, and I've covered the house, but you know, it's just one of those places. You know what I mean? You walk in, and you think, damn, this place is going to be kingdom of the spiders.' She's nodding to herself, then she repeats, 'Kingdom,' for effect.

'How many spiders have you seen?'

'None.'

'None?'

'That's not the point.' She takes a drink of coffee. 'It's the possibility of spiders. Mainly, the giant house spider. It's like walking along a dark alley at night, or whatever. It's what you don't see scares you even more than what you do.'

I take a drink. Decent coffee, ruined by, I'd say, two sugars.

'Where does your arachnophobia come from?'

'Common sense! I mean, look at them. The way their legs move. I said to the team, can you just put me in a hotel, or at least, in a modern place? So, of course, I end up in the crappiest old house, that's fifty percent nooks and fifty percent crannies.'

Can't help laughing at that, and she laughs along with me, shivering at the thought of the house as she does so.

'Anyway, I like to get out,' she says. 'And this is a much better spot than my kitchen.'

'So, it's not because you've got the missing woman tied up in the basement?'

My tone is fairly neutral, and she has to look at me to see exactly where I'm coming from. Since my face is deadpan, looking at me doesn't really help.

'Is that…? Wait, what?'

'We're not here to talk about spiders. Or your movie. There's a woman missing, and she's somewhere.' I pause, she doesn't fill the silence, so I add the unnecessary, 'And that could be the reason you don't want me at your house. Rather than spiders.'

'Oh, wow. I didn't see that coming.'

'You didn't think the police officer investigating a disappearance would ask about the person who's disappeared?'

'Since you put it like that.'

She takes a drink of coffee, looking troubled, turning her gaze across the loch.

'No, of course not,' she says, finally answering the question.

And now there's an edge to the conversation out of nowhere, which I hadn't intended. Well, fuck it, we're not on a date. Too often in the past, the audience might note, Detective

Sergeant Hutton has treated interviews with women as dates, rather than as part of a murder enquiry.

'You spoke to Constable Mara already?' I ask, and she nods. 'I know you didn't have much to report at the time. Have you thought of anything since yesterday, have you spoken to anyone about Alice? Is there anyone on the crew you specifically think I should be speaking to?'

'You want me to imply that maybe someone does have her locked in their basement?' she asks, caustically.

That's the trouble with treating interviews as crime investigations rather than casual flirtations with a side of police work. The interviewee is on edge, which is fine if they're under suspicion, but kind of gets in the way if you're looking to pick up a random piece of gossip that might lead somewhere.

'I'm just bringing logic to the party,' I say. A familiar quality of regret in my voice. There's a reason I'm on holiday for a month that transcends having been stupid enough to sleep with the chief. I need the break. I'm jaded. Not sure the last time I did a decent job. 'Yesterday a police officer turned up at your office, and it would have been out of the blue. You've had a day to think about it. People on the crew have likely been talking about it. Has anything come to mind, or has anyone said anything that might have sparked a thought?'

I take a drink of coffee, just so I can tip the mug towards her a little and nod an appreciation of the tasty beverage. A few words, a moderately kind gesture, allow a short silence, enjoy the beautiful surroundings and the perfect still of the loch, and hopefully manage to get the mood of the whole thing back on track.

'But Alice was on set a few days ago,' she says, her tone a little less defensive. 'I'd get it if she'd disappeared the night of the party, but she was reported missing, when?'

'Tuesday morning.'

'So, you know, it wasn't like she had a thing with one of the guys, or someone on Friday, and was never seen again. She was at work on Monday, right?' I nod. 'You know, a couple of us were talking about it yesterday, but nobody really knew anything. The only other person who outright remembered her was Sally in make-up. The artists are going to know everyone.'

'Sally in make-up?'

'Sure. She's at the guesthouse on the way to the glen,' and she indicates away to our right. A pause, then she adds, 'Nice view of the loch.'

'How many make-up people d'you have?'

'Three.'

'And it was Sally who did the whatever for Alice?'

'Well, you know this is small budget, right? Like, if *Twilight* was Real Madrid, we'd be Doncaster Rovers.'

'I get it.'

'So make-up is a stretch. We had four feature vampires, the ones who the team made an effort with, and everyone else, we were basically asking them to do a bit of fancy dress. Turn up on set as though you were going out on Hallowe'en, that kind of thing. Then the team went round them all just to make sure they had the right look, and to add the odd whatever.'

'And Alice wasn't one of your feature vampires?'

'Oh no. All the feature creatures are named cast members. Then we had this big set-piece, you know. Kind of a vampire orgy that turns into a bloodbath.'

'Sounds like a great movie.'

She smiles weakly.

'When you've got that many vampires, who in the audience is specifically looking at fifteenth vampire from the left, nakedly biting into the neck of a virgin? And with vampires you've got quite a lot of leeway anyway.'

'You know that Sally in make-up specifically remembers Alice?'

'Sally's terrific. She's got this, like, superpower. She remembers every job, no matter how trivial. And I don't mean she remembers everything she's done on this shoot. She can tell you the name of every actor she's ever worked with, right down to the most insignificant bit-parter on *Downton Abbey* from eight years ago. And she's only, like, twenty-five. We're pretty lucky to have her. She's doing the new Iron Man Marvel series next week. Filming in London.'

'I'll speak to Sally,' I say. 'Anyone else?'

She looks away, takes a moment. I can imagine a lot of conversations up here play out like this one. Fits and starts, interrupted by long periods looking out over the water.

'No,' she says. 'No one remembered anything particularly special from Friday night.'

'You can give me a list of all the people who signed up at the same time as Alice?'

'Sure, but I don't think that'll help. We had an open casting day a few weeks ago, just the one day, got everyone we needed. So, Alice signed up at the same time as everyone else.'

There's a quality to her voice to suggest she's not finished, but it turns out she is.

And then, just to make sure, there comes the sound of footsteps on the stones behind us, and we both turn, and there's a young man approaching.

He smiles at her, completely ignoring me.

'Abby!' he says, happily. 'Some fucking morning, right?'

She laughs. This guy is the infectious, good-humoured type.

I'm immune to that particular infection.

'Mind if I go for a swim?' he asks, and she laughs again, and indicates the loch.

'You're nuts, Randall.'

'Oh, aye!'

He's wearing a sweatshirt, jogging bottoms and flip-flops, then he stands at the edge of the loch, whips the top off, kicks away the flip-flops, whips the trousers off, he's butt naked, and then he walks quickly into the water, making the appropriate noises as he goes.

Randall is ripped, but I don't want to be here when he gets out. No one wants to see a ball-bare penis having spent any amount of time in water the temperature of this loch in November.

She's still laughing as Randall progresses quickly into the water, and then he dives forward, dunks his head, and then comes up yelping and gasping, letting it all out into the still of a Highland morning.

We watch him. He's the only show in town, after all. When he's far enough out to tread water, he turns and looks back at us.

'You coming in, Abby?'

'Maybe later,' she calls back, through another laugh.

'It's pretty fucking warm!' he shouts, then he turns and starts swimming away from shore. Front crawl, his perfectly formed butt cheeks sticking out of the water.

'Does he do that every day?' I ask.

'I've not been down here this time of the day before.'

'Thought you liked to get out?'

She looks at me. The smile that has been on her face since Randall appeared has gone. The slightly uncomfortable edge returns.

'Look around you, Sergeant,' she says. 'There are a lot of places to go that aren't my shitty little one-bedroomed.'

6

A few hundred yards away, a couple of hours later, back at the police station to catch up with Constable Mara. Sitting out front, some warmth in the sun now. This is the best weather there's been since I arrived. Would be a knockout day to be at the top of a mountain, looking out across the hills to the sea in the far distance, and back inland, down the glen, and across the sweep of the Highlands.

I take a bite from my sandwich. Constable Mara made sandwiches to share. Egg and cress. An actual homemade egg and cress sandwich. I don't think I've ever eaten such a sandwich in my life.

'Have you ever considered the paradox of *Please Mr Postman* and *Walking On Sunshine*?'

We've downloaded our respective mornings. Mara spoke to seven people, and had nothing new to add to the investigation, other than an increased sense that something untoward more than likely has happened to Alice Schäfer; while I spoke to five people, none of whom specifically remembered her, bar Sally in make-up, and even then it was more of a description of Alice's vamp outfit, and over-the-top eye make-up that required toning down.

Interestingly, Sally did note that as well as wearing about as insubstantial a piece of clothing as could still legally be called a dress, Alice had arrived not wearing a bra, poised to pop out at any moment. Despite the intended eroticism of the scene, there wasn't planned to be much nudity, aside from a couple of the principals. Alice, it seemed, wanted in on the act.

Sally had passed this information on to Carol, the cinematographer.

I'm speaking to Carol once I'm done with my egg and cress.

Mara smiles and shakes her head. The flat calm, stretching across the loch, persists.

'Not specifically,' she says.

28

'The relative position of the protagonists of both songs is the same. They're both waiting for the person they love to write to them. Neither of them knows when, or even *if* they're going to receive a letter. And yet, while the former is filled with a sense of desperation, reduced to pleading with the postman, the messenger, as though that guy's got anything to do with it, the latter is bouncing around like she's just popped a tubful of uppers, convinced her letter's arrival is imminent. What's going on with that?'

'Don't be dissing *Walking On Sunshine*,' says Mara with a laugh. 'That's my favourite song.'

'Really?'

'It's lovely. Infectious. Makes you happy just to listen to it.'

I pop the last of the sandwich. That was a damned fine sandwich, despite not containing anything that any normal person would actually want in a sandwich.

'The woman's completely delusional. She goes on and on about knowing the guy's in love with her, but where's the proof? Where's the hard evidence? There has been no letter. She has no proof that it's coming.'

'Maybe he told her on the phone.'

'Well why didn't he just tell her when he was going to visit?'

She laughs again, finishing off her sandwich at the same time.

'You can't ruin it for me,' she says.

'He's on the phone, and she says when are you coming by the way? and he says, I can't tell you, but I *have* written a letter, and that should be turning up some time in the next, I don't know, forty years or so.'

'You're worse than Alan,' she says, shaking her head. She takes a drink of Irn Bru, tipping her head back to drain the can, then lowers her arm, settles the can down on the bench in between us and looks back out across the water.

'Alan?'

Alan. You can always tell. There, with a snap of the fingers, goes any prospect of Constable Mara expressing her gratitude by inviting me round for a romantic dinner.

'My husband. He says it's code for her waiting for a visit from her dealer. Walking on sunshine is a metaphor for taking crack.'

She's shaking her head, smiling as she says it.

'Is that an actual thing?' I say. 'I mean, I've never looked it up or anything.'

'No,' she says, 'it's not an actual thing. It's a happy song, that's all. She's in love, she's happy, that's the story. Can't she just be happy?'

She finally looks at me.

'So, wait,' I say, 'I think the lassie is delusional, something we all suffer from at various points in our lives, while Alan literally thinks she's a crack addict, and I'm *worse* than him?'

She laughs again, this time getting to her feet. Fair enough, the day advances, and there's only so much time can be spent amicably chatting by a beautiful loch in the late autumn sunshine. Particularly when there's no chance of sex at the end of it.

'Good point,' she says.

'Let's be charitable,' I say, following her back into the station house, tossing the detritus of lunch into the bin, 'and imagine that *Walking on Sunshine* is the prequel to the earlier song. *Walking On Sunshine* was how it starts out, and then, when a few weeks have gone by and nothing's arrived, Katrina is left on her hands and knees, shorn of self-respect, begging like a kid to her mum for the last bag of sweets at the supermarket.'

'Yes, sergeant, that'll be it,' she says, with an amused head shake.

And then we're back, standing in front of the white board, which has been added to only with a list of names of people who've been interviewed, but with nothing of significance to the investigation. No sightings, no testimony that might point to Alice's movements or whereabouts, no clues as to why she might have disappeared.

We stand in silence for a short while, staring at the board, waiting for inspiration. Maybe Mara is waiting for me to have the inspiration. Maybe she's deferring to me because I'm the detective in the room.

'All right,' I say, to wrap it up, 'I'm afraid, bereft of inspiration, we must fall back on perspiration. Let's get to it. Meet you back here around five-thirty?'

'Yep,' she says, 'sounds good. Give me a shout if anything comes up beforehand.'

'Roger that.'

And with a nod I'm stepping back out into the sun, and notice now the first hint of a cold wind coming down the glen.

Standing in a small mobile studio unit, in between Carol the cinematographer and Danny in editing. We've been watching some rough cuts of the big vampire scene. Raw film footage. Boy, it looks shit, but what do I know? Maybe all movies look shit at this stage. Maybe rough movie footage is like any of us stepping out of bed in the morning, pre-shower, pre-shave, looking like the Borg Queen.

We're not here to judge, and the filmmakers seem happy enough with it in any case. The scene is paused on a still of Alice leaning over a young chap in a bed, fangs bared, breasts having emerged, at some stage, from the top of her dress.

'Nice shot,' says Danny, which I may have been thinking but, given the company, hadn't been going to say.

'So, you spoke to Alice about this?' I ask Carol.

'It's a little roundabout, but basically, we checked. Sally in make-up… you've spoken to Sally?' I nod. 'Sally in make-up noticed the clothing, obvs. She didn't say anything to the girl, but she brought it to me, and I took it to Karen. We all know a pair of breasts in a movie never do any harm, but Karen wasn't going to go putting someone's tits on film without asking, so she checked, and…'

She indicates the boobs.

'No one mentioned this to Constable Mara yesterday.'

'Constable Mara was here for about twenty minutes. She asked a few questions, but…' and she thinks about it, and then finally nods to herself, 'but you know what, Constable Mara and Karen and Alice here and Abigail and I, well, we all have boobs. It just didn't seem like that big of a thing. What can you tell us about the woman who's vanished? *She has tits!* I don't think so. We'll leave that crap to you men.'

'Well, that's one way of looking at it.'

Danny has gone quiet. Danny might be thinking this is above his pay grade.

'And there's another way?' asks Carol. 'It's not like men don't have this peculiar fascination with this body part that women just have to put up with.'

'We're in a little village in the Highlands,' I say. 'A film crew turns up, which must be the biggest thing in this joint in however many hundred years. Lots of locals go along with it, signing up to be in the show. You've brought your cast with you, so you're not looking for stars or even anyone to have the slightest speaking part. How is it, in the face of this, that one of these local bit-part players is to stand out from the crowd? How can she get the filmmakers to notice her? How can she get the audience watching the movie to notice her?'

Having laid it out enough that no answer's really required, I nod in the direction of the small screen.

'Oh, OK, I guess. But really, I don't know what she was expecting. That Karen would be like, wow, this woman has tits, get her a leading role in the next Avengers movie? She can play Scarlet Tit Woman.'

'Movies are one of those things that happen, they get made, everyone watches them, and most people have absolutely no idea about the process. Maybe Alice didn't know anything about it. Maybe she had no idea most of the principal crew were women. Maybe she thought that in amongst you all there might just be a man she could impress. Or a lesbian. Or maybe she was hoping one of her fellow women might just think, she's game, what else can we get her to do? Either way, it all points to her dreaming big. Wanting out of this joint.'

I'm looking at Carol, but I don't think Carol is really buying it. Not that it matters. My arguments aren't aimed at Carol. They're internal, and as I talk, I'm persuading myself. This small detail feels like the first thing I've heard today that might be of any significance.

'So, little Alice got her taste of the movies, and she's headed off out into the world,' says Carol. 'Maybe she got on a plane to Hollywood.' She pointedly, yet aimlessly, looks at her watch. 'Give it an hour or two and she'll be starting her first shift at the local diner, telling everyone who asks she's an actress. Maybe you should check flights to L-A-X.'

'Or maybe she said she wanted to leave, and someone decided to stop her,' I say, voice deadpan, to cut off the flight of fancy.

'Perhaps you're right, Sergeant,' says Carol. 'I guess that's the kind of thing that happens. But if that's what you're looking at, then it ain't going to be anyone working on the movie who wanted to stop her leaving.' A pause, and then she adds, 'Quite the opposite, in fact.'

7

Someone nearly walked into me as I was arriving at the shooting location. She slung me a filthy look, though whoever she was actually mad at, it wasn't me, then she stormed off down the road, heading back into town. I watched her for a while, decided it was possibly something worth following up if I remember, and then continued on my way here.

It's in a great spot, I'll give them that. Just up the back of the town, the scene framed to capture the loch in the distance, but no buildings in sight. Nominally the couple, currently shouting at each other, could be anywhere in the Highlands.

It's a run-through, while they get the scene set up. The light is starting to fade, and they're aiming to film at dusk. The main guy – the one who was in *Vigil* – is arguing with his love interest. This is where they get to do *acting*.

I'm a decent judge of film scripts having watched lots of films, and this one seems terrible. The argument is contrived. It's like they need the couple to have a fight (so that the woman can storm off in the night and fall into the arms of a vampire), but they failed in the basic task of coming up with a decent reason why they would argue in the first place.

I wonder if everyone involved knows it's shit. Everyone listening knows, the actors know, the writer, lurking over there in the background, a notepad beneath her arm, a pencil tapping against her teeth, knows, and there's nothing anyone can do about it. It's too late. They've all signed up, for whatever reason, and now they're stuck with it. I guess the only reason to have the writer on set would be to have her make adjustments on the hoof, but then, maybe these *are* the adjustments.

The director calls time on the scene, the two actors start wetting themselves laughing, then briefly hug in a *darling, you were amazing* kind of a way, and then they wander off set and, in unison, lift a bottle of water and take a swig, like rugby players during one of those interminable stoppages that condemn modern internationals to last three and a half hours.

These two are definitely shagging, although I don't think that's remotely insightful of me. They ain't hiding it.

'You've got me for five minutes,' says Karen, the director, approaching quickly. Even as she speaks, she turns away, casts her eye around the scene and shouts, though it's not entirely clear to whom, 'Where's Danny? We need Danny!' and someone says, 'He'll be here in five,' which is perfect, because Danny should be arriving just as the movie director has given the investigation all the time she has to spare. Nice she thinks she makes that decision.

'They say it's going to snow,' she says. 'Can you believe it? I mean, I just can't…'

'Everyone likes snow,' I say.

'Do they?'

'Your movie's going to look great.'

'Which would be terrific if we were filming linearly, Sergeant,' she says, and I start to nod, but then she doesn't know that I already know they've filmed the end of the film, and so she has to explain herself. Or maybe she just wants to movie-splain to the outsider. Kill some of that five minutes she's allotted to me. 'As it is, if this damn snow comes to anything, we're going to have a snowy twenty minutes in the middle of the film, and then… *poof*…'

'Didn't you look at the weather forecast?'

She's been looking around the set, ignoring me best she could, given that we were actually talking to each other, and now she turns sharply, and I get a wonderful look of disdain.

'Have you ever looked at a weather forecast for this godforsaken island? They're lucky if they're accurate right now, looking out a damned window. So yes, we've been looking at weather forecasts for the past month. There's been no mention of snow until last night, when suddenly, out of nowhere, chances of snow, twenty percent. And now, every damned time we check, the chances go up. They're now saying it's snowing tonight. One hundred percent. I mean, I just can't…'

Again with *I just can't*. There's something teenage about the line, and it sounds incongruous from a forty-year-old woman.

'How long have you got?' I ask.

'What d'you mean?'

'Before it snows?'

A moment, while she rolls her eyes and blesses the question

34

with contempt, then says, 'Three hours maybe.'

I'm about to glibly say, you'd better crack on then, but since I haven't actually started interviewing her yet, I manage to keep that particular comment in my pocket. Same with an aside about having to shoot the rest of the movie indoors.

'Tell me about Alice,' I say.

She shakes her head, now back to looking around the set, it being something else to distract her mind.

'You know I'm the director of the movie, right?'

'Yep.'

'So think of it as the COO of a company. On a day when a company has a hundred people working for it, you think the COO knows every one of those hundred people? You know how much work's involved in something like this? And you might think this is some low budget piece of crap, but that just increases the workload tenfold. I'm taking care of *everything.*'

'You have an assistant director, presumably,' I say, and I get another sharp glance. 'An AD.'

'Look at you. Sure, I do. Jeremy.' She tosses a hand vaguely behind her. 'Jeremy's over there. Jeremy got out of diapers last month. He's not due to get a driving licence until 2035. I wouldn't put Jeremy in charge of the coffee.'

'That's too bad, because if you don't start honestly answering the questions, I'm going to have to ask you to accompany me to the station, and Jeremy will need to direct this scene.'

'The fuck?'

'Yeah, the fuck. Tell me about Alice.'

She takes a deep breath, clenches her teeth.

'Fine. Alice. The girl with the tits.'

Ha! *The girl with the tits.* The Vermeer that got away…

'Look at that,' I say, with a certain lightness of touch, 'you do remember her.'

'We talked for about thirty seconds before the shoot. I barely remember it.'

'It was less than a week ago, so maybe you could try.'

An exasperated sigh, another head shake. I finally snap, and that lightness of touch, so evident ten seconds ago, is gone in a finger click.

'Jesus, will you cut it out? Accept it, please. A woman has gone missing. We need to speak to her family, her friends, her work. You people, all of you, are the strangers in town. She worked with you, however briefly, and consequently you need to answer some questions. That's just the way it is. No one's accusing you of anything, so there's no need for evasion or misdirection or any other movie-type bullshit. The quicker you answer the questions, the quicker I'm out your ha –'

'Carol came to speak to me about the girl. Said she got the feeling she was looking to attract attention to herself. I saw the girl's outfit, and I was like, *you think*? So I spoke to her.

'I said, you're looking a little indiscreet there, honey, aren't you, and she said some line about it being the movies, and there was no point in hiding anything. She's a nice looking girl. She's got great tits. I never had tits like that. I said, we'll certainly do what we can to get your tits in the movie. And I also said there was the possibility of another vampire movie next spring, and that we could talk about that.'

'And have you talked about it?'

'When was I going to have done that?'

'At the party on Friday evening, at the weekend, all sorts of times. It was Tuesday morning before anyone noticed she'd gone.'

'Whatever. No, I haven't. I must admit I left it rather vague, leaving it up to her to come and find me. If she's that bothered, she'll make the effort. It's not like I'll *need* her for the vampire movie. *Quick, get me the girl who's happy to get her tits out on screen! Which one? There are thousands of them.* And that movie might not even happen anyway, so that's where that one lies. So I said to her we'd talk at some point, without being specific, she seemed excited in the way young women are when the movies hove into view, I guess I saw her on set that day, although it was really up to Carol to make sure we got a good look at the tits everyone's talking about, and that's where the story ends.'

'When you spoke to her, did she have anyone with her? Like, she came on set with a friend, or –'

'There didn't seem to be. Whoever she spends her time with in this hick hellhole, they didn't seem to be on hand. Like, on the set.'

Hick hellhole. Well, that's London talking. I've been here five days, and I never want to leave.

'OK. Anything else come to mind.'

'Nope.'

'You didn't see her at the party?'

'I wasn't at the party.'

'How much detail did you give her about the movie in the spring?'

'There was no detail.'

'So, you said there was the possibility of a movie, and she just said, oh, sure, more vampires, that's cool, I'll get my people to e-mail your people.'

'Funny.' She says it, she sort of looks at me properly for the first time since we started talking, then she says, 'Yeah, you are kind of funny. Well, like I said, there wasn't much to say.'

'She didn't ask where the filming would be?'

'I told her London.'

'Well, look at that. And a more precise date than just spring?'

'I said late spring. April, maybe into May.'

'Anything else, now that you've, you know, started remembering things?'

'Really, that was all I had.'

'What's the movie called?'

'*This* movie?'

'The next movie.'

'*The Vampire Dairies*.'

'Is that a joke?'

'Yes, that's the point of the movie. It's a spoof vampire movie. But one of the best ways to sell those things is to have plenty of tits. So assuming our young heroine hasn't run away to Thailand or hasn't got herself killed or something, then there will be a place for her tits. She's got great tits. Did I say that already?'

'You did. So you told her the title of the movie?'

'Yes.'

'Anything else?'

'I think you've heard it all.'

'If one looks online, is there any info on the movie?'

'It has an IMDb page, but there's virtually no information there.'

'I'll take a look.'

'On you go.'

She looks at her watch, she looks up at the sky, she takes in the air. I find myself following her, and she's right to scowl. There's snow coming. You can smell it.

'Can I get on?'

'That woman storming off set, just as I arrived, who was that?'

'I don't know. What woman?'

She distractedly looks around the set.

'I don't know, that's why I'm asking.'

'I didn't see anyone storm off, I wasn't aware of any arguments.' A pause, and then, 'We're a happy bunch.'

She fake smiles.

It's a small place, I'll likely bump into the woman again.

'I say again, Sergeant, can I get on?'

'Sure,' I say, then I leave it a moment and add, 'You should have said.'

She turns to give me a quick slap of a word, then realises I'm joking, gives me a rueful smile at least, and then walks away and immediately starts clapping her hands and shouting.

I watch her for a moment, then look around the set, wondering if there's anyone else I can speak to, when my phone pings, and it turns out I'm leaving anyway, regardless of who else is in the vicinity.

8

Back at the station. Evening has come, the air has further chilled, the cloud is low, and the coming snow is inevitable.

There's me and there's Constable Mara and there's Sandy, Alice's boyfriend. Turns out Sandy has not been completely honest. We're all shocked that someone would lie to the police.

There's no interview room, so we're sitting in the station office. Mara at her desk, Sandy sitting on the other side, and me standing intimidatingly to the side.

Intimidation is relative. Lecter would not be intimidated. Lecter would be contemplating what wine to drink with my balls. Sandy, however, is kind of bricking it. Here's a lad who, a couple of days ago, did not think the police would be involved in his life. Comes at you fast, as they say. Of course, if he's got anything to do with his girlfriend's disappearance, then he's only got himself to blame.

'It wasn't a fight. Not really.'

'What was it, then?' says Mara. 'How would you categorise a conversation where one person shouts *There's no fucking way* and *You're not doing it* and,' Mara pauses to look at her notes, but really I think it's for effect, then continues, '*The fuck do you think you are, Alice? Scarlett Jo-fucking-hansson*?'

'I didn't… that just didn't…'

That's all he's got, and the defence rests. Not a lot else he can say, really.

'What was it you didn't want Alice to do?'

'It was nothing. We just talked, that was all.'

'It was related to the film?'

A pause, and then the nod.

Apart from an initial glance, he hasn't looked at me. Neither is he looking at Mara. Head down, staring at the desk. The old *if I don't look them in the eye they won't be able to tell I'm lying* trick. Never really works.

'You didn't sign up to be an extra?'

Head shake.

'Why not? Most other people were doing it. Seemed like a bit of harmless fun.'

'It's stupid,' he says. 'It's a stupid film. You can just tell. That director always makes low budget garbage. It's one thing… it's one thing wanting to be in a movie, but this isn't *JoJo Rabbit* or *Manchester-By-The-Sea*. This is *Space Vampires Go Jesus* or something. It's stupid. Why anyone would want to do it…'

'What difference did it make to you that Alice wanted to? Why did it affect you?'

A pause, the pause that comes before the lie, then he says, 'I didn't care. She could do what she wants.'

'I suppose this argument came after she'd done her acting stint. So, what was it you weren't happy about her doing?'

'Nothing.'

'The Scarlett Johansson line points to it being movie-related. Did they want her to play some bigger role?'

'No.'

I've been waiting for him to incriminate himself as much as possible, because I know exactly what they'll have been arguing about, but it's not really happening. And now Mara looks for my input.

'Did you see Alice the day she went filming?' I ask.

He gives me a side-eye, accompanied by a guilty head shake.

'Did you see Alice the day she went filming?'

'No!'

'I don't believe you.'

He looks hurt at the police officer seeing through his lies, but he's sticking to it.

'What d'you want me to say? I didn't see her. I wasn't interested in the stupid movie.'

'So you weren't there when Alice got herself made up for filming? You weren't there when she removed her bra, and you weren't there when she put on that slender strip of material passing as a dress? You weren't there for her to tell you that she hoped someone on set would notice, and might think, well she's game.'

This time the lie does not trip so easily from his lips. His head dips lower, eyes focussed a little further down the back of the desk.

'Sandy,' I say, and here we have a familiar line delivered by the police officer on such occasions, 'if you have something to hide, we will find it. We always find it. And if you don't have anything to hide, lying and prevaricating and hedging and bullshitting just serves to make you look guilty, even if you're not. So just tell us the truth, the quicker we can all get on. If you don't have anything to do with Alice's vanishing, then the –'

'I don't!'

'Well quit jerking us around then, kid, tell us the truth, and allow us to go and focus on what might have happened to her. Because the longer you sit there with your lying head stuck up your ass, the more time we'll spend focussing on you.'

Lying head stuck up your ass. I'm such a prick sometimes.

'Fine,' he says, the word grudgingly given up. 'Fine, whatever. Yes, I saw her.'

'And?'

'And what?'

'What did you think of the outfit?' He stares straight ahead. I give him a moment, and when he doesn't respond, I ratchet up the tone. 'What did you think of Alice basically heading off out into the great beyond to show the world her tits?'

'She didn't fucking…,' and then he snarls, and bites his tongue, cutting off the turn of his head so that he never actually catches my eye.

'Yes, she did,' I say slowly. 'The state of her attire was noted on the set, the director asked if it was OK to feature her breasts in the movie. Alice was game.' I pause again, but this guy isn't saying anything. 'Alice went there hoping to be noticed, and she got what she wanted. Furthermore, the director mentioned the possibility of another movie part in the spring. I may not be the world's finest detective, but I think we can all work out that when you made your Scarlett Johansson crack, when you said you're not doing it, given that it was after she'd already bared her chest for this film, you were talking about her next film.'

'That's…,' he begins, but once again he has nothing to say.

'Jesus, Sandy,' I snap, 'it's fine to be annoyed. Your girlfriend had just stripped off for a worldwide audience, everyone in town was going to get to see what you thought was for your eyes only, you're hardly incriminating yourself to admit you were pissed off about it.'

'Fine! I was pissed off about it.'

'There we go. And you were pissed off about the next movie?'

41

'Yes! Jesus.'

Mara gives me a look, then turns back to Sandy.

'Tell me about the next movie.'

Head shake, bitterness and anger squirming all over his face.

'That hack director was making some shitty vampire comedy. It'll be shit. She said Alice could be in it, filming in London in April. Big whoop.'

I think Alice might have made that movie opportunity sound a lot more definite than it actually was.

'And you argued about it?'

He grits his teeth, forces a, 'Yes,' through them.

'This argument started in the pub?' Nothing. 'I mean, really, Sandy, you can't have an argument in public, then pretend it didn't happen.'

'We started talking in the pub. We weren't arguing. We argued on the way home.'

'I think you underestimate how much you were projecting.'

'I'm underestimating how much people were sticking their fucking noses in.'

'You didn't go into Alice's house?'

'No. Didn't get anywhere near it. When we came to the split there, by the old church, she said I should just go home, or go back to the pub, or whatever.' A pause, then he looks angrily at me. 'What difference does it make? She made it home, didn't she? She was seen after I was with her?'

I don't answer. He knows that she went home and spoke to her mum, before retreating to her bedroom. By Tuesday morning, she was gone.

'What was the last thing you said to each other?'

He stares at the floor. Teeth clenching, jaw working, then finally he says, 'I said something stupid, I don't know, some line about her tits not being nice enough to make it in the movies. I mean, it was a stupid line. Stupid... then she said, 'Oh, just fuck off, Sandy,' and that was it.' A pause, then he adds, 'Haven't seen her since.'

He looks away, shoulders go into full slump, the awfulness of it hits him, his anger and exasperation at the police for expecting him not to lie finally vanish. Mara and I share a look, then we turn back to the kid.

'I just... fuck, I hope she's all right, that's all. Like she's just done something stupid like get on a train to London or something.'

'She wasn't on the first bus out of town, and no one's said they gave her a lift to Fort William or Inverness.'

'She could've walked to the end of the road, thumbed a lift out of this joint with someone just passing through. Young woman, gorgeous, some geezer's going to have stopped. Just have to hope he wasn't a cunt.'

Head back down. And that's pretty much that for young Sandy.

9

In an unexpected turn of events I was invited back to the
constable's house for dinner. I say unexpected, because I
initially refused, having no desire to meet this Alan character,
then she said we'd be able to discuss the case, because the guy
works in Edinburgh all week. Comes home on a Friday evening,
heads back down on a Monday morning.

Dinner alone with an attractive woman, husband out of
town? Don't mind if I do.

'It's not that unlikely a shout,' she says. 'If Alice had
wanted to leave without telling anyone, it might be the best way
to do it. There's plenty of traffic at the road end, and Sandy's not
wrong. Someone who looks like her is always going to get
picked up.'

We're eating stir fry. A packet of diced chicken, a packet of
Chinese stir fry vegetables, a packet of noodles, and she tossed it
all in with some oil, soy sauce, lemon juice and peanut butter.
Tasty as fuck, cooked in under ten minutes. Eating with
chopsticks. And there's wine. And she's stuck on Count Basie.
That'll do, Donkey.

'But why leave without telling anyone?' I ask. 'She's not
fourteen. She doesn't need to run away from home. Can't she
just say, I'm leaving by the way, I'll Snapface or whatever?'

'Snapface?'

She smiles.

'I heard someone use that joke once, and I took it for
myself.'

'Well, good for you. And to answer the question, you
should probably meet Alice's mum.'

'One of those force of nature mums?'

'Oh, yes. It would definitely have been easier for Alice to
let her mum know she was moving to London on a whim *from
London*, rather than over the kitchen table.'

'Nevertheless, it doesn't explain why she would suddenly
do it now. Whatever it was she said to Sandy about this new

movie, she made it sound far more definite than Karen Wright made it sound when she was talking to me. So, either there was some wishful thinking from Alice…'

'Or wilful blindness.'

'Yep. Or she knew fine it was entirely speculative, but she was using it to let Sandy know she was leaving this joint. But why now? For a movie that, even if it does happen, won't be for another five months.'

'Maybe the idea's in her head. She's had the argument with Sandy, she's made her stand, and she just thought, strike while the iron's hot.'

'Or perhaps someone else involved in the movie had some other thing Alice could get involved in, and said, this is happening next week. Come on down.'

'Hmm,' says Mara, 'not bad. Did you establish if anyone had left the crew this weekend?'

Put like that, it seems an obvious question to have asked. Of course, I didn't. This is one of the things that separates me from the great detectives.

There are others.

'Well, I didn't ask them yesterday either,' she says. 'We can find out tomorrow. To be honest, I don't think Alice is already in London, spending her savings on overpriced accommodation. It's not out of the question she'd do it, but I'm pretty certain she would've called home by now. Or texted, at least.'

'I'd like to speak with a couple of people from the family,' I say. 'That OK?'

'Of course.'

'Don't want to step on –'

'Don't be daft. Joint op, you should talk to anyone you think appropriate.'

'OK, good. So, Alice spent Monday at work. In the evening she ate… where? She went out with Sandy?'

'She ate at home with mum and stepdad, just the three of them, then she went out with Sandy for a drink.'

'What's the stepdad's name?'

'Alec.'

'But not Alec Schäfer?'

'No, it is. Both Alice and her mum took his name.'

'Unusual.'

'If I can quote Alice's mother, her father is a cunt. She took pleasure in the annoyance it caused him.'

'The father's not still in the picture?'

'He lives in Alicante with a twenty-year-old stripper called Tiffany.'

'Of course he does. So, Alice and Sandy are having a drink.'

'They drink, they argue, they leave, they split up on the road, she gets home, she speaks to her mum, then she goes to bed.'

'What time was that?' I ask.

'Not long after ten. Let's say she goes to her room, rather than goes to bed.'

'Then when her mum goes into her room the following morning to tell her she's going to be late for work, boom... No Alice?'

'That's where we are.'

'When Alice got home, did her mum recognise she'd been fighting?'

'Says she didn't pick up on it, and nobody's told her. Doesn't sound like they said much to each other that evening. Just a quick *hi, I'm in*, type of a chat.'

'What about the stepdad?'

'He was watching football. Didn't see her at all. He has his own room downstairs that he watches sport in. Likes his peace and quiet.'

'He has a football watching room?'

'Football, rugby, cricket, snooker. Pretty much anything. It's a man cave.'

'Does he get any of his caveman pals round to watch sport with?'

She sucks up a noodle through closed lips. Shit, that's pretty sexy.

Dammit, I'm trying not to think about that. I'm in love with DI Kallas, remember, and even though she'll never be mine, I can still be faithful to that feeling. Even if I was recently unfaithful with Chief Hawkins. And also that woman I met in the off-licence. She was buying Kahlúa, and I said, what will you do with that, and she smiled and told me, and then the next time I saw her in the off-licence we stopped and chatted, and then the next time we had a coffee and then at some point soon enough we had sex, but then I think she got the impression from somewhere that I might be a little damaged – I have no idea what was the giveaway – and then the last time I saw her in the off-licence we just smiled as we passed, and there was a look of pity on her face.

Some things escalate quickly, and fade away just as fast.

So who would Constable Mara get played by in a movie? If this was to be turned into a movie, and we can hope it doesn't get that interesting. What we need is for Alice to text her mum from London, or for Alice to walk back in through the front door, and then we can all go back to doing what we were doing this time last night, which wouldn't make for much of a movie.

I'm going to say Naomi Watts. I mean, facially she's not really Naomi Watts, but there's something about her. Naomi would be a good fit.

'You still with me Sergeant?'

And we're back.

'Sorry,' I say.

'You drift off, don't you?'

'Yeah, it happens. Sorry, where were we?'

She smiles, shakes her head.

'I think we're done with work for the evening. I'd appreciate you talking to Alice's mum and dad tomorrow, if that's OK.'

'Of course.'

'Thanks.'

She holds the look across the table, then smiles again, shrugs, and takes another bite of food, which ends with another silently slurped noodle.

I feel my noodle-eating a much more vulgar affair.

'We can do small talk now,' she says, a little self-consciously.

'Why not?'

I look at my food, take a drink of wine. I can probably be out of here in ten minutes. It makes sense to eat and run.

'You married?'

I can't help laughing at the question, even though it's not, like, innately funny or anything.

'The answer's a little involved, and might transcend small talk, but happy to go there,' I say.

'Ooh,' says Mara, 'this sounds fun.'

'Well, I guess I've only been married three times, so in the grand scheme of everything, that's not too bad, right? And the last one was over ten years ago.'

'When you think of your ex-wives, do you think of their names, or do you give them numbers?'

I also laugh at that.

'Number one was a disaster. No kids, no romance, just a mistake with a capital M. Number two... number two is Peggy, fifteen years, two kids, and I blew it. Just like I blew it when we almost got back together a few years later. I would happily still speak to Peggy, but Peggy isn't speaking to me. Not anymore. And number three lasted a month. Not my finest month.'

'Ouch.'

'Yeah.'

'So that's you done with marriage?'

'Met someone I could've married, but she was married to someone else, and then she got murdered, so there was that.'

'Oh.'

'Yeah.'

'Did the husband murder her?'

'No, he was just a prick, he wasn't murdering anyone. We caught the killer, he's in prison. Not sure how much longer for. The husband caught me at her graveside a few months later, drinking wine and talking to her. That was unfortunate. We argued. Ultimately, I never went back to her grave.'

'There's a story,' she says, and she's looking at me with the kind of pity the woman in the off-licence once gave me.

'And there's been someone else, but she's also married and not going anywhere, so we'll just leave that one there.'

I take a mouthful of food, inelegantly slurp a noodle, take a drink of wine.

'Tell me about Alan.'

'Not much to tell. We're both from the village. Met in primary school. Everyone knew we were going to get married from about the age of five, albeit we both left, and came back again before it happened.'

I've got some glib question to hand about Alan, but Alan's not some guy she loved and left, Alan's not a story. He's her husband, very possibly her best friend, and this time tomorrow evening she'll likely be telling him all about me, so I shouldn't go looking for any intimacy of conversation here.

'What does he do in Edinburgh?'

'Works on the First Minister's staff.'

I'll keep my mouth shut about that. Not that I have anything against the First Minister in particular. It's all politicians. They

---

48

can all fuck off all the way to Fuckville.

'Doesn't he get summoned to work at weekends?'

'They're kind of sympathetic to him living up here, but it happens occasionally.'

'How long does it take?'

''Bout three hours.'

Look at that. Small talk, right enough. Still, if I find myself asking which route he takes, I'm going to have to shoot myself in the face.

Another large heap of noodles on the chopsticks, suck 'em up, and there aren't too many more mouthfuls to go.

'You in a rush?' she asks with a smile.

A look across the table that I can't really read. You'd think I'd be able to read women by now, what with me being this Lothario character that women can't help but be drawn to, but no, not a bit of it.

'I should leave you to your evening,' I say.

'Oh.' She pauses, but then decides not to say anything, and shrugs. Lifts her glass.

'You're right,' she says after a while. 'Sorry, I just dragged you away from your holiday into this investigation, and now I drag you in for dinner to talk some more about the investigation.'

'It's OK,' I say.

Look, call me a shallow, twat-faced fuck-muppet, but all I really want to do is get her in to bed. And if I stay here too long, and have a second and a third and a fourth glass of wine, I'll end up making some stupid move, or saying something stupid, and then tomorrow morning we'll be working together and it'll be awkward, all because I was a fucking moron.

'You ever work at any other station?' I ask, to get over this small hump of discomfiture.

'I was in Oban for a while. A couple of years. Then this came up, and I thought, well, why not? It's such a great spot by the loch, and with the glen just up by.'

'Oban's not such a bad spot itself,' I say, and she kind of shrugs in reply, and then she lifts her glass and drains it, then lays it down and lifts the bottle, first of all hovering it by my glass.

'Top-up?'

Fuck me. I need to get out of here. I want wine. Lots of wine. And if that happens...

I push my seat back.

'Sorry, Elaine, I should… You know, I'm pretty tired. Been up early most mornings, done a lot of walking in the hills the last few days. I should get an early night.'

I look at the food, the amount that I'm leaving, and at my unfinished wine glass, and then I finally manage to look her in the eye.

'Sorry,' I say. 'I'll get out your hair. Thanks for dinner.'

She makes a *you're welcome* gesture, but seems too amused or bemused by my quick exit to actually say anything, and then I'm turning away, and heading out the kitchen. Down the short hallway, front door, and out into the chill night air.

Close the front door behind me, and then stand for a moment looking up at the sky. Deep breath, the air cold and harsh on my throat.

Low cloud, the streetlights picking up the first hint of snow.

Fuck me.

'Right then, Sergeant, home with you. There's vodka to be drunk, on your own, out of harm's way.'

And off I go, quickly through the night, romantic disaster narrowly avoided.

* * *

Several vodkas later, collapse into bed. Masturbate to take the edge off the evening's frustration. Too much information? Too much information.

Fall asleep looking at my phone. Thankfully remember to set an alarm. The alarm jolts me awake at six-thirty, and I go through the familiar routine of waking myself up by scrolling through all the shitty news of the world. War is coming, of that there can no longer be any doubt.

The room is freezing, and when I finally drag myself out of bed and look outside at the day, the land is covered in snow, and the little bit of the road I can see has several inches on it, and no car tracks. I'll be walking into the village today. That old car of mine wasn't designed for winter.

I bumble into the shower, clean my teeth, drink a long, cold glass of water, get dressed, then walk through to the kitchen. Seven-thirty, the morning still dark out there, though there might be the first vestige of daylight far to the east, if I could see it from here. I can't.

Light on in the kitchen. On the table there's a chicken, dead but unplucked, skewered to the surface with a long, thin knife through its head.

There's no note. The dead chicken is the note.

I stand there staring at it for a moment, and then check around the kitchen and the rest of the bungalow to see if there's any other evidence of the late night break-in. The house is clear, there's no sign of either the front or back door being forced. They are, at least, both locked, though no bolts thrown on the inside. It's hardly a locked room mystery. Someone either had a key, or they expertly, and easily picked the lock.

I go back through to the kitchen. Make a coffee, pour a glass of orange juice, tip some granola into a bowl. Stare at the chicken for a moment, then think, bugger it, and sit down and eat my breakfast at the table anyway.

That's it. That's my act of defiance. That's my way of saying to the clown who thought me worthy of a dead chicken warning, fuck off, you clichéd fuckweasel, I laugh in the face of your dead chicken. In fact, I do this, I sit and eat a bowl of granola in the face of your dead chicken. Your dead chicken means nothing to me. Fuck your dead chicken.

Over breakfast I have a conversation with the dead chicken, in lieu of the absence of the perpetrators of this Scooby Doo level of bullshit.

The chicken doesn't have much to say for itself.

10

'Wait. You ate breakfast with the chicken?'

I nod. Standing with Mara, mugs of tea in hand, looking down at the chicken.

Daylight is upon the land, the snow has stopped for now, but there will be more to come. The cloud is low, but the snow is giving a cold brightness to the day.

'That seems strange,' she says.

'I'm not really spending much time in the sitting room,' I say. 'The carpet's too fussy.'

The carpet is a brown and orange swirl from the nineteen seventies. No one wants to spend any time in that room.

'Of course,' she says.

She gives an imaginary documentary camera a look, then takes her first drink of tea.

I asked her to come round, rather than report the dead chicken on my arrival at the station, just so she can see the exact set-up.

'So,' I say, 'what's with the dead chicken?'

'How d'you mean?'

'Is this a common practice around here?'

'Warning people off with a dead chicken?'

'Yeah.'

'I don't think so.'

'Never had anything like this reported before?'

She looks curiously at me, then shakes her head.

'Really, Sergeant?'

'Stupid though it looks, this is a pretty serious escalation. It's hard to imagine the dead chicken is here because I'm a tourist. It must be related to Alice's disappearance. Of itself, a dead chicken, it doesn't really say much. But if there's a wider thing, some sort of, I don't know …'

'Cult?'

She smiles as she says it.

'Sure, cult.'

'No. I mean, I've lived here most of my life, been at the station for eight years, I've never heard of a cult.'

I take some tea, stare across the table at her. She smiles again.

'Are you wondering if you walked into the middle of the *Wicker Man*?' she asks.

'Maybe.'

'Chances are I'd be in the cult.'

'You would.'

'Then why would I have asked for help investigating Alice's disappearance?'

She's laughing. Some officers would have a pole up their arse about this by now.

'Then we really would be into *Wicker Man* territory.'

'I don't have you pegged as an innocent virgin, Sergeant.'

'Well, there's that.'

We share a smile. That particular conversation really could have been conducted on an entirely different, and edgier, level, but I guess that's not who she is.

'Either way,' I say, 'this is an escalation. This is someone saying, Alice has gone, and it's none of your business. So back off. Which is odd, because I'm a police officer, and obviously I'm not going to back off, so why bother?'

'They're incompetent, or they're a fantasist. Or there's a specific message they wanted to leave.'

'Which is? I mean, if it's not *bugger off back to Glasgow*.'

She takes another sip of tea, giving herself time. She looks at the chicken. At some point over breakfast I started calling the chicken Arnold. Seemed about right. I decide not to mention Arnold.

'You want me to take prints?' she asks, and she indicates the small black briefcase she brought in with her.

'Sure,' I say. 'I can't believe they'll have been that stupid, but we can give it a go. Just, you know, the knife and the door handles. Let's not overdo it.'

'OK, cool.'

And she lifts the briefcase up onto the table, opens it up and gets to work.

I watch her for a moment, and then turn away and stand at the window. From here the view looks away from the town. The loch is down to the right, though I have to stretch from here to see it. Ahead, a couple of other houses, and snow stretching away to the hills, not too far in the distance. The top of the hills shrouded in grey cloud.

'Winter wonderland,' I say quietly, and the tune comes into my head.

'Sorry?'

'Nothing.'

Behind me she goes about her business, and I start thinking about how the rest of the day will go, and that no matter how stupid this damned chicken business is on the surface, this missing persons case just got ramped up one hell of a big notch.

11

'Don't fucking touch that.'

Standing in a workshop at the bottom of Alec Schäfer's garden. I'm looking at a large, standing globe, the map of the world dating from the sixteenth century. Trade routes, and sea monster sightings depicted. The monsters add a frivolous touch to what is a beautiful piece of handmade engineering.

'How much d'you sell this for?'

I'm asking the conversational question in the face of his unhappiness at having to talk to me. Alec Schäfer thinks, or wants us to think, that his stepdaughter has fled to London, and is not happy that his wife called the police *at all*, never mind showed me back here to speak to him this morning.

The snow has started to fall again, and there was no sign of movement at the film site. This will, fair enough, be a disaster for them. Presumably they're all huddled in small rooms working out how they can use the snow to their advantage. Or, at least, complete filming without the entire enterprise being torpedoed.

Hmm, maybe Constable Mara's husband will be unable to return from Edinburgh for the weekend. That'll be a shame for him. Poor Alan, stranded in Edinburgh, while his wife is trapped in a small town, forced to work with the George Clooney of Police Scotland.

Yeah, George Clooney. Bite me.

'Four thousand, seven hundred and fifty.'

I don't turn to look at him, but the words, 'Seems a lot,' cross my lips before I can stop them.

'It's a bespoke, handmade fucking globe,' he snaps at my back.

I've never thought about globes. You see them in shops sometimes, but they're usually twenty-nine-ninety-nine with a bulb inside. An actual handmade globe seems almost Victorian. And standing here, looking at this one, and the two others that are in the works, I now want one. Four and a half grand? I can afford that. The smaller ones are probably a bit cheaper, but I quite fancy this big-assed thing here. Perhaps without the monsters.

It would be totally out of place in my small apartment, but who cares?

I imagine telling DI Kallas about it, and her coming over to look at it, and us sitting there in one of our usual silences, staring at the globe, drinking tea. And then Kallas would say something like, 'It is beautiful, I should go now,' and she'd get up, and I'd wrestle with standing close to her as she put on her coat, and I'd want to gently run my hand through her hair, and to watch her close her eyes and enjoy the moment, and she'd be right there, that beautiful face right beside me, those lovely pale lips and I'd want to –

'Are you actually going to ask any fucking questions, or are you just going to stand there all morning like an unused urinal?'

Snapped back to the present, I turn away from the globe. He's still in the same spot, but he's stopped working, and he's standing straight, tapping the top of the smaller globe he's currently creating, staring at me. Many a person has good-naturedly commented upon my tendency to daydream in such circumstances, but there's nothing good-natured about this guy. But then, his daughter's missing. And he seems like a bit of a cunt. So there's that.

Did he just compare me to an unused urinal?

'I take it there's been no word from Alice?' I begin.

'Sure,' he says, with disdain. 'She came back last night. She's in the kitchen eating bacon and eggs. She was in Oban seeing her aunt. Turns out we'd known all along, we'd just forgot.'

'Are you finished?'

He doesn't answer.

'I take it there's been no word from Alice?'

'No.'

'Can you tell me the last time you saw her?'

'Didn't I speak to the police already?' He stares at the ceiling, while he pretends to think. 'Aye, aye, you know I think I did. Sure of it, in fact.' He stares at me, then the fake whimsy leaves his voice and he growls, 'And like I told wee Elaine, naw, I didn't see Alice when she came in on Monday evening.'

'I didn't ask that. I asked the last time you *did* see her.'

'I feel like I told Elaine that n' all.'

—

56

Not from around here, Mr Schäfer. Doesn't have the attractive, lilting, Highland accent.

'Now I'd like you to tell me.'

'Fuck's sake.'

'When was the last time you saw Alice?'

'Monday morning. I was having breakfast when she walked through the kitchen.'

'Did you speak to each other?'

He holds my gaze for a moment, then he says, 'No,' with an aggression that suggests he thinks I'm about to lecture him on speaking to his daughter.

'Not even good morning?'

'We nodded at each other. She was in a hurry. Always late.'

'Had she spoken to you about being an extra for the movie?'

'No.'

'There was a movie filming in town, you live with your daughter, she was in the movie, and you hadn't spoken to her about it?'

'Thank you for explaining the set-up here,' he says, ''cause without that I'd've been totally lost, but weird though it must sound to you, officer, no, I didn't ask about that stupid movie.'

'Did you see her before she went off to do the filming?'

He says, 'No,' but there's enough of a gap there for me to know he's lying. He knows exactly how she went out to the filming, and the thought of it flashed through his head before he answered.

'Nice lie, chum,' I say, just to stir the pot, and I can see him grit his teeth. At the tone, the disbelief, the use of the word chum. Gets right under his skin. 'I've seen the footage of Alice that's on film. Quite the exhibitionist.'

'Oh, fuck off.'

'How does that make you feel?'

'It makes me feel like telling you to fuck off.'

'Did you see her before she went out to do the filming?'

'Aye! Fine! Fine, I saw her before she went out to do the filming.'

'Did you say anything?'

He swallows, he stares at the ground. It's apparent sharp words were said. Now, just because the guy argued with his daughter, doesn't mean he's automatically a suspect. And, of course, he could also have a view that what gets said at the kitchen table, stays at the kitchen table.

'If you're hiding something, I'll find out. I always find out.' *Again with the bullshit*. 'If you don't want to talk about it because it's none of my business, then you need to let that go. I'm investigating your stepdaughter's disappearance, and it's not up to you to decide what's relevant. You have no idea what else I know, what other information I'll be able to marry it up with.'

'I called her a disgusting slut,' he says, cutting me off.

Oh.

'Last thing I says to her on Friday morning. Saw each other briefly over the weekend, and again on Monday, never said a word. Now she's gone. So, sure, you want me to talk about that, fine. I called my daughter a disgusting slut, and she walked out on me.'

'What else was said?'

'I just told you she walked out.'

'So it was just disgusting slut?'

'That was the first and last thing I said to her.'

We stare across the short distance of the workshop, the globe he's working on in between us. Well, there we go. That there, if true, is a magnificent example of bad parenting. I've had a few such examples myself in my time. In fact, the only reason my relations with my daughter haven't deteriorated to the level that this guy's had, is because Rebecca and I haven't lived in the same house for about fifteen years.

'You were in the kitchen before she went off to the film set, or she came in here?'

'She came in here.' A pause, and then the regretful, 'She wanted to show me her vampire look.'

'And you lost your shit?'

'That's about the size of it.'

'Anything else?'

'Anything else what?'

'To tell me about Alice.'

He stares harshly, doesn't answer. What this guy isn't telling me about Alice could fill a library.

'What else do you do?' I ask, turning the line of questioning on a sixpence.

He pauses to readjust, thinks about it, then says, 'What does that mean?'

'What do you do in this small town other than work?'

'Huh. I don't do anything.'

'You don't go to the pub, you don't go running, you don't go out with a bunch of fifty year-old guys in a bike-pack on a Sunday morning?' Taking up all the road, and irritating the fuck out of everyone else.

'Jesus.'

He shakes his head, staring at the floor.

'Don't like pubs,' he says after a few moments. 'Haven't taken any exercise since I was fifteen.'

'What do you do?'

'I do this. This is it. I've been doing this since I had the brilliant idea I could run my own business twenty-three year ago.'

'You make enough to pay the mortgage?'

'Aye. And I'll be able to retire when I'm a hundred and six.'

'You've no friends in the village?'

He stares me down after that question. The regulation gap before he reveals something he'd rather not say, but which he's likely calculating I'll find out anyway.

'I'm in the lodge.'

Fuck me.

'The Masons?'

Another moment, then he shakes his head.

'Not exactly.'

Jesus. Something that might not exactly be the Masons has the potential to be even worse than the Masons.

'What does that mean?'

The few heavy breaths, the internal debate about whether or not to share. If it's at all Masonic related, there's a chance that what he tells me will be out there in the public domain and available for me to discover by some other means.

'There's been a lodge in the village since the early seventeenth century. At some point there was a schism…'

'A schism?'

Can't keep the smile out of my voice as I say it. Schism is such a grand word for petty or obscure disagreement.

'Yes,' he says, ignoring my tone. 'This lodge became independent of the Grand Lodge in Edinburgh. I don't know the details, but it happened, there was never a realignment. We are our own lodge, answerable to no one.'

'God, presumably,' I can't help myself saying, and he grimaces. 'So, what's your place in it?'

'What d'you mean?'

'Are you the grandmaster, the, I don't know, whatever else there is. The club secretary, the –'

'The club secretary? Fuck's sake.'

'How many people are in the lodge?'

'I don't know. I'm just a member, I don't hold any office.'

'How often does it meet?'

'I don't go often. You'll have to ask one of the others. I barely know anything about it.'

'Who's the grandmaster?'

He holds my gaze while he wrestles with whether or not to tell me. He's going to, though, so I just give him the silence and wait.

'Tom Ellis. He lives on the far side of the loch.'

'The guy in the rowing boat?'

The stare, the internal questions about how he's allowed himself to get involved in this discussion, and then he nods and says, 'Aye.'

'It's not a secret, though?' I ask.

'What?'

'The men in the village who're in the lodge. It's not a secret.'

'Of course not. We do... we do all sorts. Charity things, and dinners and whatnot.'

So, Constable Mara will likely have known already. And there was me wondering if there might be a cult in town, and her saying there wasn't. Presumably she thought it inconsequential. Just as this guy wants me to think it. Maybe, pedantically, she wouldn't call the lodge a cult.

'You got a name? I mean, if you're not officially Masons?'

'We're not *not officially* Masons. We're not Masons. We're the Lodge of St Augustine.'

'Ah,' I say, 'I dreamed I saw him once.'

His face goes blank.

'You ever threaten anyone with chickens?' I ask, and his brow furrows.

12

No one's ever asked me to join one of these organisations that are the cornerstone of middle class life in Britain. The Masons, the Rotary, the Inner Wheel, the Lions of Judah, the Holy Trumpets of Jerusalem, the Eternals, the Guardians of the Galaxy. I don't know what any of these people do. Maybe it just makes them feel important, makes them belong, though I guess that's how little Jimmy gets his start in banking, and Bungalow Bill gets the loan he needs to start his home delivery business. Connections. Who you know.

And I don't know anyone. Which is weird, given I'm in the police. There must be thousands of my lot in the Masons, and none of them ever thought to invite me. Can't think why.

Not that I've ever cared, of course. The effect of such organisations on any investigation, however, is at best frustrating, at worst, completely undermining. It makes people protective of each other. They have each other's backs. People that would otherwise have no connection, are happy to cover for their fellows. Even if they don't know any detail, they're more likely to have positive bias in favour of someone. And from the perspective of the investigating officer, you never truly know who's involved, you never truly know the inner workings of the organisation, and the interactions that take place there.

There are so many unknowns in any investigation to begin with, and the presence of the Masons paints a cloak of grey over the whole thing. We all know it, and it makes me curious about Constable Mara. She should've mentioned it, because regardless of whether or not they have anything to do with the disappearance – and I'm really not the type to think, shit, poundshop Masons, they'll be guilty of *something* – it nevertheless impacts the investigation in some way. It always does.

Having spoken to the globemaker, now I'm in with the globemaker's wife. The force of nature that is Alice's mother. I know she doesn't work, but thought I'd find her about her business. Brutally washing up, or making me conduct the interview while she vacuums. But no, credit to Alice's mum, she's sitting at the kitchen table with a glass of wine, smoking a fag.

Well, her daughter's vanished, I suppose we can forgive her alcohol and cigarettes at ten minutes after eleven in the morning. Still, she has a smoker's teeth and a drinker's complexion, so I think we know she was drinking wine with second breakfast, and very possibly first breakfast, long before Alice left.

'So, did you see Alice before she went off to shoot the movie last week?' I ask, and she coughs loudly, the classic cough of her people, vile and throaty and loud. Befitting the ex-smoker that I am, I find it repulsive. Not being an ex-drinker, being a current and ardent drinker jumping on and off wagons, I manage to pick up the scent of the wine through the acridity of the cigarette smoke. That may sound unlikely, but I'm a professional.

'We live in the same house,' she says, by way of an answer.

'So she showed you her vampire outfit?'

'Yes.'

'What did you think?'

She takes a long draw at the smoke, elbows on the table, taps some ash into the saucer by her left elbow.

'You've seen it?' she asks.

'I've seen the footage they've shot of her.'

'And?'

'And what?'

She gives me a look to indicate that I ought to know exactly what she's meaning, and I stare dumbly back so she spells it out for me.

'Did my girl get those great wee tits of hers out for the camera?'

I pause, but then I realise I'm pausing as a way to de-emphasise the description of the tits, as though a quick agreement might imply *yes, she does have great wee tits, right?* and so I just get on with it and say, 'She did. The director spoke to her first, establishing it'd be OK.'

'Anyone else?'

'Did she speak to anyone else?'

'Did anyone else get their tits out?'

'A couple of the named actresses, I believe, but no one else from the village.'

Lifts her glass, takes a silent drink, lays the glass back down. I wonder if she drinks straight from the minute she wakes up. Have been there myself, more than once. Not a happy place.

'Just my Alice, eh?'

'Just your Alice.'

'What a girl.'

'Was it consistent with who she is?'

She smiles, takes another puff at the fag, another drink from the glass.

'Nice way to put it, Sergeant Hutton,' she says, then she looks away to her side, out of the kitchen window. From here, the view down over the loch, the snowy hills on the other side.

'Snowing again,' she says.

I don't turn to look.

'Was it consistent with who she is?'

Another puff, and this time she stubs the cigarette out with slow, deliberate movements, finally pressing it down with her fingers, extinguishing all the smoke.

'She's been restless for a while,' she says eventually. Her tone has changed a little, taking on a more melancholic air. 'She was forward, certainly, she screwed most of the guys in school. Started when she was, what, thirteen maybe. Hadn't really stopped. And, like I say, she was restless, had been looking to get out.' Another lift of the glass, she engages me with a look across the table again. 'She saw an opportunity, and jumped in.' Another pause, and then the unnecessary, 'Tits first. That's my girl.'

'Does it sound like Alice to just leave without a word?'

She chews whatever remnants of cigarette smoke and wine there are in her mouth, lips going through exaggerated contortions as she does so. There's a face. I look away briefly. She wasn't wrong. That's the snow back on.

'She was scared of me,' she says.

She swallows.

She spoke forcefully, as though it's a thought she's arrived at over the last couple of days, and this is her way of getting it out there. Saying it out loud, seeing how it sounds.

'That's the first time you've ever said that to anyone.'

She holds my gaze, and nods. Glances down at the cigarette packet, doesn't reach for it yet.

'Why was she scared?'

'I was harsh. I've always been harsh. She's got her stepdad,

63

who's just… He's so wrapped up in the business, he's hardly ever here. Even though he works from home, he's hardly ever *home*. Been the same since we got married. He's barely been a father to her. So, whenever he shows his face, he has to be good dad, good parent, to compensate. And when one of the parents unilaterally takes on the role of good cop, the other parent only has one option left open to them. And here we are. I was always the one who got into arguments. I was always the one putting my foot down. I always had to be the bastard.' Another pause, then she adds, 'And that hadn't changed so much.'

All that doesn't entirely tie in with the dad calling her a slut. No one expects consistency from witnesses.

'So, you think she might leave and not say?'

She purses her lips and nods.

'When she made a point of showing you how she was going on to the movie set, she was being defiant? She was looking for you to react?'

'Poking the bear,' she says, nodding.

Having come to some sort of understanding of who she is as a parent, I can sense the change in her. She's more accommodating to the police officer's questions. More forgiving of the fact that I need to ask what I need to ask.

'You think she's just run away?'

Glass to the lips. Steady gaze. No answer. Eventually, 'Possibly.'

'If she was happy to poke the bear, why not do it again? Would you have stood in her way if she'd told you she was leaving?'

'She's twenty-two, she can do what she likes. Means nothing to me now. She's an adult.'

'So, what d'you think?'

'You know, I don't think anything. I'm worried, of course, but when I try to think, I start to panic. So, I'm blocking it out.' She lifts the glass. 'Hopefully we'll find out soon enough, one way or the other. What do you think?'

'Much too early to say.'

'You must've done this kind of thing before, this kind of case.'

I nod.

'So, what's the script? How would it usually play itself out?'

'There is no usually. And even if ninety-five percent of

cases like this ended with the girl dead or the girl walking in the front door, it doesn't mean that this time it wouldn't be the reverse.'

'I wasn't looking for percentages, Sergeant. I was looking for gut instinct. You lot work off of that, don't you? Fuck, we all do. We all have first impressions and gut instinct about everything. So, what are your guts telling you?'

'My guts are silent. I really don't know enough.' She, quite rightly, is regarding me with some degree of scepticism. I plough on regardless. 'If I worked here on a daily basis, I might have a better idea. But I work in the city, a totally different environment. This feels unfamiliar.' A beat, and then I add, unnecessarily, 'This feels like walking onto one of those Nordic crime dramas on BBC4.'

I indicate the snow outside.

'Except everyone speaks English,' she says, drily.

She knows what I think. She knows that I think her daughter is dead. Her daughter has likely been dead since, at the latest, the early hours of Tuesday morning. I shall, nevertheless, keep my own counsel on that.

'You have a good relationship with Sandy?'

'He's just a kid.' She looks unhappy about discussing Sandy, but I'm not sure that has anything to do with her daughter being missing. 'Young. Too young. It would take a particular type to date someone like Alice, and Sandy's not it.'

'Someone like Alice?'

'She's been around the village, as I said. Every time she and Sandy go into the pub, chances are he's one of about ten people in there who've slept with her. Some men could handle that, but like I say, that's a particular type.'

'What made her settle for Sandy?'

'I have no idea. Maybe he's huge.'

She says that deadpan, and then a dirty smile flashes across her face and is gone.

'Any of her previous lovers still harbour desires? Or a grudge? Or anyone left out who's always thought, how come she slept with everyone else and not me?'

She's shaking her head by the end of it.

'I don't know. I don't worry about it being Sandy, but I don't know about anyone else either.'

The brightness outside attracts me for a moment, and I turn. The light snow has turned heavy, the view of the loch becoming more obscured as we look.

'Doesn't look like the Constable's husband will be getting back from Edinburgh,' says Penny Schäfer out of nowhere.

13

Back at the ranch for lunch, after a plod through the snow. Not sure what this snow would've done to my holiday, had I still been on holiday. It looks great, but lousy for unprepared mountain climbing. I'm not really equipped for snow. I also don't have the walker's instinctive nose for direction. I've got *walking around in circles in low cloud* written all over me.

Mara is not here yet, and so I'm sitting at the smaller of the two desks, looking at my phone. Reading up on the Lodge of St Augustine. Turns out there isn't an awful lot about the Lodge of St Augustine, and what there is, is rather old. There's a history of it, some detail on grandmasters and members, but that all dates from the eighteenth and nineteenth centuries. Whoever wrote that history, did not have access to any information dated later than about 1870.

The man who led the original schism was called Donald MacDonald. There are listed a successions of MacDonalds as being grandmaster through the years. MacDonald, of course, is hardly a unique name around here. And, obviously with Ellis being the current grandmaster, it's no longer the case. Either way, there's no detail from the post-1870 period, so who knows how long the MacDonald reign survived.

I get distracted in the search by the huge amount of St Augustine lodges there are within the official Masons. St Augustine appears to have been a popular saint at some point. Probably after Dylan released *John Wesley Harding*. All these lodges were likely previously named after other more boring saints that Dylan never wrote about, like St Trinian and St Johnstone.

More recently, this lot here in the village are occasionally name-checked with a bit of fundraising, and there's an annual dinner, but that's about it. No details on who they are. No names, no photographs. I wonder why Alec Schäfer felt compelled to tell me anything about it at all.

Mara returns just as I'm at the leaning forward on my

---

elbows, rubbing my hands across my face stage of the afternoon. Seems early.

'Long day?' she says, smiling.

She removes her coat, shakes her head by the door to get the snow from her hair, hangs the coat up, kicks her boots off, and slips her feet into a pair of indoor shoes she has waiting by the coat rack.

'How d'you get on?' she asks.

She's got a bright air about her, like she's enjoyed her morning talking to the movie people, as we switched round the angles of the investigation.

'You never told me about the Lodge of St Augustine,' I say, cutting straight to it. Can't be doing with artifice and talking around the periphery of a subject.

She looks taken aback – my tone was probably a little more accusatory than it ought to have been – then she nods an acceptance of the question, and walks to the kettle.

'Tea? Coffee?'

'Tea, thanks.'

She fills the kettle, sets it down, gets it going, puts teabags in two mugs, then turns.

'You know, I thought, if I say there's this bunch of men – and they're all men – who hang out in a quasi-secret society that used to be part of the Masons, well... either, you're going to be in the Masons, because you're an officer in Glasgow, and the way I hear it, you're virtually all in the Masons, or else you might just immediately think, it'll be them, let's round them all up and waterboard them.'

'I'm not in the Masons.'

'I guess I didn't want to prejudice your thoughts about it. Left it there for you to discover for yourself, and then it could take its natural place in the investigation. But if I read your tone right, you're a bit pissed off, and so... sorry, I should've said straight up.'

I don't immediately accept the apology. Still thinking it through and whether or not that's a solid explanation.

'Not helping, huh?' she says.

'Not sure,' I say. 'You should have said.'

'OK, like I say, I'm sorry about that. But please, don't spend the afternoon looking at me like I'm part of the gang. It's strictly men only.'

'Is Alan part of the gang?'

'No, he's not. That's not who he is.'

The kettle rumbles quickly towards a climax.

'How many members in the village?'

'I'm not sure. It's a private thing, they've no need to declare anything to anyone. I know a few, but it might be twenty, might be fifty, might be a hundred. Only five hundred and seventy-three people in the village at last counting, so hard to imagine that it's too many.'

The kettle clicks off. She holds my gaze for a moment, and then turns and pours the water, continuing to make the tea as she talks.

'I can give you a few names, but unless you've learned anything that particularly points to the involvement of the St Augustine people in Alice's disappearance, I'm not sure... I think I'd rather we just left them out of it. I mean, what are you going to say? I'd like to interview you in relation to the vanishing of Alice Schäfer because you spend your Tuesday evenings at the hall talking about the Holy Grail, or whatever it is they do.'

The hall. I touch the side of my head, a small gesture to indicate my stupidity. I'd seen that hall in the village, and there was nothing to indicate whose it was or why it was there, and I presumed it was the village hall, even though it would be odd that it wasn't marked as such.

'The hall,' I say, explaining my moment of apparent revelation. 'I hadn't put two and two together. I don't suppose we can get in there without causing a stink?'

She smiles, head shaking as she turns and passes me the mug of tea.

'I mean, if you want to get a warrant, though I'm not sure what reason you're giving.'

'You ever been in?'

'The hall? Nope. Not sure that anyone has, other than members.'

'Perfect place to hide a kidnapped girl.'

She looks curious about that as she digs around in her small backpack, and then she pulls out a couple of packets of sandwiches and says, 'Tuna mayo or BLT?'

'Oh, you sure?'

'Course.'

'BLT, please.'

She smiles, tosses it across the office, then sits at her desk.

—

'You're right,' she says, 'it's a perfect place to hide a kidnapped girl. But is it any more perfect than any building? Anyone's house? We have no reason to suspect anyone here's kidnapped her. That's going to be a tough warrant to get.'

'Yeah, you're right.'

A word of apology comes into my head for my accusatory tone, but I decide not to bother. She should have told me, that's all.

'Many MacDonalds in the village?'

There's a slight furrowing of her brow, unsure why I asked, then she takes the time to think about it, and makes a small head movement as she calculates.

'Probably about fifty. Maybe more.' She smiles. 'Why?'

'Doesn't matter.'

'It's my maiden name, in case you're going to hold that against me.'

I smile, shake my head.

'We're cool,' I say.

'If you're sure. I mean, my middle name's Janet if that's going to impact the investigation.'

'OK, OK...'

Take a bite of sandwich, look out the window at the snow falling on the loch.

'Does the loch ever freeze?' I ask, deciding on a sudden small talk intervention.

'Not really. It used to when I was a kid. A little, and I mean, like around the edges in the middle of January, if we got some freezing nights, but more and more often there's nothing anymore. That's the way it goes.'

Eat sandwich, take a drink of tea, look out over the snowy, wintry wilderness, lament the passing of the seasons, the great homogenisation that's taking place, where all the seasons will eventually blend into one single twelve-month-long, mild, grey day in September.

'Not a lot about them online,' I say. 'The lodge.'

'Oh, no. Pretty much everything they do is the same as it was in seventeen fifty-six, or whenever it was formed. They don't like change.'

'No website, no Twitter, no Instagram. Not even Facebook. I thought every organisation had Facebook.'

I look at her with a small shrug.

'Did you try Pornhub?' she says with a smile.

I kind of laugh, but then I don't know if she's joking.

'Wait, what? I mean I know they're not going to have Pornhub, but is there a basis for the joke?'

'No. Well, not with this lot. I just meant, you know, secret societies and orgies and the like. That's the joke, isn't it? Like the flashback scene in *Da Vinci Code*, when Audrey Tatou remembers blundering across an orgy.'

'Yeah.'

'Hey, Audrey is gorgeous in that movie, right?' and she lets out a low whistle.

Now, if there's anything in the world to distract me from cohesive thought, it's a woman expressing interest in another woman's attractiveness.

'Yeah,' I say, because she's not wrong.

Another low whistle, then she looks away, out across the snowy wastes, as she thinks about Audrey Tatou.

Can't help laughing – as much at myself – and then I shake my head to get the conversation back on the right track.

'What?'

'Doesn't matter. I feel we need to focus. Tell me about Ellis.'

'You've spoken to Ellis?'

'I asked him a couple of questions yesterday, as he passed by, but he was evasive. He's the grandmaster of the lodge?'

'Wow, someone was unusually talkative. Who told you *that*?'

'Alec. Doesn't everyone know?'

'I guess anyone who cares, knows. Just didn't think anyone would voluntarily give up the information. Anyway, he wasn't wrong. Ellis is the boss.'

'So, tell me about Ellis.'

She makes a gesture, out over the loch, to the far side. Today, or right at this moment at any rate, the far side of the loch is swallowed by snow and mist and cloud.

'Lives over there in his isolated house. He came up from London about five years ago. Worked in marketing. Don't really know too much about what he did down there, but I guess he was loaded. Possibly burned out. Came here to escape. Bought that place, for a while there was a tonne of work getting done on it, and then that finished. Not sure many people have been over there.' A moment, then she adds, 'Nice spot, though.'

'Can you drive to it?'

'Nope. He keeps his cars parked over here. Range Rover for this kind of weather, an Aston for the rest of the time. There's a path round the loch, but it's like an hour and a bit.'

'So he rows that boat over when he wants to get the shopping in, or attend to St Augustine business?'

'He has a small motorboat. In fact, it's not so small. He comes over in that sometimes, ties it up at the jetty at the far end of town. He's across the loch in under ten minutes. I guess he rows to keep himself fit. His motorboat's there today. He must be in town. Not sure what he does when he's here. Anyway, not a day to be rowing.'

I get up out of my seat and look out at the loch. There really isn't too much to see of it, and I have to picture it as it was yesterday. The stretch of water, the isolated house on the far shore.

'Is he in to all that *Good Life* type of thing?'

'What does that mean?'

'Does he keep chickens and pigs and grow veg and do whatever?'

'My understanding is he has a large freezer. Stocks up once a month.'

'How does he come to be head of the lodge even though he's only been here a few years?'

'Not sure. I presume it's money, though it could be force of personality, or it could be that he was in the actual Masons, and he brought a lot of knowledge and a lot of connections with him.'

There's no sign of life out there. A stretch of loch, disappearing into the snow. To the right, white nothingness. To the left, the edge of town. No cars on the road, no fresh tracks in the snow, no one walking. Everyone shut in for the moment, keeping out of the cold.

'I'll need to speak to him.'

She doesn't answer. She probably has a *good luck with that* kind of comment to make, but there's no point in making it.

'I'll get his number,' she says instead.

'Is there a police boat?'

She doesn't answer. Eventually I turn.

'You mean, so you can rock up at his house?'

'Yes.'

'There's no police boat.'

'What would you do if there was an incident over there?'

'What kind of incident?'

She seems amused by the direction of the conversation. Here I am with my city values and my city way of thinking. I answer with a look.

'There are a couple of boats tied up at the jetty, as you'll have noticed. I guess I would have to commandeer one of them.'

I let out a long breath through puffed cheeks. Hands in pockets, staring out at what's to be seen of the Highlands in winter.

'I'll call him,' I say after a while, though I'm really speaking to myself. 'See where that gets us.'

She doesn't answer. Behind me I hear her settle her mug back on the desk. Outside the nothingness continues.

Fuck it, there's a sandwich to be eaten. I can give the next five minutes some direction at least.

'What are the movie people doing today, by the way?' I ask, returning to the desk, taking a drink of tea.

'They're storyboarding.'

'Yeah?'

'Reassessing the narrative. That's the phrase the director used. Considering how they can use the snow. There did not seem to be a lot of optimism.'

I try to think if there's anything else I need to ask about the movie people, but nothing comes to mind. We hold the look for a short while, and then, as though something has actually happened outside to attract our attention, we both turn and look out of the window. The snow, stretching into the far distance, stares back at us.

14

I left Mara at the office, trawling through Alice's social media posts. There are a lot of them. She's had a quick look already, but is now taking the time for the more forensic examination. Of course, one is going to assume that the most recent entries will be the most relevant, but you never know what you'll find. The way of the world now, with so many secrets happily placed in the public domain; so much knowledge, so many events, lost in the great cacophony of noise that is the Internet.

Nevertheless, from what she said before I left, Alice seemed like a product of our time. Selfies and outrage and cocktails and virtue signalling.

I've walked into town, the short walk that it is. Jacket zipped up, wool hat borrowed from Mara, hands in pockets. Stop for a moment as I pass the St Augustine Lodge hall. Looks like any old-time village or church hall. Single storey, wooden double door painted red, high windows on cither side with small stained glass panels.

There are footsteps leading up to the door, though not obviously any lights on inside. Those windows are not the type to let in much light, or to allow anyone to look in from outside. The footsteps are almost covered by the snow, so whoever is inside has been there for a while, and unless there's a rear exit, has not yet departed.

I'm on my way to speak to a man named Bill who lost a chicken. I mean, that's where we are in this investigation. That's what my holiday has come to. I'm interviewing a man about a missing chicken.

We've already established, by way of Mara sending him the photograph, that Bill's missing chicken is probably the one that turned up dead on my kitchen table. I doubt that whoever nicked his chicken and then used it as a means of threat or intimidation, left any clues to their identity, but I need to check it out.

When I get the time – it's so damned busy around here – I'll get in touch with Sgt Harrison back in Cambuslang, let her know what I'm up to. Investigating chicken theft in the Highlands. She'll be jumping in her car and heading up here first chance she gets.

I get to the door of the St Augustine hall, bang loudly upon it, then take a step back.

Rub my hands together, turn and look across the road. A row of terraced houses, at the far end a small newsagent's. That's the only one of the properties showing any lights.

What does anyone do around here? Huddle down for the long winter, and then prepare for the influx of summer tourists? Every now and again send a search and rescue team up into the mountains to bring down a body, or rescue some fuckwit who went up there in trainers and a pair of swimming shorts because the sun was shining when he set off?

The snow is thick on the road, the most recent set of car tracks becoming obscured. Soon enough, no one will be taking their cars anywhere. I wonder if the cast and crew of the movie who've travelled over from Fort William will be able to get back. They can hunker down and sleep in that abandoned hotel they've been using for filming.

I turn back to the door. Nothing. No sound from within, no hint that those footsteps in the snow belong to anyone. I bang loudly again, and just as I do, the door opens.

Ellis. Unshaven, slightly blue in the face. No heat emanates from the building. He's wearing a mustard puffer jacket, gloves and a tea cosy wool hat.

I get nothing from him, neither a hello, nor a blunt dismissal.

'Mr Ellis,' I say.

Still nothing.

'I wonder if I could ask you a few questions.'

I get the guarded look, the up and down assessment without his eyes actually moving up and down. For a moment he surprises me by removing his glove, and grudgingly extending his hand, but then I realise what he's doing.

'You're good,' I say, not accepting the handshake.

'Ha,' he mutters.

He pulls the glove back on, doesn't make any other move.

'Can I have a word?'

I get the contemptuous look, then, 'You're investigating Alice's disappearance?'

'Yes.'

'I don't know anything about it.'

We do the assessment and counter-assessment thing, eyeing each other up, making our snap judgements. There's something hardy about a guy who lives as secluded as he does, and who rows a boat across a loch just for the hell of it, but he's polished. You can see him in the city, ten years ago, bullshitting his way through million-dollar contracts. He's the kind of prick that comes up with limited edition garlic and chive, chocolate shower gel, and tells supermarkets to start advertising for Christmas in the middle of July.

'I'd be grateful if we could have a chat, nevertheless. Just trying to understand the village and the people. Get my feet under the desk. Get my bearings.'

'Don't you have Constable Mara for that?'

'It helps to get one's own perspective.'

His lips move, scowling, but he doesn't say whatever it is that comes into his head. I get the studied look for a while, then he finally says, 'You can get it elsewhere,' and slams the door shut.

Wasn't quick enough with my foot. As though I couldn't have seen that coming.

I bang on the door again, more loudly than before. Contemplate where this is going to go, think through the next few moves, and then with a low curse, I turn away and walk back down the path. I can bang the door all I like, but he knows I'm not going to stand there all day in this weather. He knows I don't have a warrant. He doesn't have to open the door if he doesn't want to, and so, having done it once to sate some little curiosity, he won't do it again.

I get to the road, stand for a moment looking in either direction, and then walk quickly across and go into the newsagent's. The chicken man can wait. Unlikely this chicken man will be getting blown up anytime soon. The bell tinkles happily, it's warm inside, I close the door behind me.

A small shop, a familiar layout. Long and thin, magazines down one side; a centre stand, with magazines and confectionary, then on the other wall, drinks and crisps. The counter is at the far end, behind which there is a woman in her fifties. Something of the Meryl Streep about her. One look at her and I know she owns the joint, the way Meryl Streep owns whatever room she's in.

'Hey,' I say, easing my way gently into the discussion.

'You've been dealt a bad hand today, I dare say,' she says as an introduction.

She appears to be English. We shan't hold that against her. After all, there are some English people who can conduct an entire conversation without mentioning the 1966 World Cup or the Blitz, though I'm not sure I've ever met one.

'How d'you mean that?'

'The snow. I understood you'd been filming in reverse order. Now you're going to have snow at the start of the film, which will suddenly vanish overnight.'

She snaps her fingers.

'I'm not with the movie.'

'Oh.'

I take my ID from my pocket, hold it forward.

'Detective Sergeant Hutton,' I say. 'Investigating the disappearance of Alice Schäfer.'

'Of course. Elaine had to call in the big guns.'

Ah, the casual put down. The side swipe. The implication that Constable Mara is not up to the job.

'I was in town,' I say. 'You know Alice?'

'Of course. *Everyone* knows Alice.'

At a guess, I'd say this woman is a seething bag of resentments and judgement.

A gold mine.

'Tell me about Alice.'

'I'm sure you've heard quite enough already.'

She's faking the reluctance to talk.

We stand that yard and a half apart, the counter between us. Mars Bars and Milky Ways and Dairy Milk and chewing gum and Lottery tickets and a pile of television magazines with a picture of a sad looking couple and the words *Maz Tells Tony He's Not The Father!* and a small display of cigarette lighters and a box of bubble gum, the whole thing that strange blend of modern life and the nineteen seventies that one finds in the backwoods of Europe.

'I'm not getting very far,' I say, deciding to press play on the gossipmonger.

'Our good townspeople refusing to speak to the copper?'

'Everyone's speaking, no one seems to have much to say. Alice was well-liked, she…' I pause for the scoff, but I'm not done. The gossipmonger likes nothing more than a raft of information to contradict. 'Look, people liked her, that's just

—

77

who she was. She got on great with the movie folk, she was popular down at the Post Office, happy family life, stable relationship…' I pause to accommodate the head shake. 'I mean, you get an impression and you read between the lines, and Alice was well-loved, and…'

This time she cuts me off with a loud *ha!*

I would've thought my acting was on a par with Gary in *Team America*, but she appears not to have seen through it.

'Look,' I say, the final reeling in of the fish, 'you can do whatever, you can be scornful, but some of us have been in the police for thirty years and we get a nose for things as the outsider. Gut instinct, if we want to be clichéd about it.'

'Gut instinct?'

'Yeah.'

'I think you might need to take some Bisodol, Detective Sergeant.'

I smile and tap the side of my head like I know shit. That pushes her over the edge.

'Have you spoken to Alice's friends?' she asks. 'I mean, her girlfriends.'

I look blank.

'No, you haven't, have you?' says Meryl Streep, with a certain know-it-all panache.

'Haven't got around to it yet,' I say, in fake defence.

'You won't find any.'

'Why?'

'Because no girl in this place would dream of being friends with Alice Schäfer. Everyone knows. Everyone. If Alice hadn't already slept with your boyfriend or husband, she would one day. She was on a mission.'

'I hadn't heard that.'

'Well, I don't know who you're talking to. I mean, good luck to her, I'm not one to judge. This isn't, I don't know, God help us this isn't the nineteen thirties. Times have moved on, and we are where we are. The girl could have as many lovers as she liked, it's not for me to comment on that, but you can't be doing that, and at the same time expect other women to go along with it.'

'Sandy seems happy enough,' I lie.

'That's the boy she's dating at the moment?' I nod. 'Well Sandy is living with his head in the clouds.'

'You think Alice continued her behaviour even though she

78

and Sandy were an item?'

She scoffs.

Just to be clear, I don't consider this *behaviour*. I too think Alice can do what the fuck she likes. But know your audience and all that, and there's no doubt Meryl Streep here thinks of it as behaviour.

'Well, I shouldn't say names, but there's one woman in the village who walked in on her husband and Alice *in flagrante* barely two weeks ago. And I don't doubt Alice'll have made a play with some of the film crew people. I mean, she would, wouldn't she?'

'Most of the film crew are women.'

'Well, I don't think that would stop someone like Alice.'

'She's bisexual?'

'Well, I don't know. She might be.'

OK, we're veering towards just making shit up now. Back to more solid ground.

'Who's the woman who walked in on her husband and Alice?'

She purses her lips, and then vocalises the gesture.

'My lips are sealed.'

'Is it well known around the village?'

'Yes, of course.'

'So, if you tell me, if you play your part in the police investigation, no one will know it was you who said it. You know, if I could've heard it from anyone.'

I got her with the *play your part* line. She's the *Hitler, My Part In His Downfall* type. When she's thinking about this conversation, it will be filled with *then I said*, and *then I told him*, and *then I put him straight*.

'Gillian Cooper. Runs the little arts and crafts studio in the centre of town.'

'What does her husband do?'

'He makes arts and crafts. They're not very good, to be honest, but they get by on the summer trade. People just want to spend money when they're on holiday, don't they?'

'Her husband's Bill Cooper?'

'You know him, then?'

'Not yet, but I heard the name.'

Bill Cooper is the chicken man. I can kill two chickens with one stone. This investigation's shaping up pretty sweet.

I mean, it isn't, at all. That's just my natural facetiousness.

———

Two days in and I have absolutely no idea what's happened to Alice Schäfer. I don't get her just running off to London and not telling anyone. Absolutely no one thinks she might have gone for a walk in the hills. Something's happened to her, and there are no good options. The only chance of a positive outcome, is that she's being held and we find her before it's too late. But if it's that, we're no nearer a positive outcome than when Mara first knocked on my door.

'Have you any thoughts on what might have happened to Alice?' I casually toss into the conversation.

She smiles, and I'm treated to the disdain of her folding her arms beneath her chest. A cold, withering look.

'Now you're looking for me to implicate someone in the village?'

Here we go again. 'I was hardly expecting a name. You know Alice, you know the village, you have an awareness of what people are thinking. You're not implicating anyone.' A pause, and then the even more casual, 'I'm asking everyone the same thing. You sound like the kind of person whose answer might be useful.'

I'm playing her like a kipper.

'She's dead,' she says without any more hesitation.

'That's definite.'

'It makes sense. Someone confronted her, and things got out of hand. They've disposed of her body somewhere. If she was going to leave of her own volition, why wouldn't she just say? That Alice was the boldest person in the village, she wouldn't have given a monkey's who she upset. And the only other alternative is that someone's got her locked up.' She pauses long enough to make the scornful face. 'That doesn't sound very likely. People don't kidnap young women, not in real life. Not in a place like this. Murder, or let's call it manslaughter, is much more like the thing. Much more believable.'

'And you're not going to name any potential suspects?' I say, deciding on this occasion to go for the more straightforward line of questioning.

'We would be here all afternoon, Sergeant. Like I said, speak to a woman in the village, and you'll likely find a suspect.'

'You?'

'Me what?'

I give her the eyebrow, and say, 'By your own definition.'

'Perhaps. But equally, I have no husband to betray me, so that would rule me out.'

Nice. Meryl Streep's scriptwriter is pretty sharp.

* * *

Leaving the store a few minutes later, Meryl pumped to exhaustion for information, I look across at the lodge hall. I stop halfway out into the cold, I contemplate turning round and going back to speak to her again, and then decide to leave it for another time. Let her delight in her participation, let her yearn for a little more involvement, then I can return when she's ready to be even more talkative.

Someone who literally stands all day looking out on the door of the lodge. She'll know a thing or two.

I close the door behind me, and step out into the snow.

15

An old cottage on two floors. Downstairs is the shop, Loch Eribour Arts & Crafts. Large windows at the front and back, bright inside, the snow outside like a beacon from either end. In the garden behind the property, with a clear view to the loch fifty yards further on, there is a small workshop to the side, with the rest of the garden given over to chickens. There are nine of them, with an elaborate-looking hutch on the opposite side of the garden from the workshop.

We're standing outside in the snow. Bill Cooper has kept the garden clear of it, shovelling it up and dumping it over the back. Doing a nice job of keeping on top of it. The only place the snow is lying back here is on top of the workshop.

'You usually have ten chickens?'

Cooper is wearing a sweatshirt and thick shorts, socks rolled at his ankles and walking boots. Mid-fifties maybe, the face of a one-time drinker, youthful good looks wasted. Clear eyes though, the look of someone who's been dry for at least ten years.

I had a quick look at some of his pottery on the way through the shop. I'm no judge. I could look at the finest pottery in the kingdom, and I couldn't tell the difference between that and something you'd get for ninety-nine pence in B&M.

The man can make a coffee mug, let's give him that.

'Aye,' he says.

'You don't get foxes?'

'The latch was lifted. Foxes don't lift latches. There was no sign of a fox. Someone opened the door, grabbed a chicken...' He pauses before completing the sentence, then adds, 'And killed it for your benefit.'

'If I wasn't here, your chicken wouldn't be dead?'

'Exactly.'

'Therefore it's my fault?'

'Maybe I should blame the cunt who took it, but I don't know who that was, so you're all I've got.'

82

'You have any idea who might've done it?'

I get a bit of a rolled eye in reply.

'Aye, sure, of course. It was Big Tam working in cahoots with Wee Jeanette.'

'Those are just names you're making up to make fun of the question?'

'You're a genius. D'you want your three bonus questions for five points each?'

'Have you any idea who might've taken your chicken?' I repeat, with that little added edge to my voice that is the hallmark of the *serious* question.

'No,' he says, deadpan.

'Everyone in the village knows you have chickens?'

'I expect so. It's not a secret at any rate.'

'You sell the eggs?'

'And the chickens.'

'Anyone ever stolen one before?'

'Ever ask the constable what she does around here? There's literally no crime, and any there is, is tourists. That lot can fuck off. But they wouldn't steal a chicken, and anyway, there aren't any tourists at the moment.'

'There's the film crew.'

'You said it.'

'But then, presumably whoever took it was someone who wants me to stop investigating Alice Schäfer's disappearance.' He's got nothing to say to that. It is kind of an obvious point to make. 'So that's what it comes down to, isn't it? It's not, who would steal a chicken, it's who doesn't want me looking for Alice?'

'You're the detective.'

Jesus.

'How well d'you know Alice?'

'What?'

'How well d'you know Alice?'

'What's that got to do with it?'

'We've just discussed, using logic that was so solid it was almost science, that your dead chicken and Alice's vanishing are inescapably linked. So, how well d'you know Alice?'

'I still don't see what that's got to do with it. I mean, if I'm guilty of something, why would I report my own chicken was missing?'

'I'm not accusing you of being guilty of anything, though it

83

would hardly be the weirdest thing for you to fake the chicken theft, leave me the pointless threat, report the theft and make yourself look innocent. I mean, whoever actually did it must have some motive other than trying to scare me off, because it was obviously never going to scare me off.'

He's got nothing to say to that, though his demeanour has darkened a little further.

'How well d'you know Alice?' I ask for the fourth time.

'Well enough. She's a popular girl around the village. Everyone knows her.'

'How well does your wife know her?'

Had a quick word with Gillian Cooper in the shop. She gave off a peculiar aura of nothingness, like she has no agency as a human being. Very odd. Maybe she's just prozacked to the rafters.

Turns out, I have seen her previously, however.

He glances into the shop. I don't turn to see if he can see her from here, or if she's watching us. There are certainly unlikely to be any customers to worry about.

'You can ask her,' he says.

'How did it play out when she walked in on you and Alice fucking?' I ask, making the judgement that the blunter the question, the better.

Mouth closed, jaw working, he doesn't take his eyes off me.

The last of the falling snow, just like that, as though someone flicked a switch. Still, cold air. No wind. A beautiful silence out over the loch.

'I think we're done,' he says finally. 'I've got work to do.'

'Tell me about you and Alice.'

'There's nothing to tell.'

'You had sex with her two weeks ago, and now she's –'

'It was three weeks ago.'

'No less relevant.'

I get the silent stare. I wait for him to say something else, but he's got no intention. Then he turns away and walks to the workshop, presumably to return to the task of making mugs.

'You a member of the lodge?' I ask to his back, as he opens the door.

The hesitation, the head slightly bowed, and then he enters the workshop, closes the door, and turns the key in the lock

I watch him for a moment, but now he's sitting at his work

bench, which is facing the loch behind a picture window, and so he has his back turned. I contemplate walking out the rear gate, going round and standing in the middle of his view, but decide instead to go back inside and speak to Mrs Cooper. A woman who possibly has far more reason to be happy at the disappearance of Alice Schäfer than her husband.

The shop is still, inevitably, deserted. There's music playing, a Highland folk band, I guess. Fiddle music, low and slow. A lament. Probably a different one to the one that was playing when I walked through the shop in the first place, but it's hard to tell. All this stuff sounds the same. Evocatively majestic, nevertheless same-y.

I stand in the shop for a moment, and despite the presence of Gillian Cooper behind the counter, it feels like I'm the only one here. Usually when one is the sole customer in a shop, there's an inherent awkwardness. The unspoken words hovering in the air, the anticipation of interaction. Something has to be said at some point, even if it's just a muttered thank you upon leaving.

But not here, because it's like Gillian Cooper isn't present. Her body is, but her mind is elsewhere.

I stand for a moment, looking around the tourist trap of paintings and pottery and artfully framed, black & white photographs and trinkets and umbrellas and tea towels and books by Colin Prior and histories of Scotland and histories of the clans and histories of the Clearances, and then there's a moment of silence as the lament finishes, but the silence doesn't last as another soon starts up, and then finally I turn to the counter to engage with the vacuum.

'Mrs Cooper?'

She's staring vaguely into the middle of nowhere, the back of beyond, then slowly the words filter through, and she turns to face me.

She holds my gaze, then finally seems to focus, and she looks at me curiously, as though I've appeared out of nowhere.

'Sorry,' she says. 'I didn't see you. How can I help?'

I don't immediately reply, waiting to see if she's actually engaged. I'm not entirely sure she's present, even though she's appeared to acknowledge my existence.

'Mrs Cooper?'

Tick-tock.

'Yes.'

'Detective Sergeant Hutton. I'm investigating the disappearance of Alice Schäfer.'

A pause, then, 'Yes.'

'Can I ask you a few questions?'

Slowly I seem to be breaking through, every word a chip at the wall she's set up to keep out the world. She straightens her shoulders a little, takes an obvious breath, there's a focusing of the eyes.

'Can I ask a few questions?' I feel the need to repeat, nevertheless.

'Yes, of course.' A beat, and then, 'We all knew Alice.'

The crack investigator notes the use of the past tense, but does not let on.

Hey, if she's thinking Alice is already dead, she ain't the only one.

'Tell me about Alice,' I say.

'Is that a question?'

Nice.

'Not exactly, if we're being pedantic, but it kind of encompasses everything I'm about to ask. How well you know her, how well you know the family, what you think of her, if you've any idea what might have happened to her, what it was like walking in on her and your husband having sex... That kind of thing.'

She holds my gaze, taking another obvious breath. Right there is the explanation for the seeming lack of existence in the world. This is a woman whose life has been shattered by finding her husband naked with another woman, and she's been medicating her way through the last couple of weeks.

Or so goes one theory, based on hardly any information.

'He didn't tell you that?' she asks. When I don't immediately answer, she adds, 'Bill?'

'I asked him, he didn't want to talk about it.'

'Not his finest hour.'

'How long had it been going on?' I ask, and she fires back with the perfect, if predictable, 'I'm not sure, but he doesn't usually last any more than two or three minutes.'

'Had they been having a relationship?' I say deadpan, like I'm the grown-up in the conversation. (In reality, as the audience knows, I'm *never* the grown-up in the conversation.)

'He said that was it. A one-off. She seduced him.'

'How did you come to walk in on him? What made him

---

think you wouldn't be home?'

'Night out in Fort William with a friend. I was always coming home, but wasn't due back until late. Kirsty wasn't feeling well, she bailed on me after the starters. Heavy period, if you want to get down to specifics. She's always suffered.'

'You didn't call and let him know you'd be early?'

A pause, then the small shake of the head. I don't ask the immediate follow-up question, but it's there. In the modern era, the mobile phone era, most couples are going to let someone know about a change of plan. Takes twenty seconds to send that text.

'Were you nervous about what you might find?'

She holds my gaze, but doesn't answer.

'Was there ever a friend in Fort William?'

'Yes.'

'Were you actually seeing her that evening?'

The question answered with silence, which is all the answer anyone needs.

'Did you suspect Bill was having an affair with Alice, or was it just with *someone*, but you didn't know who?'

A long pause, then finally, 'The latter.'

We leave it there for a moment. The depressing recounting of real life. The affair, the marriage in trouble, very possibly down the pan. Who knows how far it had already disappeared before the intervention of Alice Schäfer? The shock the woman now wears, or in fact, the shock she now masks with medication, suggests things had seemed fine until the suspicions started, and then the suspicions were confirmed.

'Twenty years doing this because of him. Growing up, I was always going to leave this godforsaken place, then he turned up, and he persuaded me to stay. Twenty years now, so he can live his dream life, sitting in his workshop, looking at the loch, making... *this*.' She sweeps her hand around the shop. 'Twenty years of sacrifice, and this is who it turns out he is. This is what I've lived my life for. Well, thank you Bill, and goodnight.'

'Have you seen Alice around town since then?'

She swallows. Rats. I think she might be about to start crying. Never helps.

'Have you seen Alice around town since then?' I toss in again, to force the issue.

'It's a small town.'

'So, how's that been?'

'How d'you think?'

'Alice has a reputation?'

'How d'you mean?'

'She has a reputation for sleeping around?'

The gaze, which has remained steadfastly blank up until this point, takes on something of an edge.

'Gee, thanks,' she says, drily.

'What does that mean?'

'Good to know that the next time I have sex with Bill, if I ever have sex with him again, I'll be sleeping with the leftovers of the village.'

'One way of putting it.'

'Tell me another.'

'You weren't aware Alice has a reputation?'

'Until I saw her naked, I didn't know that much about her. Now I know too much.'

'Seems a lot of people are saying she slept around. Common knowledge.'

'Like I say, I didn't know her well, and I never mix much. Nice to think that all those people who talk about Alice behind her back, will now also be talking about Bill. And me. My day just keeps getting better and better. Tell me something else, Sergeant.'

'Did you have anything to do with the disappearance of Alice Schäfer?'

'What?'

'You have motive for wanting Alice to disappear.'

'I, eh…'

Her words run out. There's a sound behind, laughter outside, and then the door to the shop opens, there's the loud tinkle of the bell, and then seven or eight people are coming into the shop, shaking off snow at the doorway, laughing and talking, one of them with a phone held out filming the others laughing and talking.

I recognise some of the movie crew. This is them, filling their downtime, all part of the montage scene that will go into the behind-the-scenes footage.

We watch them for a moment as they pile in, closing the door behind them, and then they immediately start looking at the inspiring arts and crafts, a couple of the young women making appropriate *oh my God, this stuff's amazing* noises, and then Gillian Cooper and I turn back to each other.

I hold the stare. The question remains unanswered. I don't need to ask it again. She swallows, she is not distracted by the sudden customer influx.

'Yes,' she says eventually, her voice barely audible above the excited chatter of young people being loud for the camera.

'Yes?'

'Yes, I'm quite happy that Alice has gone. I don't know where she's gone or what's happened to her, but if she's gone for good, then I won't be upset. Long term, it probably doesn't matter. I should go. Leave. I should leave.' She holds my gaze for a moment, then looks away. A vacant stare, however, thoughts lost, not paying any attention to the shop or the people in it. When she speaks again her voice is a mixture of wistfulness and hopelessness. 'But where is that? Where do I go? What do I do?'

She turns back, the same feeling of wistfulness and hopelessness in her eyes.

'Can you tell me about Monday evening?' I ask, not allowing the interview to wallow in her desolation. 'Into early Tuesday.'

'Monday? Tuesday?'

'Yes.'

'Why? Why Monday?'

I answer that with the look. The *think about it* look.

'Right, the night... the night Alice disappeared.' A pause, and then, 'Wait, seriously? You're actually asking what I did the night Alice was last seen?'

'Believe it or not.'

'Oh.'

'Late Monday evening, early morning Tuesday. Alice was out for the evening, she got home about nine-thirty. She spoke to her mother for a short while, then went to bed. Her parents are unaware of her having gone back out, so we can probably rule out her leaving the house much before midnight.' A pause, then, 'By the morning she'd gone.'

'You think someone snuck into her house and kidnapped her? Without anyone else hearing? And you're asking me if I was that person?'

'We don't know. The most likely scenario is she was in contact with someone, then she left surreptitiously to meet that person in the middle of the night.'

'And you think that if it was me I'm going to tell you? I

—

89

mean, it wasn't, but what actually is the point of that question?'

'The point is that you say you can prove you spent the night in Inverness, or you say that you and Bill spent the night grudgingly sleeping next to each other, but however it is, you can prove you couldn't have met with Alice, and you can be eliminated from the investigation.'

'I did neither,' she says. Her tone is coming to life, and in doing so becoming more acerbic and dismissive. This is the interviewee tone we know and love.

'You and Bill not sleeping in the same room?'

'Of course not. He's in the spare. And he can stay there.'

'Excuse me!' The cry from the other end of the shop. 'Can you tell me how much this is, please?'

I don't turn to see what she's holding up.

'Twelve-ninety-nine,' says Gillian Cooper in reply, and she gets a 'Wow!' in response, then she turns back to me. 'The price is on the bottom of the bowl,' she says, her voice a little quieter than before. 'Some people…'

'So, neither you nor Bill can vouch for the other?'

A long look, followed by the sad head shake.

'No, I'm afraid not. You're going to have to leave me on your list of suspects for now.'

A couple of the film people brush past me, as they come to this end of the shop. Eight people making the noise of eighty. This is some amount of fun these people are having looking at pottery.

Gillian Cooper and I share another long look, and then she indicates the cacophony of customers and says, 'Perhaps you could allow me to do my job. If I think of anything that'll help in your investigation, I'll…' and she finishes the sentence with a small gesture and about a quarter of a rueful smile.

'I saw you leave the film set yesterday,' I say, ignoring her request.

'Sorry?'

'I went up to the film set to speak to the director, and you were just leaving. You didn't look very happy. What was that about?'

She stares at me, a deer-in-the-headlights look, and then she shakes her head.

'I was just speaking to someone, it was nothing to do with Alice.'

'You looked unhappy.'

'Did I?'

I hold the look, but she's got nothing else to say.

'Who on the film crew were you annoyed at?'

'I wasn't annoyed at anyone on the film crew, if you must know. Plenty enough people here in the village to be annoyed about, without having to get peed off at them.'

'Who are we talking about?'

There's the question too far. You can see it coming, you push on, but eventually you get there. The question that slams the door shut.

'I think we've talked long enough, Sergeant. Please go and allow me to do my job.'

Another long gaze, more excited tumult behind, I nod, and that'll be that for the sad case of the Coopers. For now.

I step outside the shop, back into the cold of a snowy day in November. This is the kind of November day that makes climate sceptics say, see, see, where's your global warming now, you pathetic, sheep-like fools? and makes scientists and all right-thinking people respond, oh, don't be a fucking, disingenuous prick, you flatulent, moaning turd-baby.

I stand for a moment, contemplating waiting for the movie folks to leave the building, so that I can engage them, then away along to my left I see the movement of yellow in the snow, and there's Ellis, having left the lodge building, crossing the street and going into Meryl Streep's grocery store.

Immediately I start walking, the snow up above my ankles, heading back along to meet him. I doubt I'll get very far, but I can enjoy annoying him, at least. And as I walk, I make the decision that this evening, leaving footprints in the snow, I'm going to break into the lodge hall.

Sometimes, as any police officer knows, you have to take the law into your own hands.

16

'Then he told me to fuck off.'

Mara smiles.

'That's the Ellis we all know and love.'

I'd rather there wasn't snow on the ground when I make my move to break into the lodge hall tonight, it'll leave a pretty obvious trace. However, one gets a feeling, that's all, and there's just something about that place. Perhaps it's just that it stands out in this no-horse village, but there's only one way to find out.

'Anything from the film crew?' I ask.

'Nothing you haven't previously reported.'

She pauses for a moment, though I recognise she's not done. We're back, standing at the window of the station, looking out on the early evening. Darkness has fallen, the sky has cleared for the moment, though more snow is forecast for later. The loch is still, thin moonlight on the water. To our left, the lights of the village. Far away, across the loch, the lights of Ellis's house in the dark.

'I get the feeling…' she begins, 'I mean, I struggle to see how Alice's disappearance can't be related to the movie being in town. The timing seems so significant. And yet, none of the people involved in it, or at least none of those we've spoken to, give off the slightest hint of suspicion. None of them get the hairs standing on the back of the neck, none of them give off… anything. You know?' Another pause, then the shake of the head and, 'Sorry, that's not expressed very well.'

'You're right. This lot just seem interested in making a movie. There's always the possibility, I guess, that we're not speaking to the right people. We're focussing on the top of the tree, the main ones you see on the credits, when it might well be the work of someone nearer the bottom. The name that zips past at fifty miles an hour, two minutes into the end credit sequence, that absolutely no one pays any attention to. And here we are, doing the same thing, and the guilty party has so far avoided scrutiny.'

'There are only two of us.'

'Yep. I feel the most likely scenario is that some long-standing disagreement with someone close, friends or family, was brought to a head by the movie's arrival in town, and Alice's part in it. Whether that's related to individuals on set or not, though…'

Words drift away. She nods along for a moment. Silence returns, and immediately threatens to engulf the office.

'How's the snow in Edinburgh?' I ask, feeling uncomfortable, for reasons I can't place.

Oh, we all know why I'm feeling uncomfortable.

'There's no snow. Just rain.'

'Oh. Well, it is the east coast, I suppose. Is he making it home?'

'Road's closed, so no. I told him not to even try. It's not the first time. Occupational hazard in the winter. This is early, but here we are all the same.'

The silence returns, like an instant shadow as soon as she stops talking. A peculiar atmosphere rising out of nothing.

Though, really, it's not so peculiar. We're waiting for one of us to ask the other what we're doing this evening, and for dinner to be mentioned, which raises the prospect of us drinking wine together, and who knows where that goes. I mean, sure, it's possible to have dinner with a woman and *not* have sex. It's a thing. That's what some people do. But me? Doubt I can manage a second consecutive evening without doing something dumb.

I've got my break-in to consider, but I'm breaking into a hall on the main street through town, so I won't be doing it before midnight, and probably a bit later than that. And if there's no backdoor, or other means to get in at the rear of the hall, it increases the chances of me not doing it at all. I may have the finest lock-picking tool in the land, but I don't want to be caught beneath the glare of a streetlight, finagling my way into the building.

'Got plans for this evening?' she asks, finally getting it out there. Perhaps wary of the fact we were liable to stand here for the next hour.

'Not yet,' I say.

'Want to come over again? Sorry, there's not really a lot else to do around here. Especially when everyone's snowed in.'

I want to say no. The word no is on the tip of my tongue. The word no, however, doesn't stand a chance.

—

I could be reading the situation wrong of course. Wouldn't be the first time. Apparently not everyone thinks about sex as much as I do. She might just be genuinely bored on a Friday evening, and want someone to chat to. Maybe, in fact, she doesn't want me to come to dinner at all, but is just asking because she feels she should. I'm supposedly on my holidays, and here I am, helping her out on a case. She feels obliged to cook my dinner.

'You sure?'

'Am I sure?'

She smiles.

'You're not just asking because you think you owe me a couple of dinners?'

She holds my gaze, I can't help looking at her lips – she has a great smile – and then she looks back at the view.

'If it makes you feel better, I'm asking you because there's literally nothing else to do in this place. Particularly when there's a foot of snow on the ground.'

'Well, if I'm a last resort…'

Oh, we smile and laugh, and we all know what that means, and after all, I'm only ever one step away from being absolutely fucking moronic.

17

One-seventeen a.m. and the snow has just started up again. The air still and cold, with large, fluffy flakes falling. If they'd begun clearing the roads in the afternoon when the snow stopped, that work would now be wasted.

Feel like I need one of those snow camouflage outfits you see the military wear in movies. Like Richard Burton in *Where Eagles Dare*. Instead, I'm walking through town, on the way to the hall, feeling like I've got a spotlight on me.

The new snow is good. As long as I'm not busted in the act, there's a chance my footprints will be covered.

I shouldn't have done it. Shouldn't have slept with her. Can you not just, for the love of god, work with a woman without fantasising about her? Without coming on to her?

Stand at the street corner, looking along the main stretch of road through town. No one around. The streetlights are not so bright, but with the snow, the place has that illuminated winter magic about it. I move into a position where I can see the windows above the grocery store. I imagine Meryl Streep in there, keeping a look out, waiting to see who comes and goes from the lodge.

No lights on, curtains drawn. Maybe she doesn't even live in the apartment above her shop.

I take the street up by the five-foot side wall of the lodge grounds, then when I've reached the back of the property, I heave myself up onto the wall, feet scrambling for traction against the stone, and then I'm up and over. Once there, I quickly move directly behind the building, out of sight of the street. Behind, fir trees dressed in perfect white, like they've been taken from a Bob Ross painting. Happy little cold-ass trees.

Back against the wall, take a moment getting my bearings, making sure I'm not overlooked from anywhere. We're clear. Here, behind the hall, there are a few headstones, and I wonder if the hall used to be a church. That would make sense, it has the look of it. And there are hardly any churches used for the original purpose anymore, after all. The world has moved on. Albeit, this is the Lodge of St Augustine, so this crowd haven't moved very far.

There's a back door, though there's always the possibility of it being bolted from the inside, which would be a showstopper.

I take the standard issue lockpick tool out of my pocket. The Lishi. I did the course, such as it was. China's greatest gift to criminality. Or one of them, anyway. Take my gloves off, the air does not feel so cold. It's maybe minus-one, not awful for working bare-handed for a few minutes. And the Lishi will pick a Yale lock in about fifteen seconds.

Of course, I didn't just come on to Mara. We came on to each other. If I had to take a stab at her thinking, I'd say she really was just bored. That, at least, is several notches higher than any alternative, such as she couldn't resist me. I was something to do on a snowy night in November. Perhaps Alan is doing something similar on his wet night in Edinburgh. Perhaps that's the kind of marriage they have.

The lock clicks, I do that wonderfully surreptitious thing people do in movies of taking a look over my shoulder. Bob Ross's trees look back at me undisturbed. Gloves back on, I push the door open, kick the snow off my shoes as much as I can on the outside wall, then step inside. Door quickly closed behind me, and I'm standing in all-encompassing darkness.

Phone out of my pocket, torch on, lift it quickly and shine it around the small space. An entrance hallway, nothing about it. Two doors off, a coat rack with no coats, a boot rack with no boots. A window to the right, a door straight ahead, another to the left. The one straight ahead will be into the main hall – assuming there is a main hall – the door to the left will be a smaller office or meeting room.

On this wall, the coat rack, and then a painting. Also paintings either side of the door to the main hall. All three paintings are of a saint. Old fellow, long white beard, white cloak. St Augustine, one must presume. In one, sitting on a bench, piously lecturing a few students on the ways of the Lord. Maybe he was telling them about the time he got completely rat-arsed and fellated a donkey, thinking it was St Timothy, the fuck do I know? In the second, he's being serenaded by an angelic horde.

The third painting, the one to the right of the door to the

hall, is curious. In this, Augustine is being sexually pleasured. And, I mean, holy shit, Batman, is he being sexually pleasured? Seven or eight naked women, some standing to the side, three with their tongues on his erect, red and engorged penis. That's fucking weird, by the way. Augustine isn't looking at the women, however. His eyes are open, staring at God, who is looking down from the heavens.

That seems kind of fucked up.

Is it the death of Augustine? Tormented to death, or fucked to death, by a bunch of women?

History, such as it is, tells us that St Augustine died of illness during the invasion of Roman North Africa by the Vandals. A peaceful death, fading away in bed, while around him the city burned. I know this because I looked it up last night, not because I have an encyclopaedic knowledge of the deaths of saints.

So this is an interesting interpretation of dying peacefully in his bed.

Assuming the office door to be locked, I decide to leave it for last, and try the door to the main hall. It opens, and I step quickly in, closing the door behind me.

The chances of someone going past the building and seeing the light of a phone torch inside, through the few dark stained-glass windows, seem remote. Nevertheless I keep the light down, and dim it a little.

I didn't go straight round to Mara's place after work. I went back to the cottage, showered, changed. She showered and changed. It was like it was a given before we had dinner. It was a date night. I brought a bottle of wine. We didn't talk about the case *at all*. We talked about stupid shit. We made each other laugh. She was wearing jeans and a V-neck sweater.

We end up in the kitchen, clearing stuff away, and then we're standing next to each other, and I make that familiar move, the gentle touch of the face. Forward, but not outrageous, something she can shake off without it being a horror show of awkwardness, but she gave into it, and then we were kissing and she pushed me back against the kitchen worktop, her hands in my hair and on my neck and running down my body.

There's a long table in the middle of the hall, chairs around it. Two at either end, eight down either side. A table for twenty. I wonder if that's the constant number of the lodge. No new members admitted until someone dies, or is ejected for some heinous crime. Like marrying a catholic or arguing it was a positive Celtic won that game in Europe.

The backs of each of the chairs are different, carved with religious symbols and gargoyles. That would bear some inspection, but not now. Likely, not ever, of course.

Round the table, and shine the torch on the wall. A long sideboard down one side. Lots of drawers. On the wall, more paintings, and there we have it, just what you want for your society of men. They're painted in classic Baroque style, and every one is of a naked woman involved in some form of sexual activity. I walk along the length of the wall. Six paintings of identical size. In only one of them does the woman look like she might actually be enjoying herself. The others are of torment and defiling.

Jesus, these fucking secret societies. I don't linger on them, I've got the gist.

I try a couple of drawers, a couple of cupboards, but everything's locked. Quick sweep of the room, then I'll take to the task of looking through the cabinets.

At the back of the room, large tapestries on the walls, either side of the door. The passion of the Christ. The one on the left, Jesus bearing the burden of the cross on the way to his crucifixion; on the right, his Eric Idle moment, nailed to the cross. Doesn't seem that he's looking on the bright side, to be fair. Looks kind of anguished.

Either way, seems like regulation Christian schtick, rather than the weird, abusive misogyny of the other artwork.

Another door to the right, a quick look in, a flash of the torch. Toilet, sink, nothing more. Elaborate decoration on the tiling, but I don't linger over it.

Back into the main body of the hall, and over to the other side. A similar set-up, cabinets down the side, paintings on the wall. The first one shows a naked woman, an angel presumably given the wings and the fact that she's floating in air, with three men wrapped around her. One kissing her, his hand on her breast, the second licking her other breast, the third between her legs. Nothing about her to suggest she's not enjoying the attention. In the next painting, the same woman, this time being taken by three different men. The paintings continue down the line on the same theme.

I was ready to have sex on the kitchen table; Constable Mara very sensibly led me to the bedroom. Kitchen tables are all well and good for movie sex, but not the real thing. Too damned uncomfortable. She lay back on the bed, whipped her jeans and underwear off in one, and then lay there looking at me, legs parted, and then the sweater was lifted up and over her head, and before she'd finished the movement, before she'd had time to remove her bra, I was between her legs, my tongue running the length of her lips, and she was gasping and pressing herself against me, and then her hands were pushing the back of my head, and 'Oh, fuck, yes!' was coming from her lips.

While the cabinets on the other side of the hall had nothing but mats on them, and an empty bowl, this one has more elaborate decoration. A candelabra; a metal cross; a skull on a plinth, mundanely it seems with a candle inside; an instrument, that looks nautical, but whose usage escapes me; a statue of a woman in black, hood drawn up around her head, eyes staring out from the shadows.

At the far end of this cabinet, another smaller, stand-alone cabinet. I try the door. It opens.

A safe, the classic dial on the door. How terribly old-fashioned. But, of course, look the fuck where I am.

I absent-mindedly turn the dial.

There's a gentle click above me. As I whirl round, ultraviolet light starts flashing from a light in the ceiling.

The light flashes in silence. My heart races from a standing start. Throat dry, pulse at a gallop.

'Fuck it,' I snap at the room. I find my balls from somewhere, and stop over-reacting. Flashing lights, for fuck's sake. Whoever's been alerted at the other end of an alarm, they won't be here straight away. And, given the weather, I might have a few minutes yet.

Stand still, let my heart settle, slip the phone into my pocket.

It might be at Ellis's house where the alarm is ringing, and in that case, he won't be coming. Not any time in the next half hour. But perhaps he has someone in the village he calls.

Damn it, I should get on with it and get out. What is it I'm really doing here anyway?

Back out into the hall, door closed behind me. The same flash of lights out here. A moment, listening for any sound from within or without, and then I take the lockpick from my pocket and get to work on the door into the office.

Slightly harder in the flash of ultraviolet, but it's done

quickly nevertheless, and then I step into the office, and close the door behind me. In here the lights also flash.

A chair, a desk, a cupboard. Spartan. To an extent. Behind me, as I enter, another large painting on the wall. A two-faced Christ; smiling out at the viewer, while holding the mask of Satan in his left hand.

Take another moment, listening for an approach, then turn to the other wall. Here we are! Here we fucking are. Jesus. This is why you break into shit. This is why you do the stupid stuff that you know will cause all sorts of trouble if you get caught.

There are a series of framed photographs on the wall. A lot of them. Young women. Quick scan, twenty-three of them in all. Judging by the clothes and the hair, there's a clear chronology of the photographs, starting some time in the sixties, perhaps. At the bottom right, Alice Schäfer. So much for Ellis saying he didn't know her.

The fuck is going on here that he doesn't want to talk about?

And there's a kick in the teeth. A young Constable Mara, five photographs behind Alice. Well, there's a rogue's fucking gallery. What the fuck is that all about? At least the presence of Mara means that it's not the lodge's murder wall, it's not a list of women they've killed, or women they've made disappear. Most of these pictures will pre-date Ellis, however, so this isn't just about him.

Phone back out of my pocket, take a picture of the wall as best I can in this weird light. As I do so, I recognise a young Gillian Cooper in amongst the gallery. There may be others, but I can study it when I get home.

Standing still with nothing but the beat of my heart, which has settled down in any case, I can hear the sound of a car approaching, the struggle of the tyres in the thick snow. Fuck it, there goes looking in any cabinets.

Quick now, back out into the hallway, then to the back door. Open it, take a moment, can still hear the tyres labouring in the snow, and then I'm out into the cold, door closed, and then hurrying into the trees behind, and up over the wall.

18

So that happened. Managed to avoid leaving a trail all the way back to my cottage by finding my way to some previous footfalls in the snow I'd noticed earlier. Mixed them up a bit, hopefully got lost in them. Sure, if someone wants to go to some lengths on a snowy November middle of the night, but you know what? They probably already know it was me, so why bother?

Back into the house, boots and jacket and gloves and hat off, into the kitchen. Lay my phone on the table, sit back. Stare at it without opening it. Photographs to look at. At first glance I only recognised Schäfer, Mara and Cooper, but in that light, in that circumstance, I could easily have been missing something.

Two-thirteen in the morning.

Tea or wine?

Hmm, well I drank vodka last night, so there's an opened bottle of Pinot in the fridge from a couple of nights ago. If I don't drink that in the next, what, half an hour, it's liable to go off. There's your decision right there, folks.

Bottle out of the fridge, pour the glass, take a drink, sit back.

I don't feel anything about that wine. I was drinking earlier, after all, now it's two in the morning and I don't need it. There's no buzz. But here we are, the drinker and his fix.

Take another sip, open my phone. I took one picture of the wall of photographs, and as I close in on each photo, the first one I automatically go to is Constable Mara.

Photo taken in her early twenties. It's not a smiling, high school yearbook type of picture, but one taken when she was out walking in the hills. Nevertheless, a posed picture, looking at the camera. Waterproofed jacket, boots, wool hat pushed back on her head, hair down across her forehead. Smiling, happy, attractive.

That's a nice picture. That, however, is immaterial. What is it doing on that wall, and what were all the others doing on the wall?

I linger on it for a moment, glass of wine drifting between the table and my lips, then I head to the most recent picture, the one of Alice Schäfer. Alice in a party dress. Not so different, really, from the dress she wore for the vampire filming.

God, I'm tired.

Alice is pretty fit. Sure, on the one hand she's actually younger than my daughter, so there's that. But, you know, she at least has the body for pulling off what she was trying to pull off on that movie set.

Another drink of wine.

Yawn.

I stare at the wine. This one feels like it's getting to me. How much did I have at Mara's house? A lot. But then, I stopped drinking a few hours ago.

I take another drink, lay the glass heavily back on the table. Shit, must have been close to snapping the stem. That reminds me of something. A film or something, real life, a book, I don't know, a killer snapping the stem of a wine glass, burying the stem in a man's eye socket.

Must have been fiction.

God, I'm tired.

Another drink. Have to stop drinking.

And getting turned on. Jesus, you shallow fucker. Stop looking at Alice in that dress. And stop drinking.

You said that already.

Some chance. I always drink. Everyone knows it. Here comes Hutton, the drinker. That look in his eyes? They're not haunted by years of stress and horror. It's vodka. And wine. Mostly vodka.

Rest my head in my hand. Fuck me, I should just go to bed. Why am I sitting here, staring at this stupid collection of photographs when I can't even think straight?

They're not stupid! They're clues. *Clues*! There are clues here. Look at them. Just look at them for fuck's sake!

Holy shit. Here we go. The fuck is *she* doing there? Abigail Connolly, head of movie casting. Scared of spiders, likes to get out her house. She's there, twenty years younger, among the same cast of characters as Mara and Schäfer. Which means she must have lived here.

Did she live here? Wait, did I know that already? What did I know? She's scared of spiders. Did she say anything else? Did she drop a hint, or say anything that I ought to have picked up on? Fuck it, think about it.

Forehead in the palm of my hand. Head swirling. Fuck.

It would be so nice to just drop off to sleep. Shit, maybe I'm about to throw up. Sleep would be preferable. I should go to bed. That's it. Go to bed.

Moan softly, a noise from the back of my throat, blink, feel like I have to pull my eyes open. The phone has turned itself off. Fuck me, how long did I have my eyes closed? This is stupid. Go to bed. *Go to fucking bed!*

Set an alarm. I should do that. Should set an alarm. Fuck it, I can do it when I get up in the morning.

And then I'm up and out of the chair, and I'm bouncing off walls and lurching and stumbling, and then I'm falling forward and collapsing on the bed. Lying down, the room does not stop moving.

* * *

She comes to me at some point. I don't know when. Alice Schäfer, lying on my bed, naked. Undressing me. Soft fingers running over my skin. Soft lips, soft kisses, gentle bites, her tongue moist against my skin.

Must be dreaming. This is what happens when you drink too much. This is what happens. Head in a swirl, a young woman caressing you. What age was she again? Can't think. Doesn't matter. God, it's good. Her touch. Her skin.

Naked all of a sudden. I'm naked. I don't remember my clothes coming off. I must've done it when I got into bed. Her hands are running up and down my erection, and she's pressed against me, then she leans over and takes the end of my cock into her mouth. Oh my fuck, that's so nice. I'm so tired, so wiped out. Dreaming. Lost somewhere. And that feels delicious and I never want it to stop. This is why we drink. This is why we can't stop. So you can lie here, feeling like this, feeling like a billion fucking dollars.

And then she's kneeling over me, and she lowers herself onto me, and my erect cock slides inside her, and oh my fucking God, I could stay here forever. And I can barely focus on her, the face and the hair, but I lift my hands to her breasts, and this is my dream, this is always my dream, right here, and she's fucking me and moaning, and I never want this to end.

And this is why we drink.

103

19

Some might observe that drinking does not, in fact, aid sexual activity.

* * *

Wake with a freight train running through my brain. Oh, fuck me.

Eyes open. Curtains open, broad daylight outside. Close my eyes again. Too bright. Reach to the side table. Hand fumbles for my phone. The phone's not there. Hand withdrawn back beneath the covers, the room cold. This bright and cold, it must still be snowy outside. Another brief opening of the eyes, but there's nothing about the day to say what time it is.

Naked. Must have got undressed when I came to bed. I don't remember coming to bed.

What happened last night? Went to Mara's. Had sex with Mara. That was stupid. Her on top, the taste of her on my lips, the touch of her breasts against my chest. Don't think about that. No fit state. But God she was good.

Maybe I dreamt it. Maybe I dreamt sex with Mara. Did I dream about sex?

The lodge. The damned Lodge of St Augustine. The darkness and the long table and the strange, erotic paintings and the flashing light. And the photographs on the wall. And Mara was there. Mara was on that wall, along with Alice.

Fuck. Alice. There's something about Alice. What is it about Alice? I can feel her there, Alice, in my head. I learned something about Alice. Like a moment, an epiphany, a *something*. What the fuck was it?

Straight thoughts will not come. Have to get on with it. Don't open my eyes, but force myself up, swing my legs over the side of the bed. The movement makes me reel, even though I'm still sitting.

Long breath, mouth open, eyes closed, daylight jabbing at

my eyelids, head pounding.

I don't move.

* * *

Mara is sitting at her desk when I arrive. Ten-forty-nine a.m. It's not currently snowing, but the sky is low and overcast, the air cold. No hint of a thaw, only the suggestion of more snow to come. An early, full-throttle winter storm.

I stop inside the door, and stare across the short distance of the office. One's memory returns in instalments, fleeting images, shards of remembrance, creating a jigsaw to be assembled. I know I got home from breaking into the lodge hall with a photograph on my phone. A photograph of a wall with a series of women. The most recent of whom was Alice Schäfer, and in amongst the others were Constable Mara and Abigail Connolly and Gillian Cooper.

When I looked this morning, I had no such photograph. The image had been deleted. But it *had* been there. I'm sure it was. I'm sure I took it. I'm sure I was looking at it. I sat at the kitchen table, in the middle of the night, looking at it.

'How are you?' I manage, shattering a peculiar silence that neither of us seemed to have known how to deal with.

'Thought you weren't coming in,' she says. 'Wasn't really sure how to play it. You know, after…'

She smiles awkwardly.

I'm still not sure what to say. I may have got up late, but I took my time. Drank a lot of water. Showered, cleaned my teeth. Got dressed. Made coffee and a slice of toast. Sat and studied my phone and tried to remember.

'I had a late night,' she says.

'Yeah?'

'Yeah. Was just about to get into bed, then the alarm went off. Someone had broken into the lodge hall. I shouldn't have driven down. Took me longer than walking, the car slithering about all over the place. Whoever it was, was long gone when I got there.' A pause, and then the repeated, 'Long gone.'

Her look says she knows it was me who was there. I mean, I know the look. I use it all the time in the job while staring across a desk at lying criminals. And while I'd intended being up front about it from the off, now that I'm here, walking into this atmosphere, I'm not at all sure. That lodge, the photographs of those women on the wall. There's something going on in this town, and while it might be the best thing for me to be open about it and ask Mara straight up, I suddenly don't know if I can trust her.

Of course, the atmosphere might just be as a result of the sex. That's what happens.

'What did you find when you got there?' I ask, after another one of those peculiar looks across the office.

'Nothing. Place was empty, alarm going off, door locked. But there were footprints at the back. Someone had been in. Don't know, of course, if anything had been taken, but Mr Ellis should be over in a little while.'

Another pause. I need to speak to Ellis.

This feels weird. And I could have sat at my kitchen table all morning, and I wouldn't have been able to work out how to handle this. But if she has a key to the lodge hall, and has been in, and she's assuming it was me who broke in, then she knows I've seen that wall of photographs.

'You've been into the hall?' I ask.

'Well, I was in last night. That was the first time. The alarm's never gone off before. At least, not on my watch.'

'Will I be able to get a look?'

'You interested in the break-in?'

'Possibly.'

'You think it might have something to do with Alice's disappearance?'

'Did Alice have anything to do with the lodge?'

She doesn't answer straight away. More of the same awkwardness. Under other circumstances, I'd think it was regular post-sex regret. I could write the book on what that's like in the office the day after. This has a whole other dimension, and I can't tell if it's because I saw that picture of her on the wall, or if she knows I've seen it.

Jesus.

The thought just drops into my head out of nowhere. Alice Schäfer came to my house in the middle of the night. She fucked me. I was... I don't know what I was, but I remember Alice now. I remember what we did.

Or maybe, if I can just sound like all the world's worst pop songs all at once, I was dreaming.

Dreaming makes way more sense.

'Sergeant?'

She looks kind of amused/curious, which doesn't really imply she's hiding anything. But I don't *want* her to be hiding anything, which may skewer my thinking.

'My drink was spiked last night,' I say.

She looks a little surprised, then straightens and wags a finger.

'Oh, no, you're not getting away with th –'

'Sorry, sorry, I don't mean at your house. There was an opened bottle of wine in my fridge. I had a drink from it when I got home. And as soon as I had some…' I make a losing my mind gesture. 'I was just out of it.'

'You'd had a fair bit to drink earlier on.'

'No, this was different. I mean, I've been drunk often enough in my life. I know what it feels like, and this wasn't it. This was stranger, and much, much more instantaneous.' I snap my fingers.

'So what happened?'

'So what *happened*?'

'Yeah, what happened? If someone spiked your drink, what happened? Why did they do it?'

Again I stand and stare at her stupidly. I really hadn't thought this through before coming here. No game plan. Nothing.

I was raped by the twenty-two year-old missing woman, and the photo I took in the lodge hall I'd broken in to was deleted from my phone.

The door opens, snapping the moment. I could have stood there all day and wouldn't have been able to think of anything. I mean, do I really think I had sex with Alice Schäfer? A fucked-up psychotic dream seems far more likely. Someone messing with me. Don't know how, don't know why. But I certainly don't want to say that, because that's saying that this story, this thing that's going on here, is about me. The tale of the missing woman is about *me*. That's some major projection.

'Here to confess are you?'

It's Ellis, come to save me from the discomfort of the moment.

Ellis, I don't mind lying to. Much firmer ground.

'The constable says the lodge got broken into last night?'

He answers with a harsh stare, then turns his contemptuous look on Mara.

'You and me need to talk,' he says.

Mara doesn't respond. I should leave them to it.

'There are some people I should speak to,' I say. 'You know what the movie folks are doing today?'

'They've moved the entire operation into the old hotel,' says Mara, with a lovely undertone of disappointment that I'm running away. 'The people staying in Fort William came up yesterday afternoon, they're all there. Not sure, you know, if they're filming, or still in the rescue planning stage.'

OK, so that's good. They should all be in one place.

I nod without really directing the movement towards her, stare at the floor for a moment, have a brief Mitty-esque vision of having a tiny microphone I can surreptitiously attach to the underside of a desk, contemplate if there's anything I could do with my phone, accept that there really isn't, with the two of them looking at me with various degrees of bemusement and disdain, and then I ignore Ellis, look at Mara and say, 'I'll be back in a little while.'

I smile like there's nothing amiss, nod at Ellis, then turn and walk back out into the cold.

Close the door behind me, and stop for a moment. Chill air on the inside of my nostrils, the crunch of snow beneath my boots, the cold loch stretching away in front of me, snow on the hills beyond, their tops masked in low, pale cloud, the fir trees at the head of the loch piled high with snow, the feeling of more to come, the cloud of my breath dispersing in the chill, in the air there's the feeling of Christmas.

Not Christmas. Not so much. Christmas is six weeks away. The chances of this snow still being around by then, in these warming planet days, are zilch. Chances are this snow'll be gone by the end of the weekend, and it's already late Saturday morning.

Maybe the film crew will decide to sit it out, and wait for the thaw. It surely can't be far off. Not that I've looked at a weather forecast.

Have barely moved from outside the station, and suddenly I get the uncomfortable feeling of a pair of eyes on my back. I don't turn, and walk quickly away from the station, down the short flight of steps, and back towards town.

20

This looks like the shitiest film in all shitdom. I mean, we've all seen no end of bad films, right? Sometimes a decent budget and good cast might mask the shitiness for twenty minutes, but at some stage, there's no overcoming a lousy script. There just isn't. But when you get the perfect storm of low budget, bad acting and lousy script, then you're in trouble. Then you know from Scene One.

And that's what we have here. A young male vampire tries to seduce a woman using the tried and tested method of bullshitting. I mean, it's not like it doesn't work in real life, after all, so good luck to him.

'Your eyes are jewels…'

Jesus. You're a vampire, kid, just bite her fucking neck and be done with it.

I get a tap on my shoulder, saving me from the horror. Abigail Connolly, for whom I've been waiting at the back of the set. We leave quietly, she carefully closes the door behind us, we're scowled at by a couple of people, and then we're across a corridor and into the old bar. Red leather chairs, a worn tartan carpet, black and white pictures of the mountains on the walls, the deserted bar set to the side, the shelves empty, the room cold and bright and desolate and sad.

My eyes linger on it for a moment, subconsciously hoping, no doubt, to stumble across an active bottle of alcohol, and then I join the movie's head of casting, sitting in chairs either side of a low table by the window.

I can't stop myself looking out on the loch, but I guess she's seen enough of the loch and the snow by now, and she gets right down to it.

'What's up? Take it you've had no luck finding the girl?' A moment, and then she adds, 'We'd better hope she's not out there.'

'No, nothing. You haven't thought of anything in the last couple of days? No one's said or remembered anything new?'

She smiles kindly, as though she feels sorry for me. Here we are, the lost police officer, running around, pointlessly chasing his tail. She's nice, though, and manages not to be condescending.

'I'm afraid not. We obviously haven't got much done, but half the team's been focussed on converting the narrative to meet the new winter landscape, and those not involved in it mostly appear to have been acting like they're in a Wham! video.' A pause, and then she says, 'Partying,' just in case I thought it might be some other thing Wham! did in videos.

'You're from around here,' I say, tossing in the question from nowhere.

She looks a little confused, then I get the, 'What? Sorry?'

'You were brought up around here?'

'Do I sound like it?'

'Not at all.'

'Why would you think that? I'm from Surrey. Esher. One of them.'

'One of whom?'

She makes a dismissive gesture.

'Nothing. Just, I'm from Esher, insomuch as that defines anyone. What made you think I was from here?'

'You've never been here before coming for the movie? You've been on holiday, something like that?'

'I lived here for a year. Just a year. When I was twenty-one, twenty-two, that kind of age. I did ecology at uni, got myself on a year's placement at the outdoor centre…,' and she points along to the far end of the loch, 'follow the road, take a left. It used to be along there. Closed about ten years ago. I got lodgings here in the village, used to ride my bike to the site every day.' Another pause, then the wistful smile. 'Best year of my life. Loved every minute of it. Then when it came time to look for a full-time job, for reasons that no one can explain, I got a gig in a casting agency, and here we are, twenty years later. Weird how the world works.'

'It's a coincidence the movie's here, or you had some part in the location chosen for the shoot?'

A pause, then, 'A bit of both. I wasn't involved in the decision to come here, that was made way before I had anything to do with the production. But they came to my agency looking for someone, I saw the brief, and I was like, I'll have that!' Then she adds, with a hint of a conspiratorial tone, 'Despite the movie.'

She smiles, including me in her embarrassment at the awfulness unfolding in the other room, then turns to the window, makes a small gesture to the snowscape and says, 'Never saw anything quite like this when I was here before.'

'You didn't know anyone you could stay with, rather than being put in the kingdom of the spiders?'

'We're here for a month, all in. That was just too long. I still have contacts up here, a few folk I know and whatnot, but no one I can invite myself to for four weeks. No way.'

I take a couple of moments because I want her to look at me before I ask the next question, then when she engages I say, 'Were you involved with the Lodge of St Augustine? When you were here previously?'

'Why?'

'*Why?*'

'Why would you ask that?'

'We can talk about that,' I say, 'but can you answer the question?'

She stares warily across the low table. I was right to hold her gaze, as the shadow continues to grow. And then she lies.

'No.'

'Really?'

'I knew about it, I know it's still going on, but I had nothing to do with it. It's like, it's like a bunch of men, isn't it?'

'Seems to be.'

'So why did you ask if I had anything to do with it?'

'Someone said you might've done, that's all.'

'Someone?'

'You know I'm not getting into *he said she said* or anything. There's a lodge, and I heard tell that while it's basically a club for boys, there might be some women involved in some way.'

'And I might be one of those women?'

'That's correct.'

She takes a moment to assess the direction of questioning, then nods as though understanding it. I doubt she is understanding it, though. Presumably the word has gotten around that Sgt Hutton broke into the place, but I don't know that the word has reached as far as Abigail. I don't think she'd be regarding me with such wary curiosity if she'd known this was coming. She would have better prepared her face.

111

'What other women are we talking about?' she asks.

'Doesn't matter. We're interested in you. What was your involvement with them?'

'I don't think involvement's the word.'

I ask the next, obvious, question with a gesture.

'Look, it's a small place. Not many people do what I did, come up and stay for a year. I got known. I knew some of the guys. It was no big thing.' A pause, and then, 'You know, you'll find the same thing this year, with the film folk up for a while. Some of them will get to know some of the lodge guys. Doesn't mean much. Doesn't amount to a hill of beans.'

'You meant that as a *Casablanca* reference?'

Another smile.

We look at each other across the low table. I can't read her. Sure, she's hiding something, but there could be a variety of reasons for that, and none of them could have anything to do with why Alice Schäfer is missing.

I want to mention the wall of photos, but it doesn't feel right just yet. I have no idea what showing my hand to Abigail Connolly means, but that's all the more reason for keeping it to myself for now. And since she's in denial mode, all she would say is that she doesn't know what I'm talking about.

'You know if Alice Schäfer had anything to do with the lodge?'

'Why… wait, what? Why would I know that?'

'You know some of the lodge people, you know Alice…'

'Well, that seems a stretch, but no, I don't.'

'Have you caught up with your old lodge contacts since you've been here?'

I get the blank stare at that one. There's the question. This puts her on the back foot, and I hadn't even thought much of it.

'You seem unsure.'

'I don't have anything to say.'

'You could answer the question. It's fairly straightforward, and I'm not about to ask for names and places and verbatim records of your meetings. Just, have you met anyone you know to be in the lodge, that's all?'

'Yes,' she says, after another short gap.

'Who?'

'What?'

'Who did you meet?'

'You just said you weren't going to ask for names.'

'Who did you meet?'

A shake of the head. Annoyed now, rather than taken aback.

'I'm not telling you. I don't suppose it's that big a secret who's a member and who's not, but it's not my secret to tell. You can ask other people.'

Now she glances at the door. The look that says it might be time for her to be getting on with the day job.

I contemplate throwing a couple of names into the mix, but I'd quickly run up against the very short list of people I actually know in the village. That's the trouble with being an outsider.

'If you have no further questions, I should probably be getting on.'

I run a contemplative hand across three days of stubble. It's a manoeuvre with something of the Henry Cavill about it. Drives women wild. Timing not so great on this occasion.

'However it was you were involved in the lodge, and we both know it transcends you just happening to know these people… And I get you don't want to talk about that, but whatever it was, did you know anyone else who was involved in the same way? Other women?'

'You think I'd tell you if I did? That's curious.'

'I have to ask.'

'On the one hand you accept I'm protecting the men, but then you think I'd happily throw the women under the bus.'

'If nothing untoward is going on, if no one has anything to hide, then no one is getting thrown under a bus.'

'You seem pretty focussed on the lodge all the same, and as far as I know, all they're guilty of is making too many boring speeches at the Burns Supper every January.'

'You don't need to know why I'm asking. Did you know any other women who were involved with them the same way you were involved?'

She switches off the attitude now, showing the police officer a little respect for his need to investigate. It was probably the cool Cavill move that tipped the scales.

'No. We don't need to get into the way in which I was involved, but it doesn't matter anyway, not if you want to go and speak to anyone else. It wasn't the kind of thing anyone talked about.'

Now we're getting somewhere, although it transpires it's only because she's wrapping it up and she's allowed herself to be a little more indiscreet in her parting.

'You have to tell me what that means.'

'What I have to do is get back to work,' she says, getting to her feet as she speaks.

'Whatever it was you did, is it the kind of thing Alice Schäfer might have done?'

There's a knowing smile on her lips, a moment when it feels like she's about to say, 'Oh yes!' for all the world like she's David Tennant, and then she elects to keep it to herself, smiles, nods, and instead says, 'I really have to go. See you around, Sergeant.'

And she's gone.

I watch her walk from the old, deserted bar, then turn back to the snowscape stretching down to the cold loch, and away to the white slopes disappearing into the clouds on the other side.

21

'The whole zombie thing is pointless, man, right?'

Walking back through town, having interviewed a further four people on the movie set. Nothing more on Alice, and, of course, there was no one with whom I could discuss the lodge. Then I found myself leaving the old hotel at the same time as DeShaun, the props guy.

'Not sure why it's any more pointless than any other type of movie,' I say, going with the idle chat, 'but go on.'

Crisp, winter air. More snow coming, none currently falling. The snow still lies thick on the ground, killing sound. Nothing to be heard bar the crunch of our footsteps. A few tyre tracks down either side of the road, but not enough to make the road generally passable. No sign of a gritter, and word is that neither have they been out on the main road. On top of that, forecast is now for another bucketload to fall later.

'There's nothing you can do with a zombie,' he says. 'Like, with vampires, there are all sorts of options. Vampires can be sexy and urbane, they can be cool, or they can be cunts. They can be anything, really. But zombies? What are you going to do with that? They'll bite you. They eat stuff. And that's literally it. Sure, sometimes people try to give them something more, but it never works. And you know why?'

'Nope,' I say, this being more thought than I've ever given to zombies in film before.

'Because you're not being true to the concept. The zombie, at heart, is a base, brutish, vicious killing machine. Period. That's it. And he doesn't necessarily even *want* to kill you. He doesn't want anything. It's all basic instinct. Give him anything more than that, and it's like when some boring-ass politician reads a scripted joke. It's just wrong.'

'So the next movie you're doing is a zombie flic?'

'Yep. Three weeks in Suffolk, this side of Christmas.'

'Why'd you sign up for it then?'

'I didn't, as such. That's not how it works. I work for Film

Set Solutions. Basically we're available for rent. Just go where we're told, and work on whatever independent production we get that week.'

'Keeps you busy?'

'For now. I mean, seriously, there's so much production these days. There are literally like a million streaming services, and they all want original content. So many movies and shows getting made.' A pause, and then, 'Not many of them are as shit as this one though,' and we both laugh. 'Anyway, I've got a nice side-line in phone hardware when I need it. Always busy, you know, always something to do.'

'What does that mean?'

'What does what mean?'

'Phone hardware sounds a little vague.'

'It's meant to. Not telling a copper all my secrets,' and he laughs.

'Probably best.'

'Aye. Let's just talk about how shit the movie is,' he says with a smile. 'Much safer ground.'

'How come they got the guy off of *Vigil*? He must be a proper actor, right? I mean, *Vigil* had people in it, didn't it? Like the *you know nothing* lassie?'

'Sure, but they're all doing it now. Like I said, there are so many shows getting made, it's an absolute feast for actors. Once your name's out there, you're getting tonnes of offers. And actors are like dogs.'

'Don't know where their next meal is coming from, so they gorge while the bowl's full.'

'Exactamundo,' says DeShaun. 'And chances are no one will ever see this shit, so our guy doesn't have to worry about it being a career-killer. He gets a few weeks in the Highlands, he gets to shag a couple of birds, and he gets paid for his trouble. You know the basic law of low budget movie making, right?'

'I know none of the laws of movie making.'

Up ahead I can see a dim light through the stained glass windows of the lodge hall. Ellis must have gone there after speaking to Mara. Time to once more annoyingly insert myself in the lodge master's business.

'Let's say your budget's a million, right? The law of low budget filmmaking is, if you want people to actually come and see your shitty low budget movie, you need to scrimp and save on everything else, while spending as much money as possible on the biggest star you can get. If he or she's costing you nine hundred and fifty g's, then go get 'em. You can make your movie for fifty g's, no bother. A decent script'll carry you through.'

'You're not advised to spend any money on the script, then?'

'Scripts are like footballers. You can pay a lot and they're still shit, and you can find a gem in the lower leagues for buttons. And sure, you might dig up an actor that can put in a good performance out of nowhere, but the star? The name that gets your low budget movie into festivals? You *have* to pay for that. That's just how it is.'

'Actors are like dogs, scripts are like footballers,' I say and he smiles at the summation.

'That's the business. And wait, let's talk about the actresses. You know the most important thing, *the* most important thing with an actress?'

Oh, I think I do, or at least, I know what he thinks is the most important thing.

'Let's not go there, kid,' I say.

'And you know, you can always tell,' he continues anyway, smiling. 'A casting director can always tell who –'

'Sorry to cut you off, I've got someone I need to speak to. I'll catch you later.'

'Sure sure,' he says.

'Give me a shout if you hear anything about Alice, eh?' I throw in as an afterthought, and he nods enthusiastically, seemingly happy with his small part in the investigation, and then I turn away from him, cross the road, and head back up the path to the lodge hall.

Two sets of footprints, one smaller than the other. A woman's footsteps. I'm going to say that Constable Mara has returned to the hall, Ellis in tow.

Chap the door, take a step back. Turn and look behind me while I wait. No one to be seen. Not sure where DeShaun was heading, but he's already turned a corner, or headed indoors. There's no light currently on in the newsagent's, and I can't see Meryl Streep inside. All is quiet, all is white. This is like the line in that popular Christmas dirge, *In The Bleak Midwinter*, the one that goes on and on about how much fucking snow there is. We get it. It snowed.

The door opens.

117

'Sergeant,' says Constable Mara.

A moment's hesitation, and then she steps back, and I cross the threshold into the small entrance hall, pausing to kick the snow off my boots against the door frame.

'Ellis is here?' I say, as she follows me into the main hall.

I stop, taking a look around. The lighting is low, the room gloomy and dark. Must be the only room with windows in the entire town that's not benefitting from the brightness of the snow outside, the small, high, stained-glass windows having little positive effect.

'He's in the office.' She pauses, then adds, 'He's still assuming it was you who broke in here last night.'

Hands in pockets, standing in the middle of the room, looking around. Far as I can tell, nothing's changed from last night.

'Anything stolen?'

'Nope. Which is one of the reasons he thinks it was you who broke in.'

Can feel her eyes on the back of my head, and I finally turn and look at her.

'Let's go and have a chat, shall we?'

I smile, I get a cautious look of curiosity in response.

'Was it you?' she asks. 'I mean, to be fair, Sergeant, I'm also kind of assuming it was.'

'No,' I say. With a long history of lying, I'm confident I can pull it off, then I add, with that cheeky grin that always drives the women wild, 'I suspect whoever did break in, probably wore gloves, so there'll be little point in checking for prints.'

After all, the guy who broke in, *was* wearing gloves.

I get the rueful look, then she passes me, and I follow her through the door, into the small hallway at the back, and then into Ellis's office.

Ellis is sitting behind his desk, hunched forward, elbows resting on the top. There's a glass of whisky at his right hand, the room barely illuminated by a small desk lamp. I don't immediately turn and look at the wall to my right, although just standing here, looking at him, I get the sense of the change. It comes with the prickling of the skin, the feeling of unease creeping up my spine.

'What do you want?' he asks. He doesn't look at me.

'When was the last time you had a break-in?'

He doesn't answer immediately, staring darkly at an indistinct spot, then slowly he lifts his gaze.

'Is that relevant?' he asks, then when I open my mouth to answer, he cuts me off. 'Or are you hoping to imply that break-ins are a regular occurrence here, so there's no need to implicate the out-of-town police officer?'

'When was the last time you had a break-in?' I repeat, deadpan. Not in the mood for the, admittedly justified, sarcasm.

'Two thousand and four. The first flush of *Da Vinci Code* fever, and some young clown thought he could discover the whereabouts of the Holy Grail by breaking into a lodge house.'

'And you weren't in charge back then?'

'What makes you think I'm in charge now?'

He grimaces after he says that, and I get a scornful riposte to my look of curiosity.

'Who else would be?'

'The workings of the lodge are none of your business, Sergeant.'

I glance at Mara, but she has nothing to add to the conversation. Mara looks a little uncomfortable.

'And did he find what he was looking for?'

'Did who find what?'

'The whereabouts of the Holy Grail?'

Another scornful, deadpan look in return.

I hold it for a while, and then decide to act on that weird feeling I still have crawling across my skin. I look around the room, making sure to neither start, nor finish, at the spot I'm really interested in. Old, dark paintings on the walls. The large cabinet with various lodge items locked behind glass doors. A portrait of a former grandmaster. The painting above the fireplace, and then the wall of photographs.

I get that feeling of unease, and the shiver.

They're gone. In their place, another painting. Glencoe in winter, a stag on the grass, low on the moor, below the snowline. I look at the wall for another second, two, to see if there's any evidence of the hanging of the photographs, or of the evidence being covered up, then I continue the look around the room. Past Mara, past the bookcase, another cabinet in the corner, and back to Ellis sitting at the desk.

He hasn't taken his eyes off me.

'Seen anything interesting, Sergeant?'

'D'you think last night's break-in could have had anything

to do with the disappearance of Alice Schäfer?'

He straightens his shoulders a little, and the first sign of light relief – albeit scornful light relief – shows on his face.

'Do I think it might be related to Alice?'

'Yes.'

'Sergeant, you broke in here last night. I didn't see you, I can't prove it, I doubt anyone ever will, and I sure as fuck doubt you'll ever admit to it, but you know *I know* you did. You were here. So, tell me, what do you think the lodge has to do with Alice's disappearance?'

I'm not sure what my logic here is, and why I don't just tell all and ask about the photographs on the wall. Nevertheless, for now, it seems sensible to keep my own counsel.

'Let's imagine I didn't break in here,' I say, and he gives me a contemptuous look, 'who d'you suppose it would have been?'

No answer.

'Is there any reason why anyone would've thought there was a connection between Alice and the lodge?'

The same contemptuous look, the same silence in response.

I turn to Mara.

'You know of any other women connected to this place?'

She looks a little curious at the question.

'Other women?'

'There's a strong male bastion vibe about this whole thing,' I say, enjoying talking about the lodge as though Ellis isn't in the room. 'There oughtn't to be a relationship between the lodge and Alice, but someone thinks there is. I'm the outsider here, I have no idea what that might be, but maybe there's something. Do they have, I don't know, like a prom queen or some shit li –'

'Fuck's sake,' mutters Ellis behind me. 'A fucking prom queen. The fuck do you think this is?'

I raise an eyebrow at Mara.

'I'm not really sure what you're looking for,' she says.

I hesitate before saying this in front of him, then I go ahead anyway.

'Maybe there's a woman I can speak to, maybe there's someone else who had a similar relationship to this place as Alice had, and maybe that woman will be a little more forthcoming with information than this guy. Or any of the other men, for that matter.'

'What the fuck does that even mean, anyway?' snaps Ellis,

and I turn. 'A similar relationship? Alice didn't have *any* relationship.'

'Someone appears to have thought otherwise.'

'It was you! Jesus, you were literally the person to break in here, and then you're using that as an excuse to formulate some absurd correlation between Alice and the lodge. My God, the neck of you fucking police. Just get out, Sergeant, you are not welcome here.'

I stop myself making some lousy *what are you going to do, call the police?* line, hold his acerbic gaze for a little while longer, then turn and nod at Mara.

'I'll see you back at the station,' I say, and then walk quickly past her, back through the hallway into the main hall, and then slow as I go through the large room, taking as much of it in as possible as I pass through.

As I get to the front door, I look behind me, and right enough, there she is, Mara, standing at the door at the back of the hall, dispatched by the leader of the pack to make sure I leave.

We hold the look for a moment, then she lifts a dispassionate hand, and I turn away, back out into the cold.

22

So, I break into the lodge, these guys know I broke into the lodge, they'll have assumed I saw those photographs on the wall, and they removed them. Not only that, I was drugged, and someone came into my house, opened my phone, and deleted the picture. Now I have nothing to prove those photos were on the wall. And yet, they know that I know they were there, and that I'll have seen Alice and I'll have seen Constable Mara.

I guess them pretending the photographs weren't there, is no different from me pretending I didn't break in in the first place. Seems we're all lying to each other, which is not so much unlike any other investigation.

After leaving the hall, I was aiming to make another visit to Meryl Streep at the newsagents, but see that it's still closed. I'd noticed earlier, of course, but presumed she'd done that thing shopkeepers do in small places like this, like stick a *closed* sign on the door while they nip to the toilet or have a ten-minute cigarette and coffee break.

Seems odd that the shop's closed on a Saturday, but it's not like I know anything of the way this woman conducts her business, and so, after a quick glance at the door reveals no sign of life inside, I trudge through the snow, back to the warmth of the station.

When Mara gets back there, half an hour later, I'm standing at the window, drinking coffee, looking out on the vast snowscape, and the chill slate grey of the loch. Snow has started falling again, the temperature perfect for it to form and settle.

She closes the door, takes a moment to consider the situation, removes her jacket, changes her shoes, goes to the small table and pours herself a coffee from the percolator, and then comes and stands beside me at the window.

If there wasn't a troubling missing person case to investigate, this would be pretty fucking idyllic. Trapped in a small Highland village for the weekend with an attractive woman? You'd get a ninety-minute movie out of that on some lousy Freeview film channel.

'Sex was great,' I say, after a while.

She laughs, comes out of the laugh smiling.

'Yeah, it was,' she says.

'You feel guilty?'

She takes another drink, doesn't look at me while she considers the question.

'Why'd you ask?'

'Married people do. I've been married and had sex, and I felt guilty. The last married woman I slept with felt guilty. She still feels guilty.'

'That's the woman you're currently in love with?'

A beat, then, 'Yeah. She feels guilty.'

'Do you want her to leave her husband?'

Well, that turned on a sixpence. I'd just started a casual conversation about sex, and now we're talking about *this*.

'I don't know,' I say, and suddenly my inner angst, given an unexpected outlet, decides to spew forth. 'As I said, I've been married three times. I won't say I completely ruined the lives of those three women, but I certainly ruined the marriages, and I made them miserable for a while. And I wouldn't want to do that to her.'

'Maybe you wouldn't.'

'History suggests otherwise.'

'You seem like a decent enough person,' she says, and I can't help laughing.

'I'm a fucked-up drunk. I have sex with people I shouldn't. And if she left her husband for me, I'm sure I'd be great for a while, and I'd do what I should, and I wouldn't do what I shouldn't. But one day, however... one day it would come.'

Well, that'll do it for my inner angst. Said enough.

There's a pause while we drink, then she says, 'Sounds like you're hiding.'

'Really?'

'Yeah. You're looking for excuses. Classic man, scared of the commitment.'

'I've committed three times in the past.'

'You get married, you get scared, you sabotage the marriages. A self-fulfilling prophecy.'

'You're the married woman who just slept with another man,' I say, in the kind of straw man argument that politicians embrace on a daily basis.

123

'We're talking about you,' she says.

'We are, aren't we?' and that glib remark is thankfully the end of the conversation on my relationship with DI Kallas. Of course, being in love with Kadri Kallas as I am, I *want* to talk about her. But at the same time, I feel uncomfortable talking about her, and I doubt she wants me discussing the two of us with another officer, regardless of how detached Mara is from the situation.

'Sex was great,' I say, with a slightly comic, let's-start-from-the-beginning tone, and she laughs again.

'Yes, it was. And looks like we're going to be stuck here for a couple of days.'

'Yeah.'

'Though did you see the forecast for Monday?'

'Never look at the weather forecast.'

'Interesting. Twelve degrees and raining.'

'Ah. There goes the snow.'

'Yep. Going to snow the rest of today, and by tomorrow afternoon it'll be sleet, and by tomorrow evening, the warm front from the south-west will be in full force. Come Monday...'. She snaps her fingers. 'There goes the snow.'

'Do the movie people know? They could wait.'

'They have to wrap by Tuesday. The *Vigil* guy has to be in Thailand for the filming of *Mission Impossible 8*.'

'Really?'

'Bit part, I heard, but you don't want to miss out on the chance to get punched in the face by the crazy Scientology midget.'

I can't help laughing at that, and she laughs with me, and then the laughter goes, and once again we're standing in silence, staring out at the bleak midwinter, drinking coffee. Wait, it's not midwinter, is it? A couple of days ago, in fact, it was still autumn, and it will be again by Monday.

'Either way, I'll be free this evening,' she says, with a lovely lightness of touch.

I smile, I let her see me smiling, I don't reply. Nevertheless, I get that weird feeling in my throat, and suddenly, because it's who I am, I could have her right now, and the thought of waiting until this evening, and the concern about her photograph being on that wall, and her potential involvement in the case, and the worry that while I'm looking at Ellis with suspicion, she's working with him, she's on his side, all that goes flying out the window, out there into the cold wastes of a chill November day in the Highlands, and I just want to take her in my arms, and kiss her and run my hands all over her, and undo her jeans, and pull them down and sit her on the edge of the desk and then part her legs and thrust my head between them, and listen to her moan as I bring her to an orgasm. Right here. Right now.

'What are you thinking?' she asks.

'I'm free this evening too,' I manage to say.

I swallow, though not because I've just drunk coffee.

'It's a date,' she says.

We need an emergency change of subject.

'Is the newsagents' usually closed on a Saturday?'

She glances at me, a little curious, then looks back towards town, in the direction of Meryl Streep's place, though from here all we can see of it is the back of the building, which looks out onto the banks of the loch.

'You mean Margaret's?'

'Yeah. If Margaret's the one who looks like Meryl Streep.'

A moment, and then the nod. 'Yeah, I see what you mean. I noticed it was closed too. Just assumed she'd stepped out for a moment. She lives above the shop, so it's not like she'd have been unable to get to work.'

'Doesn't look like she's opened at all today.'

'Don't know. Maybe she just decided there would be so few customers there was no point. That's a long day standing behind a counter, in order to sell one magazine.'

'I don't know Margaret well, obviously, but she doesn't strike me as the kind of person who'd choose not to open because there'll be no custom. She has a here-to-serve vibe. One can imagine her equating keeping her store open with the guys playing Schubert on the Titanic.'

'You're right. Bang on, in fact. I'll call her.'

She turns away from the window, and walks to her desk. I look out over the bleak, wintry land, and in an instant the lightness of conversation has gone, the desire that was raging a minute ago has gone, and been replaced by a familiar sense of unease, and the awareness of the coming of the storm.

23

We're standing outside the door to the side of the newsagent's, which leads to the flat above. Snowing heavily now, and we're both slightly hunched in the cold. There are several sets of footsteps evident around the front of the building, but then that could easily have been people coming to the shop and finding it closed.

'This isn't good,' says Mara, a few seconds after her third rap of the door.

'Nope.'

'I'm getting a bad feeling. You getting a bad feeling?'

'Had it since before we walked down here.'

She knocks again, then takes a step back from the door.

'I don't really want to break in. It'll be pretty embarrassing if she's just gone out for a long walk or, you know, fallen asleep in the bath. But… God, I don't know, she could've had a heart attack, so we'd better do something.'

That bad feeling I've got is nothing to do with her having a heart attack.

I produce the familiar lockpick from my pocket, and get to work. I can feel her looking at me, a combination of curiosity and amusement. The sure and certain knowledge that this is how I so seamlessly broke into the hall.

A simple lock, and the door opens in a little over twenty seconds. A very small hallway, and then stairs leading straight up. A couple of coats on hangers, a couple of pairs of boots placed neatly side-by-side. I indicate the snow boots. That's not a good sign. No idea how often you're going to need snow boots in a place like this, but today's the day if ever there was one. Meryl Streep hasn't gone anywhere. The odds just rose dramatically on the heart attack. Or, as we all suspect, the other thing.

'Crap,' mutters Mara beneath her breath.

I walk up the stairs in front, knock sharply on the door at the top, and then enter the house without waiting.

The door opens to a small hallway with four further doors off. Directly in front, a small kitchen, in which there's no sign of her. Quickly along the hall, and into the room at the front. The sitting room. Hesitate when I get to the door and see what's waiting for us, and then I enter the room more slowly, Mara following.

'Fuck,' escapes her lips in a low voice.

Meryl Streep is blue, her body long gone cold.

I should probably stop calling this woman Meryl Streep. The actual Meryl Streep, far as I know, doesn't currently have a knife buried in her eye socket.

'Should check the rest of the house,' says Mara, and she turns away, and walks quickly back out into the hall. I don't follow. Whoever did this is long gone.

I step forward and place the backs of my fingers gently on the side of her face. Margaret is sitting in her seat, in front of the television, as she will have done so often in her life. She's sitting upright, better posture than I ever have when watching the TV, (and I'm alive), her hands resting on her legs. A slightly unnatural position, but one that looks serene and calm. Peaceful. I can picture her sitting like this, watching *Midsomer Murders*, marrying up dubious characters on the show with people she suspected of getting up to no good in the village.

The hilt of the knife has been rammed right into her face. There's not a huge amount of blood. Some has run down her cheek, dripping off her chin, disappearing into the dark blue of a thick, woollen jumper. Three large splatters on the white collar of whatever top she was wearing beneath the jumper. Still, not much blood to show for such a brutal, and instantly fatal attack.

Turn and look across the road. All that can be seen from here is the top of the hall, and the roofs of a couple of the buildings to the right. Hills stretching away behind, a few small cottages lost in the snow. No one else would have been looking in on this.

Hands in pockets, I start walking around the room, aimlessly checking it out. Nothing to be seen or found here, and I shouldn't touch anything at this point anyway. A sofa; three small side tables from a stack, individually placed around the room; a familiar panoply of ornaments and nick-nacks and paraphernalia; a couple of paintings not by Jack Vettriano.

A magazine on the sofa. The Economist. OK, we all have our first impressions, and I'll admit I had Margaret here down as a Woman & Home or a Scottish Life or Shit TV Weekly type of a gal. But the Economist? Didn't see that coming. In the way of the shallow, first impression, instant judgement specialist, I immediately have a little more respect for Margaret.

In one of the other rooms I can hear Mara on the phone. I go back over towards Margaret and take a look at the knife.

A broad kitchen knife. In the panoply of kitchen knives, it would be somewhere in the middle, somewhere between the bread knife, and one of those little-assed knives you use for cutting up cucumber. Will need to look in the kitchen to see if the killer just grabbed something out of Margaret's knife set, or whether they would have come prepared. Unless there's an obvious gap in a knife block, it will likely be hard to tell for sure.

'Hey,' says Mara, and she comes to stand beside me, looking down at Margaret.

'You speak to Fort William?'

'Yeah. We're on our own.'

'Really?'

'Road's blocked. Helicopters aren't flying. Looking at the weather forecast, they say we're unlikely to get anyone before Monday. Late Sunday a possibility, but don't hold your breath.'

'Epic,' I say, then I leave it a moment, before adding, 'Well, it's been nice working with you, Constable, but I think I'll go back to my holiday now.'

Unused to the high quality of my dry humour, I get a quick glance from her, then she sees I'm joking, and shakes her head. There's been a murder on her patch. She's not in the mood.

'We need to do as good a job as we can, under the circumstances. I'll call the doc, get her over here to take a look, and I'll nip back to the station.'

'You got a P-73?' I ask.

The P-73, the do-it-yourself forensic kit for the police officer in need of a SOCO team.

'I used it on your place after the chicken.'

'Of course, sorry.'

'You ever had to use one?'

'Nope,' I say. 'We always have people to hand. Still, I did the course seven or eight years ago, so I should be able to remember which way round to hold the magnifying glass.'

This time I get the rueful smile, then she walks away, takes the phone from her pocket, and makes her next call.

24

The village doctor, Catriona MacDonald, stands with her arms folded, staring down at the body of Margaret Wills. Or, as they keep saying in the newspapers, Meryl Streep. For the sake of narrative consistency, where we're assigning actresses to the bit-part characters, the doc is being played by Judi Dench.

Yep. Judi Dench. We'll leave it at that, shall we?

The three of us are standing in a line, looking down on the corpse. We've been in this position for a couple of minutes now. I guess Mara and I are waiting for the doctor to pronounce. Or do something.

Finally she addresses this very point.

'I'm not sure what it is you're looking for from me,' she says.

'At the very least,' says Mara, with what I know to be her familiar practicality, 'in the first instance I just need you to pronounce her dead. Regardless of how...' and she finishes the sentence with a gesture towards the corpse.

'Oh, she's dead, all right,' says Judi Dench, with a lovely delivery, and I can see the slight movement of Mara's eyes in response.

'Given that there's zero chance of getting a team or a pathologist here in the next twenty-four hours,' I chip in, 'we were wondering if you could just make a quick examination. I know you're not a pathologist, but just a rough stab at time of death, or if there any other marks on her body that might tell us a little more of the story.'

Well, I'm not wrong, this is why she's here, but even as I say it, it sounds utterly unconvincing. Chances are I've seen far more murdered corpses than she has, and I'd likely be no worse off making a guess at the things I just asked of her.

'*I know you're not a pathologist*,' she says, this time with an added scathing quality. 'I know you're not a pilot, but we were wondering if you could have a crack at landing the plane in a hurricane.'

She gives me a side-eye, and I, with the steely I've-had-enough-of-your-snash look of the true professional, return the look, and she nods, reluctantly accepting her assignment. And, presumably, accepting that it's not that unreasonable a request under the circumstances.

She steps forward, takes a moment, and then removes her coat, lays it on the carpet a couple of feet away, then takes a pair of latex gloves from her bag, and kneels down beside the corpse.

'We'll leave you to it for now,' says Mara.

'I won't be long. Then we should get the body to the surgery, leave it there until Monday. I'm not cutting her open, though.'

'Wouldn't want you to, Catriona,' and Judi Dench grunts, then turns her full attention to the corpse.

Mara makes a gesture to me, and then I follow her out of the room, back along the short corridor, and into the bedroom, with its window overlooking a short stretch of snow-covered grass, leading down to the loch. Neither of us can help glancing at the bed as we pass it, just as I can't help saying, 'Not really appropriate, Constable. There'll be time later,' and I get the same look she's probably given me about ten times in the last three days.

The glib comment passes into history, then the two of us are, once again, at a window, looking out on early winter, as the snow falls.

'I shan't lie, Sergeant,' says Mara, straight off the bat, 'this is way out of my league. I've never seen anything like this before. You?'

'Yeah.'

'Really?'

'This kind of thing has followed me around like a shadow my entire career.'

Silence, one that extends from one second to the next, and on.

'Jesus,' says Mara, after some time, then she adds drily, 'You couldn't have gone on holiday to Aberdeen?' and I laugh lightly, as demanded by the line.

'You've actually seen someone stabbed in the eye, or you've been witness to a murder victim? Or victims?'

'Yes, I've seen that, and a whole lot worse besides, but really, we don't need to talk about it.'

'Jesus,' she says again. 'Any insight into who might have

130

done this? Is there a recognisable personality trait you can point to? A *something*, so you can say, well we need to speak to *that* guy?'

'It's rarely so straightforward. You'd think there might be, murder being such an outlandish and unusual act, but no. Perhaps a profiler might be able to come up with something, but if I tried to do that, it'd be not unlike me cutting open Margaret's gullet and trying to decide what time she ate dinner last night.'

Another silence, but it's time that I told her what's on my mind, rather than hiding behind throwaway one-liners.

'Here's the thing,' I say. 'I spoke to Margaret yesterday.'

'When? Why?' She looks curiously at me. Out on the water, to our left, we can see a white motorboat leaving the small pier. Ellis, on his way back across the loch to his home.

'I'd been across the road, didn't get anywhere with Mr Ellis, thought I'd speak to the shopkeeper. Shopkeepers know things.'

'And did she tell you anything?'

'You know, I didn't think she'd been particularly forthcoming. Nevertheless, I got more out of her than I have done anyone else, and I was thinking that if I played her right, there was more to come too.'

'And you think...?' and she lets the sentence go, as she turns and looks back out into the hallway, in the direction of dead Margaret.

'We have a missing person, we have something sinister going on, Margaret talks about it, and then Margaret's dead. First rule of detective club, there's no such thing as coincidence.'

'What did she tell you? I mean, really? And you didn't even tell me you'd spoken to her. Did you tell anyone else?'

'Nope.'

'So, if it was that bad, surely Margaret wouldn't have told anyone either?'

'I presume not. Which means, whoever did this, knew what she was like, suspected she'd talk too much, and decided to permanently close the floodgates of the reservoir before she properly got going.'

I look at her, as I can feel her unease.

'What?' I say.

'That just sounds... I mean, that's crazy, right?'

'Why?'

'All we have here is a missing person. That's it. You just used the word sinister, but where's that even coming from? Maybe Alice just went for a walk, late at night, to clear her mind, and fell over and banged her head or something. Maybe she had a massive bust-up with her parents, then left, and they don't want to admit it because they don't like airing their private business in public. They could save us wasting our time, but they're not going to care. They'd be putting themselves first, and it's not like they'd be the only people on earth to do that. I mean, really, where does sinister come from? Alice could currently be snuggled up in front of a fire with a Swedish masseur, having the time of her life. This, all this, everything we've done up until now could actually have been a waste of time.'

'And now Margaret's dead with a knife in her face, and it's completely unrelated?'

'I don't know. I mean, I'm not saying that, but I just don't think there's enough information to tie the two together.'

'What was rule one of detective club?'

'I'm not buying it.'

'Then, what are you buying? Anything like this ever happened here before? On your watch, or before you arrived?'

She shakes her head, an almost imperceptible movement.

'A stabbing in the eye is an outrageous act. People don't get stabbed in the head in their own homes, not in everyday life. So, where has this come from? Is there anything else going on in town that might point to a similar level of peculiarity? Not the vampire movie, that's just a bunch of people dicking around. What then? Well, hasn't a young woman gone missing with zero explanation? Does this woman have a reputation for sleeping around? Yes, she does. As a result, isn't she a divisive figure? Maybe it's a stretch from divisive to kidnapping, or even murder, but there has to be some explanation for her disappearance that goes beyond her running off with a masseur. So we potentially have something sinister happening to Alice, and now we definitely have something sinister happening to Margaret. If this was Glasgow, if this was *anywhere* and the snow wasn't falling like this and the road wasn't block, there would be a team of two hundred getting thrown at it, and the lead detective wouldn't be a bum sergeant like me. That in there,' I say, pointing back through to the hallway, 'is linked to Alice disappearing, and we need to spend the next two days working on that basis, and have as much as possible to hand over to Fort William when those fuckers turn up here on Monday.'

Are the detective branch in Fort William fuckers? I have no idea. And it's not like I'm blaming them for not being here. Sure, they'd be all over this joint if we were living in Sweden or Finland, but the year Scotland spends the money on the equipment required to clear this kind of snowstorm from the roads, is the first year of fifty when it never snows at all.

'Nice pitch,' she says. 'Not entirely convinced, but let's say, for now, we work to this premise. Margaret speaks to you, you speak to some people, Margaret gets killed. Who did you speak to, and would they have known you'd spoken to Margaret first?'

'The couple at the pottery shop.'

'Bill and Gillian?'

'Yeah. I was speaking to Bill anyway because of the chicken, then Margaret told me Gillian walked in on Bill and Alice having sex a couple of weeks ago.'

'I heard that. What did they have to say about it?'

'Not a lot.'

'And given that everyone in the village heard about that, there would've been no reason for them to suspect Margaret told you.'

'Correct.'

'Anyone else?'

'Nope, not yet.'

'So, who knew you spoke to Margaret? D'you know if you were seen?'

'Like I said, I'd just left the lodge. I crossed the road. I never saw anyone else at that point, I never saw anyone when I left.'

I look at her, one of those significant looks to indicate that I'm not saying the significant thing, that I'm going to let her say the significant thing.

'Mr Ellis might have seen you go into Margaret's place,' she says, resignation in her voice.

'All roads lead to Ellis.'

'Yep.'

We share a glance, and then look back out onto the loch. The boat has advanced quickly out into the middle of the expanse of grey, now getting lost in the snow and the wintry mist.

———

133

'Well, let's just wait and see what mum says, and we'll take it from there,' she says after a moment.

That remark kind of sits there for a while.

Mara's maiden name is MacDonald. The doctor is called MacDonald.

'Catriona's your mum?'

'I'm afraid so,' says Mara. 'It's that kind of a place.'

'She's still dead,' says the voice behind us, and we turn to Dr Judi Dench, the constable's mother, in a traditional doctor scene, removing her gloves and shoving them in her pocket.

'Anything interesting?' I ask.

'Nothing major. She was killed quite some time ago. I'd venture yesterday evening. There's nothing to suggest Margaret was wrestled with in any way prior to the fatal blow with the knife. And that stab in the eye,' and here she mimics the movement, 'was the single blow. I'd say she was sitting there watching television. She maybe let someone in, maybe they even sat and watched TV together, then the killer rose, produced a knife, and thrust it into her face before she could move.'

'Boom.'

'Yes, Sergeant, boom. But, really, I feel I've been forced into an act of wild guesswork by your need for something positive. Be that as it may, that's what I *think*. We should get the body moved. The weather, at least, is in our favour. We have a room at the rear of the surgery. We can place Margaret's corpse in there, I can have a closer look at it for you, although I don't think I'm coming up with anything further. I'll make sure the heating is off in that room, and perhaps leave the window a little ajar.'

She glances from me to Mara and back, and then says, 'That's all I've got. We should get on.'

'We should. Right, we'll find some blankets, then try to manoeuvre her out of here. How far to the surgery?'

'A couple of hundred yards,' they say in unison.

'You all right to get the Land Rover?' I say to Mara, and she nods.

'OK, cool,' I say, and the easy part, the moving the already dead body part of the day, is put into action. 'Is there anyone in the village we should be telling first?'

'I'm on it,' says Mara, and once again she turns away, phone to her ear.

And so the next stage, the straightforward logistical work,

begins.

* * *

An hour and a half later I get back to my house for a quick break, and that's when I find the death snowman.

Yes, the death snowman. I mean, seriously, what the fuck is going on with people?

25

'You ever read Calvin and Hobbes?'

There's a pause. There are a lot of pauses in the conversations Constable Mara and I are sharing.

'Nope,' she replies after a few moments.

I called her ten minutes ago, said she should probably come round to my house. I wasn't sure what she'd think about that, so rather than leave it as a surprise – in case she turned up butt naked under her coat, clutching a tube of sex oil – I tossed into the conversation that someone had been in my house, and they'd left another threat. Or, at least, what was supposed to be a threat. Since the target of the threat does not feel threatened, can it actually be called a threat at all?

'Six-year-old kid, imaginary tiger?'

'Nope,' she says again. 'That was a TV show?'

'American cartoon strip, never licenced to TV or movies.'

We all have our cultural references, right? For some it might be Dickens or Austen, it might be Orwell or Hemingway, Iris Murdoch or Kafka. Mine is Calvin and Hobbes, and that's just how it is.

'There was a kind of running snowman gag. Every winter Calvin would make snowmen, but they wouldn't be the regular kind of a boring-ass snowmen you get in real life. He'd create grotesque masterpieces. Twisted forms, horror snowmen, huge holes in their bodies, or holding their decapitated head in their hands, contorted faces, hunchbacks and monsters, jagged teeth and wild eyes. That kind of thing. Difficult to create in real life.'

'Right,' she says. 'Calvin and Hobbes. Now that you mention it. My roommate at uni had a couple of those.'

She sort of indicates the snowman that's been constructed in the sitting room. Face contorted in pain, head tilted back, a knife embedded in the eye, blood running from the wound, and blood running from its mouth. The rest of the snowman, while slim by snowman standards, is a fairly regulation snowman construction.

'You think this is influenced by Calvin and Hobbes?'

'I'm not sure. In fact, I doubt it. It's more that this reminds me of Calvin and Hobbes, that's all. Perhaps, as a consequence, what is obviously supposed to be a threat, just looks like childish stupidity. I mean, whoever did this can fuck off.'

She rubs her hands together, her breath clouds thickly in the frigid air.

In order to ensure the death snowman didn't melt, the perpetrator turned off the heating, and opened all the windows in the house. The temperature in here is the same as out there. I haven't closed any of the windows yet. Wanted to get all the photos taken, and have Mara take a look, before moving the evidence outside. Maybe he'll still be standing by the time the Fort William squad arrive to take over on Monday morning.

That, I've already decided, is what's going to happen here. I just need to tread water until then, then I can hand it over to someone else and get on with my holiday. Whichever prick did this stupid snowman stunt can then start directing his dumbass death threats at Detective Inspector Heid The Ba'.

'I take it that's food dye or paint or something similar,' she says, indicating the blood.

As it is, I've already checked. The blood ain't faked. I shake my head. Her eyes widen.

'Wait, what?'

'Seems to be real.'

'How'd you know? I mean, you didn't…'

'Wasn't sure how else to check. Didn't take much. Wasn't like I licked it, or anything.'

'What *did* you do?'

'Put a tiny amount on a fork.'

'And it tastes of blood?'

'Far as I could tell. I didn't, you'll understand, want to take too much.'

'What d'you think… I mean, the blood? Whose blood? You can't tell. It's just blood. Sorry, stupid question.'

'I think there's too much to have used their own. I mean, that's more than a finger prick. It could just have been squeezed out of some mince. Or…' and I make a small head movement back towards town.

'Margaret.'

'Margaret. Or a rabbit or a whatever. We'll need to get it tested.'

137

'And that ain't happening any time soon. What d'you want to do?'

Since this is her patch, I'm inclined to defer to her, but I have to remember that I'm the senior officer here, I'm the one with the burden of murder inquiry experience.

'We photograph our bloody, white friend here. Every angle. We try to establish how the perpetrator broke in, but I think we already know they likely have a key. We'll take a substantial sample of the red snow, stick it in the freezer, and then move the fella back outside. Recreate him out there.' A pause, and then I add, 'Close the windows, turn the heating on. Alternatively, we leave everything as it is until the cavalry arrive, and I go and find somewhere else to stay for a couple of nights.'

There are options, and that's not intended as a coy, *I could move in with you*, and neither does she take it as such.

'I think Mr Craven might lose his shit if he found out his house was left like this for an entire weekend,' she says, a light laugh in her voice. 'I don't think there's anything to be gained from leaving dead Frosty *in situ*. We'll do as you say, get him outside, get the place warmed up.'

And with that, she takes her phone from her pocket, and starts quickly taking pictures of the scene.

Dead Frosty. Lovely.

* * *

'You're a funny man,' she says.

Inevitably, afternoon has turned to dark evening, and equally inevitably, the wine bottle has been opened.

The gentle fall of heavy snow has turned into an ugly blizzard, and the village has bedded down for the evening. We split up to do some more of the rounds, speaking to as many people as possible. Hurried conversations on doorsteps, for the most part. There's been a murder. Have you seen anything or anyone suspicious? If you see anything, or have any concerns, call this number. Some variation on the delicate balance between 'be vigilant' and 'there's no need to panic'.

From it all, nothing substantial, nothing to add to the investigation. Margaret Wills is dead, and we're no nearer finding out why.

Three days in, and I have one suspect. Ellis. That's it. And what are the suspicions based upon? He's head of the local

---

138

equivalent of the Round Table. He's surly. He had photographs of young women on his wall.

No motive, no witnesses, no suspicious movements. Little but gut instinct, and even that might just be because there's no one else for my guts to get suspicious about.

So, here we are, in a small village with a road running through it, no more than twenty minutes from the next town, and a bit less than an hour from the next major police presence, and it's as though we're in an Antarctic station, detached from the world, left to our own devices.

'You think?'

'I don't mean, you understand, that you're funny hilarious.'

'Obviously.'

She smiles.

We're sharing a healthy meal of wine, olives and black pepper Kettle chips. Maybe some actual food will get made at some point, but no one seems in any rush to do that.

'This is a horror story,' she says. 'Margaret literally had a knife buried in her eye. I can't believe I've seen that. I can't believe that's what I've spent my afternoon investigating. When I called Alan, he was like, oh my fucking God, what is going on up there?' You know, if Alan cared, he'd have found a way to get home. Alan can fuck off. Alan deserves for me to be banging his wife. 'That's the kind of thing... I mean, I haven't remotely processed this yet, but I'm going to be waking up five years from now in a cold sweat, still thinking about seeing Margaret in that chair. And Alice is missing, and you've had these threats, and this is where we are. This awful shitshow, this horrorfest. I admit it, even after Margaret died, I still wanted to be in denial about it. But this... just everything. You're right. It's all tied together, and it's as sinister as anything. And...' and she makes a kind of flippant gesture, 'you seem to be like, whatever. This is just what's happening. No biggie. Someone's missing, someone's dead; we'll get it sorted, you can go back to your holiday and I can go back to making sure Mr Reynolds stops locking the gate on the public footpath at the bottom of his garden.'

'Reynolds locks his gate? What a prick.'

I get the smiling eye roll again, then she raises the wine glass. A sip, the glass lowered, the tip of her tongue touches her moist lips.

'But seriously, what's the secret? I mean, I know you say

you've seen this kind of thing before, and worse, but how can you not be even more of a basketcase, the more you see of it? How can every extra murder not just send you plummeting even further into the abyss?'

She looks earnestly across the table. I mean, this woman is no DI Kallas, but she's got something. If I wasn't such a lovesick fool with Anders Kallas's wife, I'd certainly be falling for that tube Allan's wife.

Always the wives.

Doomed to fall for women all the time. I don't think that's addiction, it's more just something that happens. But it must have a name. It must be a recognisable psychological condition. The love addict's relationships will always end in disaster, because either the love will be unrequited, or else it will be fulfilled, and then he or she will find themselves falling in love with someone else.

I'm not going to fall in love with Constable Mara. But there's worse than that, particularly in relation to the investigation. I want to keep my distance, because her photograph was on that wall with all those other young women, and she hasn't mentioned that she's had any connection with them, and there simply must be.

Logic says those pictures are not specific to Ellis, which means they're lodge specific, which means that when we're discussing the lodge, Mara knows more than she's saying, which means she's hiding something, and I really ought to be keeping my distance.

Except I'm crumbling, and I have no idea if I'm being played.

'You're drifting again,' she says. 'Wow, you just... Where do you go?'

'Oh, I'm not answering that. *Where do you go* is this season's what are you thinking?'

'Ha.'

'I was in Bosnia in the nineties. It was shit. Jesus, it's almost thirty years ago, and it's still there, imprinted on my brain. Some part of me shut down after that. I dealt with it with alcohol and sex. Still am, while other people suffer along the way. And... I don't know, the part that I shut off is still shut off. It'll remain so until I die.' A pause, and then, 'Shouldn't be too much longer.'

Half-smile, shrug it away, take another drink. The second

glass of wine of ten. Or fifteen.

She reaches her hand across the table. She looks at me like so many women have looked at me.

Fuck, I hate it when the conversation's about me. The conversations about me have to be confined to my own head.

I don't touch her hand. Instead, 'Tell me about the photographs on the wall of Ellis's office.'

She stays in the same position for a moment, and then slowly withdraws her hand. Pulls herself away a little. Swallows.

'What photographs?' she inevitably asks.

Fuck. I mean, I really was determined not to say anything. And I likely just fucked the evening, didn't I? There goes casual flirting over a couple of bottles of wine, before retreating to the bedroom.

Take a drink, let out a long sigh from puffed-up cheeks, give myself a moment. All the time she stares at me across the table. Waiting.

'OK, no one's shocked to hear that it was me who broke into the lodge.'

She gives me an unchanged expression, that admission such an obvious one it's not even worthy of an *I know*.

'I entered the office. On the wall to the right of the door, a wall that had today been largely cleared, was an array of photographs of young women. Twenty-three of them in all, dating back, one could tell from the hair and the clothes, to the late sixties. Seventies at the latest.'

I pause, she still doesn't speak, and so I decide to forcibly hand the ball over.

'What can you tell me about those photographs?'

Now she takes a drink, then lays the glass back on the table.

'I stuck my nose into the office last night, but it was just a quick check. I didn't see the photos. You're going to have to tell me about them. Did you not take a picture of them on your phone?'

'I told you I got drugged last night. When I awoke this morning, the picture had been removed from my phone.' She stays silent. Another drink. 'D'you know why Ellis, or the office itself, would have twenty-three photographs of young women on the wall?'

'What were they? Who were they? Were they, I don't know, were they posed, were they naked, were they… Was there anything suspicious about the photos themselves, or was it just their existence on the wall that you're questioning?'

'The latter. The pictures were just pictures. Nothing professional, a lot of them taken when the subject was out and about. On a boat, up a hill, wherever. Really, a random selection, no significance to the individual photographs.'

'And who were they? Did you recognise any of them?'

Another pause, but we've come this far. Now I just have to say it. Now, if there's a trap being laid, or there's mischief being played, I just have to walk right into it, at least trying to have my wits about me.

'Alice Schäfer.' A beat. One second to the next. Come on, man, spit it out. 'You.' Another pause, trying to read something into the expression. 'Abigail Connolly, the movie's casting director. Gillian Cooper, and maybe another couple of faces from around town. I needed to get a longer, better look at it.'

We hold the gaze for another few moments, now beneath the suffocating weight of suspicion. Fuck, I can't be doing with this. Now it's out there, we just need to crack the fuck on.

'What's the connection? What are all these women to the lodge? I presume you know, given you're there. The list goes back, as I said, several decades, so there's no way it's Ellis's private fiefdom. It must be related to the lodge, not him.'

Finally the spell is broken, she makes a small head shaking movement, then lifts her glass, taking a quick drink.

'Why didn't you say?' she says. 'I mean, you say you saw my picture on the wall last night, and you haven't said anything.'

'Nuh-huh,' I say, with a small finger wag, which I quickly stop in case I suddenly resemble a teenage American girl. 'We can come to that, and we can come to issues of trust and suspicion in due course, but first, you need to tell me what's going on with those photographs. Because there's a link between the lodge and Alice, and there's a link between the lodge and someone on the movie, which means Alice and Abigail have something in common, and, whatever it is, it seems you too have that in common.'

All that without repeating the question, which I ask with an open-hand gesture. She's nodding by the time I finish talking, accepting that an answer has to be given. But, like a politician waving away an accusation of corruption or inappropriate shaggery, her facial expression immediately seeks to deescalate the conversation.

'I should have said, sorry, and really, it's nothing. So little, in fact, that it was barely worth mentioning. And I didn't, to be fair, realise that Alice had been involved in it. They have this thing every year, their grand dinner, which is in the lodge hall, so, really, not so grand after all. And it's based on some ceremony or other from, God knows, the Templars or the whatevers from the twelfth century, I really haven't a clue. And at the head of the table there's a man and there's a woman. At some point in the lodge's long history, there was some old guy without a wife. So, rather than sit there on his own, he started the tradition of inviting a young woman from the village.' She pauses to further emphasise how stupid and inane this is, tossing another throwaway hand. 'I mean, it wasn't a prom queen type of a thing. It was literally sit at the head of the table eating your dinner next to a guy. It's… yep, it's pretty outdated, but unsurprisingly they clung on to it, and it seems they were still able to get the women to go along and get a free meal. But really, that was it. Dinner. No prom, no parade, no mass orgy, no gangbang, just a bullshit dinner listening to a bunch of boring speeches.'

'And you did this?'

'Oh, yes, I had my turn. It's not, necessarily, a different person every year, but I just got asked once. Maybe that was because I didn't put out at the end of the evening.'

'And you didn't know Alice had been asked?'

'You know, I really didn't pay any attention to that place anymore. They keep themselves to themselves and don't cause any trouble. I work during the week, my friends from the old days have all moved away, Alan's here at the weekend and we do our own thing. I'm kind of detached, unless work demands that I not be.'

We hold another long gaze across the table. From outside, the howling of the storm, the wind not letting up.

'Why did he take the pictures from the wall? Why did someone come into my house, drug me, and then remove the photograph from my phone? If it's some innocent dinner, why not be happy to explain?'

'I don't know, Tom. I didn't know he had the pictures. You said none of them were salacious?'

'They weren't salacious.'

'Maybe he was just embarrassed they were there at all. I mean, it's a pretty weird thing to have. I was there, and I had no idea. Maybe none of the others had any idea, and Ellis didn't want people finding out. Maybe it's one of those things where he's been thinking, I probably shouldn't have all those pictures on the wall, I really ought to take them down, then he suddenly thinks, ah, now's as good a time as any.'

'Now's as good a time as any? Leaving it to the point where doing it will make him come under suspicion? Coupling that with drugging me, and tampering with my phone.'

'Did you really take the picture? Maybe you just thought you'd taken in.' A pause, and then, 'I mean, you were pretty drunk.'

'I wasn't that drunk, and I looked at it when I got home. I sat at my kitchen table, studying the picture, drinking wine.'

'OK, then I don't know. I don't understand that. Maybe Mr Ellis is involved with Alice's disappearance, I really don't know. Maybe he just thought, crap, if you see that you might make an association he doesn't want you to make, and so he gets rid of them.'

'I'd already seen them.'

'I don't know,' she says. 'That's all I've got. But if what all those other women did was the same as what I did, there really is nothing to see here.'

'And you're a MacDonald,' I say. Can't stop myself, and might as well get it all out there now that we're here.

'I'm a MacDonald?'

'Yes. Seems the history of the lodge is jam packed with MacDonalds. Now it transpires the doctor is one and you're one, and I'm just wondering if there's a connection.'

A rueful smile, a shake of the head.

'I don't know what to say to that. Honestly, like I said, there are fifty of us in this town. Fifty of *them*, as I'm not even one of them anymore. I mean... Jesus, Sergeant, I've given you reasons not to trust me, I'm sorry, but that's not one of them.'

I lift the glass, tip the rest of the contents into my mouth, close my eyes for a moment in the tell-tale sign of someone who loves the taste and its effect just a little too much, and then rest the glass back on the table.

'Do you need me to leave, or can I have another?' I say.

She sits back, gives me another meaningful stare across the table, which ends with her shaking her head, and unable to stop the smile.

'You have your way about you, don't you, Sergeant?'

'An irresistible combo of glibness and superficiality? Drives women wild.'

'Yeah, sure it does.'

She leans forward, lifts the bottle, pours me another glass and tops up her own.

26

She produces the handcuffs in the middle of sex.

I've had sex with a few police officers in my time, and at no point have any of us ever suggested handcuffing anyone. Kind of figure it's for fetishists and folks playing dress-up.

She smiles wickedly as she does it, and I wonder, just as I'm supposed to wonder, if this is nothing to do with sex. And it's certainly nothing to do with blackmail, as she's the married one, I'm on my holidays, and I have no one's soul to crush.

I'm lying on the bed, suddenly a little on edge, tensed to move quickly if I think I need to, and she kneels beside me. Her unshaven pussy is glistening, her breasts are small and uneven and beautiful, and she teases me with a look, the handcuffs dangling from her fingers.

'Do you trust me, Sergeant?'

Well, Constable, I don't know that I do.

Thirty seconds ago, I was still flush from a bottle of wine, Mara was sitting on top of me, grinding her pussy into my face, moaning and gasping and coming to a wonderfully loud climax, and the rest of the world, and this dumbass investigation, could go to hell. And now comes the wake-up call.

The little voice in my head, the one I rely on for pretty much everything, says she's genuinely teasing. The look on her face says it, and I really believe she's not involved in this bloody awful business. Nevertheless, she could be. And her photo was there, and I'm an outsider in a small town, and maybe she came looking for me in the first place because they were looking for a fall guy.

She leans over me, looking at me the whole time, her eyes wide and bright, and she takes the end of my damp cock gently into her mouth, running a soft finger down the length, then caressing my balls. Oh my fucking God, that is so good.

She gives herself in to the job for a moment, and I, weakly, typically, instantly forget about the handcuffs, head back on the pillow, moaning softly, my hand on her blonde hair, and then she quickly raises herself, smiling all the while, takes my unresistant hands and cuffs them together against the metal poles of the headstand.

Snap of the fingers, and there I am, cuffed and naked and erect and helpless.

She smiles again, then lies on top of me, pressing my erection against her thighs, her breasts against my chest. She leans forward, her lips to my ear.

'How does it feel, Sergeant?' she whispers. 'How does it feel?'

She reaches down, and slides my cock inside her. Lying flat on me like that it's uncomfortable and wonderful at the same time, then she sits up and starts grinding herself into me, her movements slow and delicious. Her hands pressed against my chest, her lips parted, her eyes fixed on mine.

Jesus, it's glorious.

Let me stay like this forever. Let her never leave, let me never come, let me be cuffed, and let them all be murdered around us, let the world collapse beneath the weight of the storm.

She speeds up, the excitement of it showing on her face, and I want to reach up and hold her waist, I want to feel her breasts, I want to sit up and take her nipples into my mouth, but I'm chained and frustrated and liberated and euphoric, and I can't last like this much longer, my cock thick and full and ready to explode, then she gasps suddenly, pressing down, pushing herself against me, and she leans forward and starts kissing me, her lips moist and harsh, and we're moaning into each other's mouths, then she breaks off, pulls away, as my cock is aching, desperate to finish, and she starts biting my chest, still fevered with passion, down across my stomach, gasping all the time, still in the throes of an orgasmic high, then she comes to my cock and takes it harshly into her mouth and starts sucking quickly, her lips and tongue all over it, up and down the length, and Jesus, this won't take long. 'Fuck!' bursts loudly from my mouth, as the wind rattles the windows and the whole house shudders with the storm, and she gasps, 'Oh, God!' with her mouth full, and I want to grab her hair, and I want to kiss her and slide inside her and lick her breasts and fuck her and keep fucking her and fucking her and the phone rings.

The phone rings.

She gasps, her teeth catch the end of my cock and I gasp

with her, she takes me into her mouth again.

The phone rings.

She pauses, sucking me deep in her throat, barely able to breathe, calming down as she does so. I'm coming. God, I'm coming, the peculiar, magnificent intensity of a fellated ejaculation, Jesus fucking Christ.

'Oh fuck, don't stop, don't stop. Fuck!'

The phone rings. Still ringing. She pulls away, three seconds too soon.

'Fuck!'

She lets go, and it's agony, that awful agony, and I'm desperate just to grab my cock and finish it off and I can't, and she looks at me, strangely, distantly, as she reaches over to the bedside table and lifts her phone, and my cock is twitching, and I know I'm going to come anyway, I can't stop it, a strange, unfulfilling ejaculation, and as I start to come, my damp erect cock spurting unspectacularly, and I moan with the release of it, she puts her fingers to her lips as she looks at me, gets up from the bed, turns her back and answers her phone.

'Mara.'

The semen pulses slowly from my cock, white and insubstantial after last night's sex, running down its length into my pubic hair. A jerk, a soft moan, and a little flies from the end and lands on my stomach, then the slow pulse of release continues.

'Where?'

Another pause. I'm staring at her legs, her buttocks, her back, her shoulders, then I close my eyes and rest my head back on the pillow. 'Jesus,' softly escapes my lips. Not even thinking about what this might be, who this might be. I don't care. I don't want to know.

'I'll be five minutes.' She hangs up.

She pauses briefly, then turns and looks at me. Her face has lost all the expression it had a minute ago. She may be naked, she may still be damp, but she's already working.

'There's been another murder. Gillian Cooper.'

There's a coldness to her voice.

'Oh, fuck,' I manage. 'We should get round there.'

She stares at me, and then turns away, and walks through to the en suite. Door closed, and then I hear the sound of the shower running.

27

The storm rages, the wind against the window, rattling the roof.

Mara left some time ago, but I can't be sure when that was. No clock in view, can't reach my phone, which, in any case, is on the floor, in the pocket of my trousers.

She didn't speak to me again. She was in the bathroom for no more than a couple of hurried minutes, then she emerged, still drying herself, and she got quickly dressed. I asked her if she'd undo the cuffs, and she said, 'I don't think so. Not yet.' She stopped at the door, she said, 'I'll try not to be too long,' and then she was gone.

Gillian Cooper is dead. That means two of the people I've interviewed in the last couple of days have been murdered. I'm trying to work out if Mara might think I'm involved. That I might have committed the murders. Certainly, the opportunity has been there. We were apart for a couple of hours this afternoon, and it was me who spoke to Cooper.

Crucial point, needless to say, is that I didn't kill her, and I'm not really sure why Mara would think that I might have done. Maybe she's thinking it's an *Angel Heart* type of situation, me going around, interviewing people and then taking them out in my wake. Maybe she thinks I have some connection to the lodge, and I'm here to wreak my revenge.

Then, of course, there's the possibility she's plain and simply complicit in some way, and doesn't want me there for this one. Can't think how this makes sense either, but it's a possibility.

And that's all I have for now, trapped here, naked on a bed. The euphoria of earlier long gone. Feeling cold. The duvet was pushed off, and so I lie here naked, flaccid, goosebumped, wide awake and uncertain.

But you know what? I don't give a fuck. What's the worst that can happen?

Hmm. She frames me for the murders, I get incarcerated, name in ruins, never see DI Kallas again, then I get gangraped every day in prison because I'm an ex-copper. Yeah, OK, that would be bad. But that's not going to happen.

And really, my name in ruins? Wheel out the hysterical laughing emojis.

She'll be back at some point, hopefully not with a camera, and we can talk about it. If there's worse than that – that I'm to be killed, that Ellis shows up, that some other unimagined horror is to be visited upon me – I'm not lying. I don't care. The stupid shit someone's been pulling here, the chicken and the snowman, that pointless nonsense, it means nothing to me. This could literally be what happened to Midge Ure in Vienna. Means nothing, don't give a fuck, do what you will, you bastards.

I should be able to think straight. I mean, I'm lying here doing fuck all else. I should be trying to weave together the different strands. I am supposed to be a detective, after all.

The vampire movie people. The lodge. The photographs on the wall. The most recent of those women has gone missing. One of the earlier ones has been found murdered. I've been left lying here, chained to the bed, by one of the others. Another of them is involved in the movie.

I try to picture those photographs that I looked at so briefly. Is it possible Margaret Wills was on there? It would have been one of the older ones, and I could easily have failed to recognise her. It makes sense, in fact, that she would have been.

Whatever Mara's part is in this, and I'm not yet condemning her for leaving me here, I don't buy the innocence of these young women all being guests at the annual dinner. Sounds too neat, too convenient, too easy, too straightforward.

If it is related to them, then why now? Why does it start now? It has to be the arrival of the movie. Every sequence of events needs a catalyst, and that's the obvious change in town. And if it's related to both the movie and to the wall of photographs, the link is Abigail Connolly.

Not that I got any particular feel for her when conducting those interviews. Nothing to get the alarm bells ringing, nothing suspicious other than the vague evasiveness we see with roughly eighty percent of the people we speak to.

There's someone I need to see tomorrow to get help on those photographs. Just an idea, which might come to nothing, might not even get started. But it's worth a shot.

There's a key in the lock, and I tense for a second at the sound, then instantly relax. Relieved, more than anything else, that she's back, confident she'll release me, and that I can have a shower to clean up and warm up. Fuck, it's cold.

A moment or two longer than expected, and then the door closes, and I know straight away. It's not Mara. Jesus, here we fucking go. For a second I wonder if it's the husband, but there's no way it's that guy. Not now, not in the middle of the storm.

A peculiar tension comes over me, I mean, for a guy who supposedly doesn't give a fuck. But here we are, my doom awaits me, and my body tenses and the adrenalin starts pumping.

The door opens, and in walks Dr MacDonald. Mara's mother. Judi Dench, her face stuck somewhere between a grimace and a look of questioning horror.

'My God, I thought she was joking,' she says.

She stands just inside the door, staring at me, not making any effort to release me.

'As we can see,' I say, 'she wasn't. But really, Elaine dispatched you to… I don't know, what? You have the key to the cuffs?'

'Obviously.'

'So, you're here to release me?'

'I have one job. I didn't realise I would find you like this.'

'She said.'

'Like I say, I thought she was joking.' A pause, and then, looking uncomfortable, she says, 'I suppose I'm going to have to come over there.'

'That would be nice, Doc, thanks.'

'Don't call me Doc.'

She approaches me, that wonderful look of disdain on her face, and unlocks the handcuffs.

Fuck, that's a relief. I'd been trying not to think of the discomfort of having my arms chained up like that above my head.

'Thank you.'

'Let's never do this again.'

I push myself off the bed, contemplate wrapping the duvet around me and decide it's too late for that and really not worth the effort, then walk quickly to the bathroom.

'I'll be in the kitchen. Don't be long,' she says.

She leaves, and I close the door and get the shower running.

28

She's sitting at the kitchen table, waiting for me. I stand for a moment, take the temperature of the room, ascertain that Mara has not returned in the five minutes I was in the bathroom, contemplate making myself a cup of tea, acknowledge that I'm lying to myself and what I'd really like is wine or vodka, and accept that I am cowed somewhat by the presence of the grown-up in the room, and that I really need to go and find the constable.

'I hope I haven't embarrassed you,' she says.

'Might sound hard to believe, but it really would take more than that.'

'Well, I do find that hard to believe, but I don't want to know. I waited for you, though there was no particular need for me to. We should get along there.'

She pushes her chair back, and gets to her feet.

'Tell me the story.'

'Bill said he and his wife had been fighting a lot recently. Seemed quite open about that. Way too much information, as far as I'm concerned. It had been his turn in the shop, and she'd gone out to the workshop to work on a couple of small projects. That's what he called them. Small projects. Maybe she was making a mug. I don't know.'

'It was a mug. I was out there earlier on.'

'Fine, you'll know then. She was neither the potter, nor artist, that Bill is. She was gone a long time, he didn't really care. That's what he said. Presumed she was out there all that time just to avoid him. It gets to nine at night, he finally thinks, this is a bit weird, I didn't realise she was *that* pissed at me. He goes out, she's been stabbed in the eye.'

'Exact same m.o.?'

She nods.

'How long d'you think she's been dead?'

'A few hours. The heating had been turned off in there, the body is cold. She's sitting in the same position as Margaret, hands resting on her thighs.'

'Fuck me,' I say, than hold up an apologetic hand, as though this doctor might be offended by ill language, though she's clearly not.

'Meanwhile, Bill is, as they say, losing his shit. Elaine thought she should stay with him, and asked me to come here. She explained how I'd find you, and I thought, as I said, that's a bit of a weird joke to make, and here we are…'

'Well, I think I should be apologising to you for the embarrassment rather than the other way around, though ultimately, I'm not sure what I could have done about it.'

'Not letting yourself be handcuffed by my daughter springs to mind,' she says, and I can't help smiling.

I lift my jacket off the back of the chair and head for the front door, where my permanently damp boots are waiting for me.

* * *

Gillian Cooper sits in position, hands comfortably placed on her knees, knife buried in her eye, at the back of the small workshop. Away from the window looking out on the loch, out of sight of the house and shop behind it.

'She would've been sitting out here for several hours, like that, and Bill didn't notice?' I say. 'He didn't notice there were no lights on? He didn't notice she hadn't gone inside to use the bathroom or make a cup of tea?' As I say that, I notice the kettle and the unwashed mugs, and I wave away the last remark.

'He said he knows it sounds odd,' said Mara, 'but he just didn't want to talk to her, and ignored the peculiarity of it. Wondered if she'd gone off somewhere else, and that he'd missed her. When he closed the shop, he went upstairs, stuck the TV on and fell asleep in front of the football. Seemed happy to ignore her when he woke up.'

She glances back towards the house, although she can't see it from where she's standing, never mind being able to see Bill and Dr Judi Dench, who is in there administering a sedative of some sort.

'I think he's now experiencing full blown you don't know what you've got until you lose it.'

'We've all been there.'

She acknowledges that with a small nod, we stare at each

other for a moment. I barely know what I'm thinking right now so I sure as fuck don't know what she's thinking.

'Was it still daylight when you spoke to her?' she asks.

'Just about. And really, that was a very short conversation. She didn't have much to say.'

She holds my gaze. I wonder if there's something else she's wanting to say, but if there is, she ain't saying it.

'No sign of a forced entry?' I ask.

'None. Of course, the door wouldn't have been locked. Perhaps we can presume the killer was someone known to her, but even if it wasn't, they wouldn't have had to force their way in. The door would've been open. Maybe they even knocked.'

On the worktop there's a small mug, on the side of which there is a half-painted stag's head. Beside it, a brush with dried-in paint, a small palette. I wander over, look at the mug without lifting it, cannot note any discernible difference between the quality of this work and anything else on display in the shop, and then turn back to the room.

She's watching me, with the continued air of suspicion she's had since I got here. Time to address that particular elephant, while the doctor is otherwise engaged.

'You left me manacled to a bedpost.'

Nothing. Certainly no apology.

'That seemed an unusual decision,' is how I finally put it. I don't really want to fall out with her, although it might be for the best. This isn't *my* case. I don't actually have to be working on it. I don't have to be here. And I certainly don't have to continue the relationship, which also isn't really my relationship to have. We stumbled into it, and it shouldn't be too hard – indeed, it would likely be sensible – to stumble back out again.

'Spur of the moment.'

'Based on?'

She's hesitant. It being apparent what she's thinking, I decide to help her along.

'You've got a sleepy little village in the Highlands, I turn up, and suddenly a young woman disappears. And then people start getting murdered. You're drawn to me for whatever reason. I mean, it happens between people, so that doesn't have to be a mystery. But you get a bit of a feeling about me, I have a bit of history. Maybe you made some calls. You know I broke into the lodge hall, and then happily lied about it. You know I'd started to doubt *you*. You start to think, wait, what's the story with this guy? Nothing happens for a hundred years in this place, then he shows up.' I pause for a moment to let her jump in. She's doesn't, so I go on talking, even though I've pretty much said it all. 'Interesting, if that's what you were thinking, that you chose to have sex at all. Or was the plan to just leave me manacled until the cavalry arrived on Monday? Hmm, can't be that, why wouldn't I still be manacled?'

I'm done now, and I give her the raised eyebrows of curiosity.

'Not bad, detective,' she says. 'I mean, I don't really think you're involved in this, but I don't know. I'm lost here.' Right enough, she *looks* lost. And what small-time, backwoods officer wouldn't be? 'This is way out of my league, way over my head. I cannot believe these two things have happened at the same time. Double murder and a white-out snowstorm.'

'Maybe it's not a coincidence. Whoever did it can read the forecast. They know there are unlikely to be reinforcements before Monday. They have freedom to run amok, commit mayhem, and then, possibly, get the fuck out of Dodge on Monday before the cops arrive.'

'I don't know how we can watch the roads. And there are so many rough tracks that a good driver in a good car might well be able to negotiate, even in this.'

She finishes with a head shake, starts to say something, then the futility of whatever it was takes her, and she makes a gesture of hopelessness.

'I don't know,' is all that comes out.

'OK, we need to start doing what we can,' I say, struck with a need to be the team leader, even though the only other member of the team very recently left me chained and helpless. 'It's cold in here, I say we cover the corpse, lower the blinds, lock the door, and leave everything as it is until Monday. We'll need Bill's agreement, of course, but if he's reluctant, we need to persuade him.'

'Yes.'

'Now, we need to talk about that parade of pictures on the wall in Ellis's office.'

'What? Really?'

'Alice Schäfer was up there, and she's missing. I think, in fact, we might be moving into *missing presumed dead* territory. Gillian Cooper too was on there, right?'

'She might have been, I don't kn –'

155

'And what about Margaret? She would've been a while ago, and I'm not sure if she was there. I didn't get to see the photographs for long enough.'

'I don't know. I mean, she's lived in the village since she was, I don't know, sixteen maybe. She might well have been one of the older photographs. As I say…'

And she shrugs again, a hopelessness about her.

'So, whatever this thing is, we have two women dead, one missing, and two, if not all three of them were part of this same thing, related to the lodge.'

I wait for the objection, the protest that it's just a trivial matter, that it really was nothing more than an annual dinner. And it's a small village, with all sorts of connections between everyone who lives here. We'll probably find the women have far more than just the lodge in common.

She says none of that. She swallows. She looks uncertain.

'And if it is related to that wall of pictures, that puts you in the firing line.'

'I'm not in the firing line.'

'You don't know that.'

How the fuck do I know what she knows? That was just the kind of automatically spewed out line you get in one of those low budget, garbage horror movies like *Spidersaurus vs Gigantafrog*.

'This thing, this meal thing, or whatever the connection is between you ladies and the lodge, you know who else in the village is involved?'

She looks uncertain. She looks like she has something to say. Something to tell me. I think for a moment I'm going to get it, but she shakes her head, and I feel that's her turning her back on the explanation, and instead says, 'The whole lodge business is just a bunch of men playing at being a secret society. That's just it. They're playing. They like it to be secret. But what they do with the women, you know, she's not a gala queen, she's not a, you know, it's not a thing…'

It's not a thing. Well, I disagree, it's some kind of a thing.

'Would someone know the names of the other women?'

'Mr Ellis, I guess.'

'Someone other than Ellis. We need to tell these women, we need to get round to them right now and let them know they're under threat.'

'They're not under threat.'

156

She sounds agitated for the first time.

'They're under threat, Constable, they are clearly under threat. If nothing else, I've been concentrating my investigation on that lodge, and someone out there doesn't want me here. I haven't given anyone else any reason to get me to back off.'

'Well, maybe Ellis sent you the chicken and Ellis did the stupid snowman, but it doesn't mean that he's also committed murder. He might just want you to back off investigating his business. Who knows what secrets he has there, but it doesn't mean they're necessarily criminal.'

'What about Bill Cooper? Was he in the lodge? Can we ask him?'

She shakes her head, then lifts her hand to enforce the gesture.

'Mum's giving him a sedative, anyway.'

'Alice's stepdad, then. He told me himself he's a member.'

'I think we should just leave it for tonight –'

'Dammit, Elaine, if you want to get somewhere here, I need to speak to people. I need names, I need to warn people. We need to start being specific.'

'It's almost midnight, let's just... Even if Alec could tell us, I'm not doing anything with that information *now*. I'm really not comfortable randomly phoning people in the middle of a night like this and warning them that... Jesus, I don't even know what we'd say. The bogeyman's out to get you?'

'It doesn't matter what we say, getting them awake and paying attention is a start.'

'Look, I don't know what tomorrow's going to look like, though at least we know this snow isn't going to have gone anywhere, but we've had no other phone calls, as far as we know no one else is currently in trouble. I say we go out, we sit in the Land Rover, we park it on main street and keep watch on the town. At this time, in this weather, no one is likely to be about, and it'll be easy enough to stop anyone we see.'

'Your plan is to spend the next eight hours sitting in the car?'

'I'll keep the engine running and the heating on, and we can take it in turns to sleep.'

Fuck me.

Dammit. She might be right. What else are the two of us going to do at this time of night? Wake everyone up, tell them a killer's on the rampage? Really?

'OK,' I say, 'we'll do it.'

'My sitting in the car plan?'

I can't help smiling at that, and finally she relaxes a little.

'Sure, your sitting in the car plan. First, however, I'm going to try to talk to Mr Cooper.'

'Good luck getting past mum.'

A nod, an acceptance that that won't be easy, then I think of the other thing that needs said.

'You seriously sent your mum to undo my cuffs, when I was lying there like that? Your mum?'

She stares at the ground for a moment, eyes a little wide.

'I don't always think straight,' she says eventually.

You and me both, darling.

29

'No.'

'I need to speak to him.'

'I didn't give him a mild sedative, Sergeant Hutton,' says Dr Judi Dench. 'I knocked the man out. He'll be asleep for several hours at least, and quite possibly given the time of night, eight to ten hours. You can talk to him in the morning if you must.'

'You really had to give him that? What if we suspected him of his wife's murder?'

'I gave him a sedative, not a one-way ticket to Buenos Aries.'

Nice. This woman has a terrific bluntness about her.

We're in the shop downstairs. The handmade wares in low lighting, the blizzard loud and thrilling against the windows. Fortunately, the constable drove her car down here when she left me tied to the bed. We don't have far to walk.

'We should go,' says Mara. 'Let the doctor get some sleep. Who knows what tomorrow brings.'

'Sleep?' says Judi Dench. 'I don't think so. Much too wide awake for that. I'm going home to a bottle of port and another awful Dan Brown. God knows why I allowed myself to get addicted to that nonsense.'

'What d'you know about young women and the lodge?' I ask, and I can see Mara wince to my side. She keeps her mouth shut.

'Young women and the lodge?' asks Judi Dench, and it's hard to tell which one of her derisory tones it is she employs for the question.

'The Lodge of St Augustine, and the involvement of young women,' I say, spelling it out.

'I didn't know they had any female members,' says Judi with a straight bat. She looks at Mara as she says it.

'You never had anything to do with them?'

'You just said *young* women, didn't you?'

159

'I'm guessing you were young once.'

'It's been a long time, but I've never wanted anything to do with the lodge.'

'You had the option?'

She answers this with a look, the mouth in a thin line of regret that we've stumbled into this conversation.

'MacDonald?' I ask.

'You've done your research,' says Judi Dench. 'Running that place had been in the family for a long, long time. Fathers to sons. My dad, bless him, was cursed with a daughter and a wife who had three miscarriages. I suppose we should all be glad he didn't turn into Henry VIII. At some point he might have mooted the possibility of my involvement with them, but I made it quite clear. Quite clear. I wanted nothing to do with it. Then I brought shame to the family by having Elaine as a single, unmarried mother. You'd have thought it was the nineteen twenties. And here we are, our own place within the community, and nothing to do with that particular ship of fools.'

'You ever hear anything about them?'

'I used to hear stuff, but not in a long time. I really don't want to know.'

'What kind of a thing did you use to hear?'

'Nothing that I'd want to regurgitate to a police officer in the middle of a murder investigation.'

'Why not?'

'It's all hearsay and speculation and gossip. You may want to be the arbiter of what's important and what's not, but I'm afraid I'm not prepared to give you that option. I don't think I know anything that should be factored into a murder inquiry, so I'm going to keep my mouth shut. I think you might find a lot of others doing the same, but you never know. There may be some who are willing to talk.'

'So you don't know about your daughter's involvement?'

I get a raised eyebrow from Judi Dench, a slight head shake from Mara, the doc glances quickly at her, and then says, 'I do not want to know, thank you very much. Now, you have my number, you can call if you need anything. As I said, Mr Cooper will likely sleep through the night, though you might want to check on him at some point. Good evening.'

And with that and a courteous nod, she turns and walks away. She pauses at the door, looks out at the white squall, lifts the collar of her coat, and then opens the door and steps out into the storm. A rush of wind and sound and fury, and then the door closes, and we're once again standing in silence.

The still of the night returns to the shop, though the wind swirling around the building keeps the silence at bay. Little point, however, in standing here like this any longer.

'I don't suppose you'd care to share any of the hearsay, speculation and gossip she's talking about.'

Mara doesn't reply. I give her a moment, then turn to look at her. Another one of those edgy glances. Jesus, this has been a weird as fuck relationship.

'We should go and do the plan,' she says.

Fine. Might as well do the plan. The sitting in the car all night plan. Maybe boredom will finally loosen her tongue.

* * *

She is not of a mind to talk. She tells me I can sleep first, and I take her up on it. Not really tired enough at the moment, but happy to close my eyes.

There may have been two people murdered, but I think I've had enough of this small town drama. Monday cannot come quickly enough. Indeed, perhaps tomorrow the wind will have calmed down sufficiently to allow a helicopter to fly, and they can land some support troops. Let an Inspector come, let her be annoyed that there's a Glasgow copper sticking his nose into their Highland beat, let her ask me to step aside, and I gratefully will.

I called Abigail Connolly, the least I could do. Didn't want to say too much, didn't want to get into interviewing her over the phone. But I told her about the murders, and told her she should be careful. She noticeably didn't ask why I was singling her out, albeit she would not necessarily have known she was being singled out at that time of night.

I said I'd see her in the morning, although I'm not sure when that's going to happen. The morning already has a list written for it.

I've never sat in an electric car before. Seems odd. The tsunami of carbon neutral vehicles that we're promised still seems light years away. But here we are, the constable and I, in a car in near silence. The wind from behind must be hitting us at such a perfect angle that it's virtually silent. All we have in the car is a whisper of the outside, and the low hum of the heating

---

161

and the engine.

Tip my seat back and close my eyes. I start to think of the doctor walking in on me, manacled to a bed, naked, cold, (shrivelled), the remnants of the lovemaking dribbled through my pubic hair. I ought to be mortified. And sitting here, eyes shut, my attempt at an empty mind inevitably straying into self-loathing and regret, I manage to come to the conclusion that yes, I am mortified. Maybe the worst of it is that I'm a fifty-six-year-old detective sergeant, and I let myself be that vulnerable. That embarrassingly open to humiliation.

I feel the heat of embarrassment and awkwardness. Sleep has zero chance of coming.

Constable Mara is not my friend. However, wine and vodka are not my friends, and it's not as though I can stay away from either of them.

'I'm sorry,' she says, out of nowhere.

Here was me thinking I was pulling off a decent pretence at sleep, but people can always tell. Nevertheless, I don't say anything. And I'm certainly not going to tell her not to worry about it, and that it's fine.

'I shouldn't have sent mum round. I was annoyed, I was... I'm freaked by the whole thing. I'm completely out of my depth here, and just not thinking straight.'

'I want to go and see Ellis in the morning.'

I don't open my eyes, though I can feel her turn and look at me.

'I'm not sure how we do that,' she says.

'We get a boat, we cross the loch.'

'Have you seen the loch? I can't go out in that. No one will give us a boat to do that, and even if they did, I have no experience of handling any kind of craft in this weather. Do you?' She lets me not reply, then adds, 'I know you don't.'

'The forecast is for a little less wind. Maybe the loch will be navigable.'

'We'll have help on Monday.'

'We can't sit here waiting for the cavalry to show up. Two people have been murdered today, God knows what tomorrow brings. We can't just sit tight, no matter how much we want to.'

I'm clearly not very good at detaching myself from the drama when I'm right in the middle of it, despite my determination to not give a fuck about anything.

'Who can I ask?'

'Sorry?'

'Who has a boat I can commandeer? Is there someone to whom the request wouldn't be a complete surprise? Someone you're used to asking?'

A pause, the kind you know is going to be ended by a positive answer, though one she is reluctant to give, then she says, 'Mum.'

'Mum? This really is a one-horse town, isn't it?'

'No one's claiming otherwise. You could also ask Mr Craven. In fact, given the weather, that might be a better idea. His boat's a little bigger.'

That makes sense. The guy who owns the croft I'm staying in. Another one of those who'll have his finger in all sorts of enterprises and ideas.

'I take it Mr Craven is in the lodge?'

She doesn't reply, and this time I don't get a feel for her hesitation. Finally open my eyes and glance at her. She has her hands on the wheel, as though we might be heading somewhere, staring straight ahead.

'You don't know?' I say.

'You'd have to ask him.'

'You really don't know?'

'You're really going to have to ask him. You can do it when you're sitting on his boat tomorrow morning.'

There's that tone again. Dismissive or contemptuous or gently mocking or God knows what. Something negative, that's all.

I look at her, I wait for her to return the look, it doesn't come, and I turn away.

Close my eyes, fold my arms, allow myself to slide a little further down in the seat. Sleep will not come, but I need to rest all the same.

Searching around for a happy place to which to disappear, I do not have far to look. That wonderful early evening when Kadri came to my house, and she held me and she kissed me and she came to my bed. I'll be going to that place for the rest of my life, even if it never happens again.

30

Up with the dawn.

We finally abandoned our watch over the town at six a.m. I came home, fell into bed, slept for ninety minutes, woke with the alarm. Teeth, shower, dressed, water, coffee, toast, and then I'm trudging through snow and knocking on Craven's door at a little after eight-thirty, second stop of the day. Lack of sleep be damned; in this cold, snowy morning, I feel wide awake and ready to grab this crap by the balls.

The snow has stopped, but it lies thick on the ground, maybe two feet deep. Am not surprised, as I arrive at the gate of his bungalow, to find the path leading to his front door cleared, glistening wet in the morning, covered in sandy grit. No footsteps go beyond the gate, however, so it's not as though he was clearing his path because he was going anywhere.

Up the garden path and I knock on the door. As I wait, I turn and look out over the loch. It remains a sea of restlessness.

I already woke DeShaun at his cabin in the snow, him and Randall sleeping in the same caravan.

'Can I ask you a favour?' I said.

He was standing in the door in his thick red puffer jacket, boxer shorts and thrown-on trainers.

'Shut the fucking door, man,' said Randall from somewhere, and DeShaun emerged onto the steps, closing the door behind him.

'Fucking Baltic, man,' he said.

'What are you doing today?' I asked, it being a straight down to business type of situation.

'Got a little bit to do down at the hotel, but not much. Mostly set up. Starting filming at like ten or something, so I'll need to be down there by... wait, what's the time?'

'Just after eight.'

'Crap, I should be getting my shit together. What's up? Fuck it's cold.'

It wasn't even *that* cold. Still, the guy was standing there in his boxer shorts.

'You said you had a line in phone hardware.'

His constant movements, aimed at keeping himself warm, stopped dead, and he looked at me suspiciously.

'What? Wait, what are you accusing me of?'

You've got to love the innate suspicion of the police.

'Wondered if you could help me.'

'Go on,' he said, voice still wary.

'I deleted a photo from my phone a couple of days ago. Would you be able to do some, I don't know, like phone hacking magic, and retrieve it?'

'You deleted it from deleted pictures as well?'

'Yeah.'

'Sounds like someone was a bit careless.'

No comment.

'Sure, I should be able to do that.'

'It's easy?'

'Might have to do a bit of searching, but I'll plug it into my Mac, and get it sorted for you. What am I looking for?'

I took the phone from my pocket and handed it over.

'Seven-three-zero, six-three-zero. You got that?'

'Seven-three-zero, six-three-zero.' He tapped the side of his head. 'I won't forget.'

'Tell anyone else that code and I'll arrest you for impeding an investigation. Minimum five-year sentence.'

I was just making that up, but he nodded seriously.

'When can you do it?'

'I need to do some stuff down at the hotel, or Karen will like completely lose her shit, but I'll take my MacBook and I should be able to do it in the next couple of hours. Good enough?'

'Yep. You'll be at the hotel all day?'

'Yep. What am I looking for?'

I hesitated for a moment, but then why else was I there? The whole process involved letting him in on this side of the investigation, and I didn't know of any other option.

I told him. And now I'm here, and my phone, and all that it contains, is in the hands of a young guy I barely know, who can do whatever the hell he wants with it.

The door opens, and I turn.

'Good morning.'

Craven, naturally, looks unimpressed, but then he has done

any other time I've seen him in the past week.

'What's the matter now?' he asks, getting straight to it. If I'm at his house at this time on a Sunday, there must be something wrong.

'You have a boat?'

Craven holds my gaze, with the same kind of look of suspicion with which Mara has been regarding me much of the last two days. Ever since we were stupid enough to start sleeping together.

He ostentatiously looks round and over my shoulder, and then indicates the loch.

'You want to go out in that?'

'I understand your vessel's big enough.'

'You've got much experience?'

'None. I'll need you to drive it.'

'You'll need me to drive it,' he says deadpan. 'What if I'm doing something else this Sunday morning? Are you going to pull some crap about police requisitioning, and compel me to do as I'm told?'

'You know I can't compel you to do anything, Mr Craven. I'm asking. You'd be doing me a favour.'

I get a disgruntled whatever look, then he steps to my side, so that we're standing next to each other on the doorstep, and I turn and follow his gaze out over the loch.

'Weather's turning,' he says. 'Bad enough now, it'll be terrible again in a couple of hours. Hour and a half maybe.'

'We should get going then.'

He grunts. Noticeably he doesn't ask where it is I want to go, but then he likely already knows. It's not as though there are too many other options.

'I'll be recompensed, shall I?'

'You can submit an invoice to the police station, if that's what you usually do. It's not the first time the police have requested the use of your boat, right?'

Another grunt, and then the grudging, 'Fine. Wait here, I'll be ten minutes.'

He closes the door in my face.

* * *

This is why I'm not in the Navy, or working below decks on the luxury yacht of some Russian billionaire oligarch crime supremo.

We're on a fifteen-minute boat journey across a loch in fairly inclement, but not catastrophically tempestuous weather, and I'm bricking it. Fuck me.

We're on a motorboat of a certain length. It's white. It's raised at the front, with the cockpit and the steering wheel, and a small cabin beneath it. I'm saying small cabin, but the door's closed, I haven't been in, and maybe it's just a cupboard. That's all I've got. Maybe there's a nautical word for steering wheel and cockpit, but that's of no interest to me. All I care about is getting to dry land.

What a stupid thing to be scared of. What's the worst that can happen? The boat capsizes. Big fucking shitshow, Batman, who cares? So I'd be stuck in the middle of a freezing loch? I'm not actually scared of that. Probability of rescue, low, probability of death, high. Don't give a fuck. Bring it on. It would save me from all the shit that flows through my head every single day.

And yet I'm terrified. Who knew? Nice to add another fear to the list. Fuck me backwards.

'You feel sick?' asks Craven.

First thing he's said since we started. He's standing at the wheel, and I'm just to the side of him, down a step, clinging on to the rail that runs around the cockpit. Every few seconds the bow of the boat hits a wave, my stomach lurches and spray cavalcades through the air and covers us. Nice of him not to offer me a life jacket, and I didn't ask because I had my *what's the worst that could happen* hat on.

'No.'

I swallow. I don't feel sick, though I thought I would. I thought feeling sick would be the worst of it.

'That's because you're shitting it, son,' says Craven. 'Your mind's too preoccupied with the fear to realise your stomach's in turmoil.'

He laughs.

I don't care. And I have nothing to say. I just want to feel land again, even though it's less than ten minutes since we left it.

Already wondering how long it'll take me to walk back around the loch, and whether I can afford to not give a fuck if it's two hours.

The boat lurches, my stomach lurches, fear races, spray flies.

31

At least Ellis's boats are tied up, tight against the small jetty. No guarantee he's not out and about in the surrounding hills, but it's early on a Sunday morning, and there are no obvious signs of footfalls through the snow.

Still, he is not answering repeated bangs on the door. I turn and look back at the small boat in which we just crossed the loch. The fear has gone, forgotten now that the ground is firm underfoot. Craven remained on the boat, and stands in the same position as before, clutching the steering wheel to keep his balance, watching me with a familiar irascibility.

I turn back and give the door another knock, then take a step back.

There are possibilities. He's in the shower, or somewhere else in the house, and hasn't heard. He's heard and decided to ignore it, or will get here in good time. He saw me coming and thought, that guy can fuck off, I'm not answering the door to him. Or the other thing. There's always the other thing. The possibility that plagues every murder enquiry. That Ellis – who I've been assuming all along is involved in some way with the disappearance of Alice Schäfer, and very possibility complicit in some way, if not downright guilty, of the murders – turns out himself to be a victim.

Won't that be a pain in the arse?

Give it another half minute, aware that the cold is seeping into my blood the longer I stand here, then finally I fumble for the Lishi, and get to work. Third time in two days. If the Daily Record could see me now.

Outrage At Boozy Copper's Break-In Spree.

One Rule For Them, As Cop King-Pin Takes Law Into Own Hands.

Love Rat Cop Shags Holyrood Wag In New Outrage.

God, I wish I could shut my brain off sometimes.

Into the house, close the door loudly behind me. I'm not looking to sneak in after all, I'm not looking to surprise him. The list of things he could be doing in his own house that I don't want to know about is long. Long and squalid.

'Mr Ellis!'

Stand still in the dark wooden hallway, listening for sounds of life.

A long runner on a wooden floor, stairs immediately to the right. Two doors off to the left, another beneath the stairs, another straight ahead. All the doors are closed, not much light in here. Not getting any particular sense of the house. Don't feel his presence, though neither do I feel the presence of death. Perhaps he's just out.

Last chance, before I get on with it.

'Ellis!'

Once again I stand still, listening for any sound.

Nothing.

'Fuck it.'

Room to room, and be quick about it.

First room, the sitting room overlooking the loch. Would expect to find a telescope in here, but then, perhaps it's more likely to be at the upstairs window. Perfect place from which to keep an eye on the town.

Nothing to see in here, and I barely make any mental note of the place. I'm looking for Ellis, period, dead or alive. Have no desire to spend time searching through drawers, looking for clues, like I'm fucking Velma or something.

Next room along, a small dining room, table and chairs and an old-fashioned hi-fi, and a quite horrible chandelier. Devoid of life. Hallway, open the door beneath the stairs, the expected cupboard, rammed full of coats and shoes and fishing gear, and nothing to suggest there's a body hidden in amongst all that crap, then into the kitchen at the back of the house.

A large room, brighter than all the rest. A long kitchen table, cabinets around the walls, to the left the kitchen area. A couple of doors to the right, presumably to a pantry or a washing machine. On the other side of the table, double doors leading out onto a patio.

There's a radio playing, talk radio, but it sounds like Radio 4, rather than one of those outrage-powered stations where people shout bile into their phones in the name of freedom.

'What do you want, Sergeant?'

Ellis doesn't look up. His right hand holds a spoon over a bowl of granola, his left rests on the handle of a coffee mug.

There's a cafetiere on the table.

'You never answer your door, or you knew it was me?'

'Craven called. Said he was bringing you over.'

Well, I really ought to have worked that one out. I'm the stranger in a town where everyone knows everyone else.

'You can pay me for any damage you've done to the lock.'

I don't bother with the defence.

'It was me who broke into the lodge hall on Friday evening.'

He stares into his bowl of granola, having not moved since I came in, and then he grimly smiles.

'You're funny, Sergeant Hutton. Did you have to launch an inquiry? You're like that fucking moron Johnson having to investigate himself to find out whether he committed fraud or shagged the wrong person or attended a booze-up in his own fucking garden. Well, at least you were fairly quick to conclude who the culprit was. Going to lock yourself up now?'

I suppose I can hardly begrudge him the sarcasm.

'Let's talk about the photographs on the wall.'

At last he moves, slow and deliberate, spoon to his mouth, noiselessly takes the food and starts chewing. Spoon back in the bowl, lifts the coffee, takes a drink.

'What photographs?' he says eventually. 'There are lots of photographs in that hall.'

'The ones you'd removed by the following day.'

Silence.

On the radio they're talking about Brexit, one of the many great plagues upon our times.

'How many people use the lodge office?'

A small movement of the eyebrow. He still hasn't looked at me.

'It's my office.'

'Do others enter the office? Do you have meetings in there? Guests? When you have lodge meetings, are there others who use the space?'

Now he lifts his eyes, but not his head, and looks pokerfaced across his breakfast.

'Would that be your way of asking if there's anyone else you can speak to?'

'Who else uses it?'

'Most members will have been in there at one time or another. It's not a secret lockdown room. It's not a *fucking*

170

bunker. It's just an office.'

'So what happened to the photographs?'

'I took them down,' he says. 'It's my office, I'm allowed to change the décor sometimes, right? That's a thing I can do, I believe. Or are you in fact here as a delegate from Freemason Central Command, with instruction to bring the lodge back under the control of the centre, starting with taking charge of which photographs I can display in my office?'

Fuck off, you prick.

'Why did you take the pictures down when you did?'

'You bullshitted me for a couple of days, Sergeant, maybe I'll just bullshit you.'

'There have been two murders in the last twenty-four hours.'

His eyes narrow a little, the classic shadow across the face. Either concern, or acting, always so hard to tell.

'So, now we have Alice Schäfer, whose photo was on that wall, missing. And we have Gillian Cooper, whose photo was on that wall, dead, and we also have Margaret Wills dead, and I have no idea if her photo was on the wall.' A beat, let him look curious and concerned for a moment, yet still unforgiving, 'Was Margaret's photo on the wall?'

'Yes.'

'Who else?'

'Who else what?'

He takes another mouthful of food, as though an act of defiance.

'Who else in the town was on that wall?'

'You really think those two women got murdered because their pictures were on a wall?' he says through the food.

'I don't know, but I don't like coincidences.'

'Gillian and Margaret would've gone to the same school. They would have been signed up to the same GP's surgery. Maybe they both played golf or they were in a book group or they both went shooting or fishing, or fuck knows what. Maybe all sorts of things. You're clutching.'

'What were the women to the lodge?'

'What?'

'Why did you have those pictures? What link did those women have to the lodge?'

'The fuck does it matter to you? It's none of your business, Sergeant. Alice's disappearance, these two murders, have nothing to do with us. Nothing to do with the lodge. So the fact that their pictures are on the wall is completely insignificant.'

'Constable Mara was also on that wall.'

'Was she? Why don't you ask her, since the two of you are getting on so well.'

I get the sly, knowing look, and feel the familiar guilt and shame of the addict and his curse.

'I did. She told me. I want to know if you give the same answer.'

'You're a funny man, Sergeant.'

'Yeah, I know. Why'd you have the pictures of the women?'

More food, a slurp of coffee, the cup placed firmly back on the table. Making the calculation. If there's nothing more to tell than what Mara told me, then why bother keeping it a secret? It's more about asserting authority. His house, his lodge, his town, he shouldn't have to defer to an out-of-town police officer. Does he look weak by answering? That's what he's thinking. Like I give a fuck about some stupid power dynamic.

Or else, of course, he's hiding something.

'It's a trivial matter, Sergeant. A ceremony steeped in history, dating back to long before the Lodge of St Augustine broke away from the centre, now reduced to little more than a dinner with a couple of speeches. The women are guests of honour, nothing more.'

'Why take the pictures down then, if you've nothing to hide?'

'You annoyed me by breaking in. You stuck your nose into lodge business, when it was of no concern to you. It was inevitable that you'd see the picture of Alice on the wall and jump to the wrong conclusion. I elected to remove them from view.'

'And then you broke into my house and removed the photograph from my phone? And you drugged my wine?'

'No one broke into your house.'

He can't help himself, the vague look past my shoulder in the direction of outside, the loch, the boat tied up to the jetty. No one broke into my house, because it was just a matter of Craven letting himself into his own house.

'What was the point?' I say, not bothering to look for confirmation of Craven's part in proceedings.

As I think of him, I suddenly wonder if he's still going to

172

be waiting for me out there. Would this all be part of their obstruction? Take me across the loch, then turn around and go home, leaving me to walk back.

If that's the case, I'm stealing this fucker's boat.

Yeah, that'd go well.

'I saw the picture on the wall. I saw Alice. You can't wipe my memory.'

He doesn't answer. The eyes don't leave me, but he goes on eating his damned granola in silence.

'It's not about Alice, is it? It's about the others on there. It's about me taking that photograph on my phone and showing it around town. It's about me showing that picture to others, asking them to identify the women. That's what you don't want.'

'Like I say, it is a matter of little consequence, like so much in life. We have our secrets, we have our rituals, passed down from generation to generation. What does any of it mean? Why does anyone care? But there's little in life, beyond hunger and security, that cannot be reduced to such questions. Why make a film about vampires? Why make any film? Why write books? Why go to church? Why walk along a road in an orange sash playing a flute? There's little that can't be reduced to the insignificant. And so we have our insignificant secrets. Nevertheless, secret they are, and secret they will remain. The identities of the women on that wall are not generally known. The women themselves are sworn to secrecy every year. The origins of this are long since lost in the history of the lodge, but we continue it for traditions' sake.' A pause, and then, 'Humour us if you will, Sergeant.'

'No.'

A withering look this time, and then the dismissive wave.

'I'm bored, and I have things to do this Sunday morning. You can leave.'

'I'm not done.'

'Well, I am, so there's little point in your being here. Goodbye, Sergeant.'

'What about the stupid chicken, and the even stupider snowman? That was you, was it? What happened to the horse's head in the bed?'

He holds my gaze for a moment, then flicks open his phone and uses it to turn the volume up on the radio.

Unavoidably, together we listen to ten seconds of some obfuscating fucker of a Tory, and it's a Sunday morning, so it can't be Today, and I wonder if there's no escape, then I turn, and walk back out into the hall. As soon as I'm out of the room, the volume of the radio is substantially lowered.

I stand with my fingers on the front door handle. I contemplate the classic bluff, which I've employed in the past, of faking my exit, opening and closing the door without actually leaving, but I know that within five seconds of the door closing, Ellis will be marking my movements, making sure I've actually gone.

There's a noise upstairs. Nothing much, but a definite bump. A movement, rather than the creaking of an old house.

I look up the stairs, as though I might be able to see something.

'You're still here.'

Ellis is at the kitchen door.

'Who's upstairs?'

'My God, Sergeant, are you paid by the suspicion? Do you get a bonus every time you conjure up some absurd theory or wild speculation?'

'There was a noise upstairs.'

The long stare, and then his hand moves to the wall heater at that end of the hallway.

'The boiler has just come on. Likely because the temperature dropped with you opening the front door a few minutes ago. The boiler is as old as the house, which may not be old for a house, but it's old for a boiler. It does little without letting us know about it. Would you care to check my boiler, or do you want to go and get a warrant, so you can get a certified plumbing engineer to check the boiler?'

We stand in silence for a few moments, which is about him attempting to assert himself, and me trying to listen for any other sound from upstairs. There is no doubt, at least, that the heating has come on.

Fuck it.

Up the stairs quickly, two steps at a time. Ellis does not follow.

I go room to room. Four bedrooms of various sizes. One, the obvious master, at the front of the house, a large picture window looking across the loch to the town, an elegantly furnished bathroom off. Three other bedrooms, none of them currently in use, little of note in any of them. Another room, an upstairs sitting room, to the side, looking down the loch in the direction of the glen. A small telescope by the window. Nothing to be seen at the moment, of course. And there's a bathroom and there's a large, walk-in cupboard off the hallway, and that's that.

No one. No other sound, no sign of someone having scurried off to hide in a cupboard.

I walk slowly back down the stairs, cursing quietly. Back into the hall, Ellis remains exactly where I left him a minute ago, leaning on the kitchen doorframe.

He looks as though he's going to make some glib comment or other, but it doesn't make it all the way to his lips, and instead I get a withering look.

I turn, open the door, and walk quickly through the small porch and back outside.

Oh, fuck off.

Craven's small boat is already halfway back across the loch.

I'm standing there, staring at the cold, dark waves against the cold white of the land and the cold grey of the sky, the small boat several hundred yards away moving with the swell, when I feel Ellis come and stand silently beside me.

And so we stand together for a while, Ellis in whatever triumph he feels, waiting for me to ask, and me, grinding my teeth, feeling stupid for having trusted Craven in the first place, wanting two things. A glass of vodka, and fuck all else to do with this stupid case.

'In case you're wondering, I pre-arranged with Mr Craven for him to leave, just to fuck you off. So, no, you can't get my boat. And you can't stay.' He makes a gesture towards the rough track that leads away from his house to our left. 'You'd better get walking, they say the storm's coming back.'

He turns away, firmly closing the door behind him.

I stand and look out over the cold. The loch stretches away from me. For a moment the small boat disappears in the swell, and I hope briefly that it's sunk and that Craven might be drowned, but the water moves, the up and down of the waves in the wind, and there he is, still motoring slowly back to the other side.

I turn and start walking.

32

I start the trudge back to the village, despite myself, trying to think about the case. By the time I'm about halfway there, and my mind is giving into the cold and the drudgery of the walk, and the snow has started to fall again, and the chill of the wind whipping across the loch has intensified, I've persuaded myself that Alice Schäfer isn't dead. Alice Schäfer, in fact, is the murderer, and she's currently hiding out in Ellis's house. She came to the town to kill Margaret Wills and to kill Gillian Cooper, and before that she came to my house, and I wasn't dreaming, and she really did make love to me in the middle of the night.

That's how fucking cold and how fucking scrambled my mind is. The missing woman is the killer.

I walk along, talking out loud, practicing my pitch to Mara. And what would she say to all that?

By the time I get to the station, which I stumble across before getting back to the house, I can barely think or move, I've lost the feeling in my feet and hands, I'm frozen and covered in snow, and the storm is picking up once more, the wind howling, the snow whirling.

Mara's sitting at her desk. She straightens, looks worried and curious and bemused.

'Sergeant? What the…?'

I stand there for a moment. The office is not too warm, and I don't get the shock of the heat yet. Had already, through the fug, been thinking this through. Was I getting hypothermic? If I was, or if I wasn't, how would I know? Should I just walk inside and sit on a heater, or would that cause some kind of a shock?

Not having the answers, here I am.

'Jesus,' she says, and then she's up out of her chair and leaping into action.

* * *

Fifteen minutes later, huddled in a seat, cup of tea in hand, blanket wrapped around my shoulders, functions beginning to return to normal.

What was the stupidest part of the morning so far? Not realising that Craven and Ellis would be working together, or setting off into the snow for a ninety-minute walk, improperly dressed for the occasion?

Fuck, it wasn't as though I was wearing shorts and sandals and a T-shirt.

'What did you learn?' she asks.

She looked at me as though I was about to die for a few minutes, but that has eased as I've thawed out, and now she's looking slightly perturbed that I set off with Craven and without telling her what I was doing, and that he abandoned me on the other side of the loch.

'Confirmation of your explanation of why there was a gallery of young women on the wall of his office at the lodge, should I choose to believe the two of you.'

She looks like she doesn't really know what to do with that, so she just kind of shakes her head.

'And I think there was someone else in the house with him, but I have no way of knowing for sure.'

She looks a little curious.

'I wouldn't know. I don't know of anyone else who stays out there.'

'You don't suppose it could be Alice?'

'What? Why? Why Alice? You mean being held prisoner?'

'I mean, hiding.'

She seems confused by the notion, and eventually shrugs. I'm back, deep in my suspicions, not believing anything she says or does.

Take some more tea, the drink getting to the kind of temperature that allows it to be taken quickly. Can still feel the glorious warmth of it going down, still being revived by the mouthful. I've thrown on an old pair of trousers and a jumper from lost property, my boots and clothes drying on a variety of heaters throughout the building. I'm giving it another twenty minutes and then I'm going to see DeShaun.

'Anything to report?' I finally ask.

It occurred to me, at some point on the walk, that perhaps I'd return to news of another murder, but I guess that's something she would have told me already.

'Nothing,' she says. 'Fingers crossed the storm keeps the killings at bay, and then tomorrow morning…'

She makes a take-off motion, and I can't really argue with that. It will be a blessed relief when the big dogs arrive. If they arrive, and if they're big.

'Yeah,' is all I say.

More tea, almost finished the mug. Stare at the floor, feel her eyes on me. Don't want to look at her, because we'll end up just doing another one of those curious stares, that I don't think either of us really understands.

'You check in on Bill Cooper this morning?' I ask.

'He looks wiped out. Combination of events and the lingering effects of whatever knockout mum gave him last night.'

'Anything to contribute?'

'Nope. Our conversation was brief, but he basically said the same things as he said last night. Nothing that could help us.'

I have every intention of checking in on him myself, but I won't mention that. Everything has to be measured against my level of suspicion with the constable. It was her, after all, who suggested I get the boat from Craven.

'OK, thanks,' I say. Polish off the tea. Stare straight ahead, into the unknown. Time passes from one minute to the next. Soon enough, I'm going to have to go back out into that snow, with my boots still damp, and I really, really don't want to.

* * *

'Didn't she say? I handed it in about an hour and a half ago. It didn't take me long. Piece of piss, tbh.'

'You handed it in?'

'To the police station. I gave it to the lady policewoman. Officer. The policewoman officer. Oh, wait, that's from a film. Policewoman officer. What it is? What is it?' He snaps his fingers.

'*Hot Fuzz*,' I say with no enthusiasm. Already cursing Mara. Fucking hell.

'That's it.' He laughs at the thought of *Hot Fuzz*. 'Wow, you're good. Got it just like that.'

'What did you tell her?'

'Who?'

'Constable Mara.'

178

'Right, right. I said you were looking for me to dig up some photos from it, and I thought I'd found what you were looking for. I mean, I think I did.'

'What'd she say?'

He stares at me with a peculiar intensity – though perhaps it's just him illustrating how much thought he's giving it – then he nods. 'She asked if I could open the phone for her, and I said I couldn't. She asked how I'd worked on it if I didn't know the code, and I said I did know the code, but I couldn't tell her. She kind of nodded at that. Thought she might pull some bullshit police manoeuvre, but maybe she's just not like that. I don't know. You should go and see her.'

Well, maybe she didn't pull that particular bullshit police manoeuvre, but she certainly pulled another one.

'You find the photo that shows a lot of other photos on a wall?'

'Women? Yeah. I mean, it's not a great shot. I cleaned it up a bit for you.'

'Thanks.' Above and beyond.

'Let me know what you think, or if there's anything else you need looked at.'

'You recognise anyone on the photo, by the way?'

He's been nodding, mostly in agreement with himself about how helpful he's been, and he keeps nodding for a second.

'Some,' he says after a few moments.

'Go on.'

'Wait, is this part of the police enquiry now?'

I give him the appropriate look.

'What?' he says.

'Yes! I'm the police officer, and this is me asking questions. It's part of the fucking enquiry.' A moment, then I make a small apologetic gesture. 'Sorry. But you know, DeShaun, there have been two murders and there's a missing woman. So, yes, police inquiry.'

'I'm not a suspect though?'

'Jesus, I literally gave you my phone.'

'Good point.'

I ask him the question again, this time with a suitable look of exasperation. I am not, as we all know, psychologically designed to interview the younger generation.

'What was the question again?'

'Did you recognise anyone?'

'Right. Alice, right? She was one of them?'

'Yep. Anyone else? And this isn't a trick question, kid, I only got a quick look at it. I don't know everyone who's on it.'

He looks a little unsure, like he doesn't want to admit to any others, then he finally says, 'Was the policewoman there?'

'Yep, good spot. Anyone else?'

He perks up a little, accepting my minimal throwaway words of praise, and getting more enthusiastic for the discussion.

'You know, it's hard to tell 'n that, but there were a couple of other folk I think I might have recognised from around the village. Someone else who turned up for the vampire gig, right?'

'You can't think of the names or where you might have seen them in the village?'

'Not off the top of my head. Maybe if I saw the photo again.'

'I'll bring it back, if I have the time. What about anyone from the film crew?'

He gives me the familiar *I have something to say but I'm going to pretend there's nothing* look.

'What?'

'Nothing.'

'Tell me, DeShaun.'

'I'd need to see it again.'

'Who do you think you saw?'

'Look, I think there was someone, but I don't want to get anyone in the shit.'

'Why'd you think you're getting anyone in the shit, son? It's just a photograph on a wall, it's no big deal.'

'No big deal? That's why you're giving a complete stranger your phone, that's why we've been sitting here talking about it for the past ten minutes.'

'Abigail Connolly?'

'What?'

'Was it Abigail?'

'Was it Abigail what?'

'Whose picture was on the wall?'

'What? No, oh no. I mean, I didn't see *her*. But there was someone else… But don't do that thing, man, of listing everyone here to gauge my reaction. Lips are sealed, man.'

'Jesus, DeShaun. Who did you think you saw from the film crew?'

He holds up a pair of defensive hands.

'Look, I really need to get back to the shoot, Carol's got a couple of things she needs doing. Bring me the phone back, and we'll go through it together.'

'Is Abigail here?'

'I need to go, man.'

'Fine, go. But is Abigail here?'

'Don't think so. I mean, she's head of casting, and I think they're done with that. See you, man.'

It doesn't matter whether he talks, and right now, it doesn't really matter about Abigail Connolly. Either way, I have to see that picture again, and I have to confirm that there really was someone else from the film crew amongst them. One person from the film coming back to revisit an old haunt is one thing. Two, and both of them part of this peculiar group of young women who are linked to this strange lodge business, begins to look even more suspicious.

I leave DeShaun to his film shoot, stand in chill silence at the doorway of the old hotel for a few moments looking out on the blizzard, suddenly feel consumed by self-doubt, wondering if all my thoughts about the lodge and its connection to these crimes are way off the mark, and then tell myself that either way, this time tomorrow my part in this will all be done, the snow will be melting, and I can return to quietly drinking wine on my own at my kitchen table, and then I open the door, take the cold blast full in the face, and step out into the raging storm.

33

Mara is gone when I get back to the station. Even with just a few minutes back outside I can feel myself starting to shiver again, and I stick the kettle on and make a large mug of tea.

Mug in hand, coat still on, I sit down at Mara's desk and stare out at the storm. Give myself a couple of minutes to warm up.

So, Mara must really not want me to see that photograph. If she hadn't wanted me to know she was on it, for one reason or another, that might have made sense. But I already know she is, and she knows that I know. Which means there's someone else she doesn't want me to know about, which means she's tied up in the whole thing.

Although, if that's the case, it doesn't make sense she asked for my help in the disappearance of Alice Schäfer in the first place.

I drink the tea quickly. I drink everything quickly, which is fine with most things, but not so great with wine and vodka. Feel like I want to go to bed, wearing the kind of warm, fleecy pyjamas that I haven't possessed since I was eight, snuggle beneath one of those expensive-ass duvets you come across in expensive-ass hotels, and go to sleep. And it's not my case, so why shouldn't I, lack of pyjamas and duvet notwithstanding?

Fuck it, I wish I could.

There's a high probability that Mara took my phone with her, of course, but on the off-chance she put it in a drawer, I need to start looking.

The two desk drawers are locked, but fortunately they're the kind of lock that gives way to the picking tool in seconds.

Top drawer, the obvious one for the phone to have been placed in, and it's not there. And so it begins, and I start raking through the files and detritus of Mara's small town station life, not in the slightest bothered if she walks in on me while I'm about it.

All the while I have to consider the possibility that the sex was just a distraction tactic. That she wasn't interested in me for that Ryan Gosling-esque raw sex appeal I've got going on. Perhaps she heard Alice was missing, had no idea what was going on, and asked for help. Then someone – and by someone, obviously I mean Ellis – said what the fuck are you doing? We don't need some pesky copper on hand. Take his mind off it. Sure, she could have asked me to stand down; instead, she took a different route. I guess that's where the Ryan Gosling thing came in to play. I mean, who can blame her, right?

Ten minutes later, having established that the phone has not been casually placed in a drawer or cabinet, I'm back sitting at her desk looking at the one thin file that I came away with. The paperwork relating to the various applications to film the movie in and around the town, all of which had gone through Highland Council in Inverness, and had been copied to Mara. There's nothing from Mara herself, although as the local police officer presumably she just had to be kept informed, rather than issue any actual approval.

There's one name all over it, and that's Petra Hunt, the film's producer. All the movie correspondence came from her, and hers is the only signature from the film company side.

Fuck it, I didn't speak to her. Not that I spoke to everyone on the damn film set, but I should have got around to speaking to the person in overall charge of the whole shebang.

Since Hunt is Finnish, would she really have been around this place long enough to get her picture on the board? I guess Abigail Connolly isn't from around here. Perhaps the route she took, of working at the nearby outdoor centre, is a well-trodden one. If Connolly could have gone from studying ecology to working in film, then why not Petra Hunt, from ecology to finance to film. People end up in all sorts of places, regardless of where they start out.

I stand up again, walking to the window, looking out once more on the white squall. I want to speak to Mara, and I need my damn phone. Cursing DeShaun for handing it over, mainly cursing myself for being so stupid.

Fuck it, need to get back out there, out into the storm, though I could barely want to do it less. And so I go through the routine, putting damp clothes back on, pulling on damp boots. Take another minute at the window, and then with a curse and a head shake, open the door, feel the force of the wind and the snow in my face, then walk out into it, not bothering to lock the door behind me.

* * *

I knew the inevitability of this before I got here.

Abigail Connolly is dead, a knife buried in her heart. Perhaps, at the moment of her murder, she held her hands aloft in horror, and the killer's familiar eye socket approach was denied them. A knife in the heart will do the same job.

I stand for a moment, looking down at her stricken body – she's sitting upright in the familiar position in an armchair – then I step forward, place a light hand against her skin, still some residual warmth in her body, then I step back and take a look around the house.

She wasn't wrong. It's old and speaks of spiders. If you don't like those leggy little bastards, this is not the place for you. Windows are small too, with no view down to the loch.

The door was unlocked when I arrived, no sign of anyone having forced entry. A familiar look to the crime scene. Quite possibly the door opened and the unsuspecting victim-to-be invited her killer in out of the cold. I think of how this all started for me, when I did exactly that with my late night visitor. Recognised the look of the police officer, and asked her in.

I'm fifty-fifty on whether Mara is involved, but so far pretty damned sure she's not murdering anyone. Fuck, that would be a plot twist, I suppose. A shitty one, but a plot twist all the same.

I need to get back to the film set. I need to establish if anyone else is missing. I need to establish who else DeShaun recognised from the wall of photographs, even if I have to beat it out of him. Hopefully, with the news of Connolly's death, and the real possibility that whoever else was on that wall is also under threat, his tongue will be loosened, and beating will be unnecessary.

There's no sign of her phone, which is unsurprising, and no sign of a laptop. All evidence removed, very possibly disposed of. I make a search of the house, looking in drawers, checking behind doors. There's nothing to find. The killer turned up, they buried a knife in Abigail Connolly's chest, they left.

Soon enough I'm back at the window, looking out on the storm, a position I seem to have spent much of the day in. Moving from one place to the other, pausing every time before embracing the cold.

184

Abigail Connolly rests in death behind me. I thought of getting a blanket and draping it over the corpse, but there are a lot of conventions going out of the window now. I need to get back to the movie set, but it's entirely about attempting to head the killer off at the pass. It's not about informing people of Connolly's death, although obviously there will be people who need to be informed, and who will care. I don't intend to make any attempt to establish whether she has family who should be told. The quick fly round the premises aside, I'm doing none of the regular crime scene activities. And I'm about as detached from the victim as I could possibly be, considering we're in the same room, and it's a woman I've spoken to a couple of times.

It's no time to be caring. She's a cipher. A thing that happened. But this story is not *about* her. She was caught up in the maelstrom, and now she's dead. Now I need to find out what the story *is* about, and hopefully before anyone else I care nothing for gets killed.

So, I'm a heartless bastard. In my defence, at least I'm trying to sort this out before it gets any worse.

'Fuck it,' I say to the world, and then out the door, close it unlocked behind me, and start walking quickly through the snow in the direction of the hotel.

Notice it straight away. With a snap of the fingers, there's been a change. The wind has shifted, and although it's still snowing, and although it's still damned cold, there's a feeling in the air. Maybe the snow is a little less dry, there's a hint of warmth somewhere.

I walk to the hotel, head down, not looking over my shoulder. Despite the death, despite the fact that whoever's committing murder is not going to welcome my involvement, I do not fear attack. Perhaps I don't think they'll go that far; perhaps I just don't care. My passing would not be lamented by many.

Wait? If this isn't about Abigail Connolly, it sure as fuck ain't about you, you narcissistic cave dweller.

Get to the hotel in ten minutes, without seeing anyone else abroad. No one else stupid enough, no one else with any reason to be out. More than likely there aren't too many about in this place on any Sunday, regardless of the weather and the murder spree.

Into the hotel lobby, stand in silence for a few moments. There's no one here, and I feel the temperature of the hotel trying to gauge where they're likely to be. The door to the dining room is open, but there's no sign of anyone in there. Finally, a creak of a floorboard upstairs, and so I quickly make my way up there.

A few people in the corridor, biding their time. There are a few open doors, a couple of folk milling in and out of rooms, but the centre of attention is a closed door, behind which they are presumably filming.

'DeShaun around?' I ask the first person I come to.

Despite the fact that I'd lowered my voice, I still get the censorious finger to the lips, and she indicates the closed door with a nod.

'He's on set,' she whispers.

'I need to speak to him.'

'You can't.'

'I'm the police, I'm investigating a triple murder, and I need to speak to him.'

I spit the line out, with far more feeling than my level of determination warrants. Naturally, in the face of talk of a triple murder, she blanches quicker than boiled cabbage. She looks at the door. She's now trapped, in between the police and the movie director.

'It's OK,' I say, deciding to give her a bit of breathing space. 'I can wait a minute or two. How long will they be?'

'Any time now.' She glances at the door, as though expecting something to happen. I notice the red light. That's what she's looking at. As we watch it together, like anxious lovers watching the sky to see if the Spitfires will return from dogfights over the Channel, the light switches from red to green.

'Bingo,' I say, a little less quietly. 'I can go in?'

'Yes. But be circumspect. Quiet.' A moment, then to my back, 'Please.'

I open the door, quickly step inside, and close it behind me.

Wow, this was a big fucking hotel room. This must have been the high-priced, executive suite. There are ten to fifteen people in the room, with two cameras and all the attention centred around the bed.

There's a woman on the bed, naked, bar a sheet which looks as though it's just been tossed over her. There are four men around her: three of them standing, one of them sitting on the bed, leaning towards her, chatting.

'Derek?' says a voice I don't recognise. 'The fuck's

Derek?'

'He went with Randall to look for the cutter,' replies another detached voice.

'That was fifteen fucking minutes ago.'

'Five. They'll be back in a minute.'

'K, K. Can we just go through this again. Benny, that was terrific, fucking nailed it man. Jan, you OK?'

'I'm good,' says the woman.

'You seemed a little –'

'No, no, it's good, really.'

'And you're all right with the sheet all –'

'It's fine, Jeremy.'

She smiles, she whisks the sheet away, tossing it onto the carpet. Someone, a runner or a prop guy or a something, scurries over and takes the sheet, moving it out of shot. The actress, who I'm imagining I once saw in a thing, is now naked on the bed.

'Let's go,' she says.

This'll be why it's so warm in this room. Must have the heating cranked up full.

She's gorgeous, looks wonderful naked. No wonder she's happy using her body like this. I turn away. Look around the room. DeShaun's there, back of the room, out of shot, looking at me. I make a gesture towards him, indicating the door.

'Right, people,' says the voice.

I open the door, and immediately feel about fifty pairs of eyes on me, and a, 'Jesus fucking Christ,' fills the air. I step back out into the corridor, leaving the door open until DeShaun has followed me. The inevitable, 'Will someone shut the fucking door?' comes just before DeShaun steps out of the room behind me, then the door is closed, they can go back to their scene, and I lead DeShaun away from the small crowd. We find an empty room a couple of doors along, go inside and close the door.

We gravitate towards the window, and look out on the storm, and the loch, and the tumult of the waves. Ellis's house must be directly opposite here, but it's lost in the snow and cloud.

'I really don't have a lot of time,' he says. 'Things are getting pretty stressy in th –'

'Can you keep a secret?'

He looks a little taken aback by that. He doesn't answer, seemingly too uncomfortable with the idea. He doesn't want to have to be the keeper of secrets.

'I don't know,' he says when I give him a harsh look.

'Well, let's see how you get on. Abigail's been murdered.'

He swallows. Eyes widen.

'Fuck.'

'Yeah, fuck.'

'When?'

'I don't know, but she's dead. That's all that matters for Abigail now. This isn't about when it happened, this is about making sure it doesn't happen to anyone else.'

I stare at him harshly, but all I get is the wide-eyed stare in return.

'Jesus, DeShaun. There have been three confirmed murders. Each of the victims was featured on that wall of pictures. I need you to tell me who else from the film crew was on that wall.'

'Didn't you get your phone from the lady?'

'I haven't seen her, she's out and about. Out there, somewhere. Tell me who else?'

'I don't… I mean… I don't want to say.'

'Fuck me, DeShaun. Where's the director?'

'What?'

'Whoever that was in there shouting stuff, shouting directions, who *was* that? That wasn't Karen.'

'No.'

'So, where's Karen?'

He swallows again. DeShaun is not mentally built to cope with talking to a police officer under any sort of duress.

'Where's Karen, DeShaun?'

'I don't know. She's just… you know, she's gone missing. No one knows where she is.'

'So, who's that in there?'

'That's Jeremy, the AD. Petra said we have to crack on. Time's short, 'n all, only got two days left of the shoot.'

I stand and look at the wall in the direction of the filming, two rooms away, as though I've got some sort of Superman-level shit going on with my eyes.

'I need to know where Karen is.'

I can feel the shake of his head next to me. I don't look at him.

'Was it Karen's photograph you recognised on the wall?'

Nothing.

'Fuck me, man,' I say, turning towards him, 'enough,

already! Was it Karen's photograph on the damned wall?'

'Yes! Jesus. Yes.'

'Oh, for fuck's sake. Anyone else?'

'What?'

'Anyone else from the wall, from the wall of photographs, anyone else from the movie on there?'

'I don't think so.'

'But you're not sure?'

'I don't think so. I'd need to see it again.'

'Well, if you hadn't given it to someone else.'

'Whose side is she on?' he more or less yelps, and I have to back the fuck off. He's not wrong. Perfectly reasonable of him to give it to Mara, since I didn't bother telling him otherwise.

'What is this movie about?'

I can feel DeShaun's agitation, his keenness to get back next door, back to the familiar.

'Like, vampires and stuff, you know this.'

'But that, in there. A woman naked on the bed, and four men around her? Is that a gangbang scene? I mean, this isn't a porn movie, is it?'

'Of course not. It's got your man out of *Vigil*.'

'So, what's that scene about?'

'I don't know. They have some sort of weird sex ritual going on.'

'Weird sex ritual? Can you be more specific?'

'Something about, I don't know, like keeping a woman in a state of near-orgasm for like hours and stuff.'

'Where do the vampires come in?'

'It's their ritual. They take it in turns drinking her blood and like keeping her aroused.'

'And this isn't a porn movie?'

'I just… I mean, there is not a single act of penetration in sight, man. It's kosher.'

'I need to speak to someone about the movie.'

He makes a gesture, a simple *that's what you're doing* movement of the hands.

'I need to speak to someone in creative. I need to speak to someone who knows what the film's about.'

'I just told you what it's about.'

'Does it have an underlying meaning?'

'Fucked if I know,' he says, almost laughing at that.

'Terrific. I need to speak to one of the creatives. Who else is there?'

'Julie, I guess.'

'The writer?'

'Yeah.'

'Fine. I need to talk to her. And Ms. Hunt. Can you get them in here, right now, please?'

'I can't just... I mean, you saw what it's like in there, people are literally –'

'DeShaun. Go and get them. Julie and Petra. Right now. If they don't want to come, tell them I'm coming in there to shut down the whole damned picture.'

He swallows again. He continues to stare.

'Go, DeShaun, and have them back here in under a minute.'

And now, finally, he turns away, the same look of concern on his face, and runs out into the corridor.

34

'Vampires come in cycles. They are up, they are down. But no matter how far they are down, or how long they are down, they always come back. I thought merely that a vampire film would be a strong bet. That is all.'

'That seemed quite explicit what was going on in there.'

My voice has an insistence to it that is not shared by Petra Hunt. She is deliberate without being slow, but certainly has no sense of urgency. On the other hand, I've yet to tell her that Abigail Connolly is dead, or that there's real reason to be worried about Karen Wright going AWOL.

'Explicit?'

'Pornographic.'

'No, it is not pornographic. It is a naked woman. This film is being made in English, but I envisage selling it more widely across Europe than in the UK. There is a more sophisticated audience, better able to deal with the naked human body without making absurd over-reactions. There is an underlying feel of eroticism in the film, but do not confuse that with pornography.'

That's me and my Britishness put in my place. It's a fair cop, and I can hear DI Kallas saying exactly the same thing.

'So, what is the underlying... I don't know, message of the movie? Does it have layers? What is it actually about?'

'That is a good question. I think it is open to interpretation. I like that.'

She looks at Julie, the writer, eyebrows raised. *You wrote it, what do you think it's about?* I follow the look. *Yeah, Julie, that's why you're here.*

'Desire,' says Julie, without missing a beat.

'Desire?'

'Yes.'

'That's it? Desire? *Die Hard* is about desire. *The Muppet Christmas Carol* is about desire. What about desire? How does it relate to the title? *Endless Crazy Love* sounds like, I don't know, like an American teen movie, or a twentysomething romcom, not a vampire movie.'

'Yeah, I never really understood that.'

She gives Hunt a quick, sheepish look at she says it.

'You never understood the title?' I say. 'You wrote the damned thing.'

'Karen came to me with the idea. She had the title, she had the narrative, she just needed a script. The story fleshed out with dialogue, and a fresh perspective. But she had this basic idea.'

'And whose idea was it to come here? To this village?'

'Karen was insistent,' says Hunt. 'She had already scoped the area, she really came to both Julie and I, who are obviously at different ends of the filmmaking team, with a fully-formed concept of what she was going to do. This is a nice location, so I did not complain. Being so remote caused some difficulties, but this hotel was an invaluable resource.'

'Did Karen say how she knew about this village?'

'She said she had toured the Highlands and this was her preferred location.'

'She never said she'd lived here?'

'She did not mention that. Do you think she lived here?'

'She must have done, I'm sure. When she was younger. I don't know for how long. Abigail Connolly also lived here for a year.'

Hunt holds my gaze, expressionless, for a few moments, and then nods.

'That makes sense. Abigail seems unusually involved in the process for a casting director, as far as my understanding goes. She and Karen are obviously familiar with each other on some level, although I believe they have only worked together before on one previous film.'

I look at the writer, who sort of shrugs in agreement.

'The treatment I was working from was credited to both Karen and Abigail.'

'Treatment?'

'The synopsis of the film's narrative. They'd worked on it together. You know, so they presented me with this, like, twenty-page document. Here's the story we want to tell, this is how it goes, can you, you know, flesh it out?'

'And you never asked why it was called *Endless Crazy Love*?'

'Sure, I asked.'

'And?'

'Karen said it was all part of the process.'

'What did that mean?'

She shrugs again. I look at Hunt, and get a blank look in response. It really is like talking to Kallas, minus the painful levels of attraction.

'You know there have been two murders in the village in the last two days?' I say.

The writer visibly shudders, though it is slightly affected.

'Of course,' says Hunt. 'I do not believe they can be related to this production, even though our presence is obviously a change to the usual routine of the village.'

'Abigail's dead,' I say with the kind of curt brutality I've learned from Kallas.

The writer's eyes widen, her hand goes to her mouth.

'Abigail is dead?' says Hunt.

'Murdered, in a similar fashion to the previous two victims.'

'Oh, Jesus,' gasps the writer. Both mouth and eyes even wider than a second ago.

'You are being serious?' asks Hunt, deadpan.

'Yes, I'm being serious. Abigail, who stayed in this town at one point, is dead. You don't know this, but I've already learned there is a specific connection between her and the two previous victims, and with Alice, the missing woman. That connection also exists with Karen Wright, now missing. I need to find her. No one knows where she is?'

'Oh, Jesus fuck,' says the writer, expanding her repertoire of shock. 'Is there anyone else?' And then, the inevitable, 'I don't have the same connection with this place, do I?'

I give her the appropriate look, then back to Hunt.

'Karen?'

'I do not know. I spoke to her this morning about an hour before filming. She said she was going for a quick walk before the storm returned, as there was someone she had to speak to. She did not say with whom she would be talking.'

'You weren't worried when she didn't arrive?'

'Of course I was worried. I have already spoken to the police constable and alerted her to the fact.' *Jesus*. 'I wondered if perhaps Karen had got stuck in the snow. But the storm had returned, and I did not want to risk any more of the crew by asking them to go and look for her. There seemed little else I could do. Meanwhile, we needed to complete the filming on

———

193

schedule, or else the entire production would be in jeopardy.' A pause, and just as I've started to think that she's got the cold-hearted movie executive schtick down to a T, she says, 'With this new information, it seems the production has gone beyond jeopardy. It is time to close it down, and to focus on the well-being of the crew. For now, I need to establish if anyone else has gone missing. Do you know of any such people?'

She asks the question of both me and the writer. I shake my head, the writer looks panicked at being put on the spot, then says, 'I don't know. Like, I haven't heard anything.'

'I should get everyone together in the main dining area downstairs,' says Hunt. 'Once there, I should make sure no one goes anywhere unaccompanied. Do you suspect anyone from the crew might be involved in the murders?'

'Other than as victims, no,' I say, which sounds glib as soon as it's out of my mouth. Feel, again, like I'm talking to Kallas, and that I really need to get the big boy trousers on.

'Now that I've told you this, have you suspicions about anyone?' I ask.

'Jesus,' says the writer again, incredulous.

'No,' says Hunt. 'But I will give it some thought, because it is not something I have previously considered.'

'OK, I should leave you to get on with it. Damn, I don't have a phone. D'you have any spare, like, movie set phones you could let me have. Something, that I can –'

'Of course, we can supply you with something,' says Hunt.

Fuck me. This woman is good. Sensible, focussed, unruffled. This is the kind of woman you want in charge of the country, while the Etonian spunkweasels are making shit vampire movies. It's always the other way around.

'OK, thank you.' Last look at the writer. 'You have anything else you think I might need to know?'

'Like what?'

The lassie still looks like she's inadvertently walked onto the set of *Squid Game*.

'Is there anyone else who was involved in the scriptwriting process? Anyone else with a finger in the creative pie who might have some idea about what's really going on here?'

'What does that even mean, *what's really going on*?'

'Karen and Abigail got together and came up with a story, which they then specifically wanted to film right here. In this village. Now, sure, if nothing weird was happening, maybe it's because it's just a nice location. But one of them's dead, the other's missing. Two other women are dead, another missing. We're at five victims now, and it starts with Karen and Abigail wanting to make this movie. Whatever it's about, it's worth killing for.'

She's breathing heavily. The writer is giving off solid *my part in the murder spree* vibes. She's probably already factoring it in to her autobiography.

'I just, I don't know, I don't know. I remember, I think, you know, there was a thing once, but I mean, really, it was... it was just a thing, you know. I don't know.' *Holy fucking gibberish, Batman, will you just get to the fucking point?* 'You mentioned the title. I got the impression, and you know, I can't even remember why, but the title had something to say, that was all. Now that I think about it, but it hardly seemed important.'

I ask the obvious question with open palms.

'I really don't know. Something about the initials. Like that's what the title was about. You know, like, I don't know, they say *Lucy In The Sky With Diamonds* is about LSD, right? Something like that. You know, L is for Lucy and S if for Sk –'

'Yeah, I got that. So, what does ECL stand for?'

She lifts her shoulders. We look at Petra Hunt.

'I have not heard such a thing,' she says.

'You can give me a phone I can use for the Internet?'

'Yes, of course,' says Hunt, in her familiar way. 'I will have someone bring you something appropriate immediately. Now, if you do not mind, we have much to do.'

I nod, I include the writer so she knows she's dismissed, and then they walk quickly away, and once again I'm on my own in this small, ghost of a hotel room.

I look around at the bed with a sleeping bag dumped on top, a holdall and some tossed-aside clothes on the floor, and then go and stand back at the window.

Through the mist, on the far side of the loch, Ellis's house is now visible. And there, tied up to the jetty, is Craven's small boat. Fucker's gone back across there.

'Fuck,' I spit out into the day.

35

The weather is turning. No longer so bone-shatteringly cold. The snow is wetter, turning to sleet, on its way to becoming the promised rain. Ahead of schedule.

I'm in a small wooden motorboat, crossing the loch once again, heading for Ellis's house through the soaking blizzard. The indefatigable Dr MacDonald, or Judi Dench as she's known to the audience, is at the rudder, as the boat careers wildly in the waves, ill-matched for the tumult. I have my head down, leaning forward, with a small pail, scooping water out from the bottom of the boat. On the one hand it hardly seems to be making any difference: on the other, if I stop, we definitely ain't making it to the other side.

We pitch into a trough, a wave breaks over the bow, more water washes over us, another couple of gallons fill the bottom of the boat, the small vessel rights itself, we continue to plough on, about halfway across. And I scoop and I scoop.

Feel like shit, the sea sickness hitting me in a way it didn't previously. Smaller vessel; rougher seas; unable to stare at the horizon; all of the above; I don't fucking know. Haven't exchanged a word with Judi Dench since we headed out. The wind is howling and freezing and soaking, the loch is turbulent. We both have our jobs to do. Conversation is not an option.

By small amounts, or racing towards a climax depending on how one chooses to measure it, the story emerges.

I stood at the window of the hotel, knowing I had to follow Craven's boat across the loch. I didn't want to. I wanted to stay there, in the warmth. I wanted this whole thing just to go away; or, at least, my part in it to go away. And that would've been so easy to do. All it would have required, was me deciding to go back to my cottage. Get in the shower, warm up, make myself a vodka tonic, or pour a glass of wine, and Bob's your fucking uncle, I would've been back on holiday.

But it's not like I need any more reasons to hate myself, so as soon as I had a phone in my hand, I called Mara, she did not pick up, then I called Dr Judi Dench, and asked if she was willing to take her boat out on the loch in a storm. 'Have you seen my boat?' she said.

Nevertheless, here we are. I rather wish she'd just said no.

In between the phone call and coming out onto the loch, I had the time for fifteen minutes of haphazard Google searching. Came up with something, but God knows if it is right. It ticked the required boxes, and that's all I can have at the moment, limited as my knowledge of this is.

Not thinking about it now, though. Not thinking about anything. The boat judders as another wave crashes against the bow, and I swallow my fear, the taste of the loch on my lips. Trying not to think about the possibility of the boat breaking apart, sinking instantly, rather than this lingering, seemingly inevitable horror.

I hear a voice in the wind, and turn, looking up at her from my crouched position. She's shouting, but I can't make it out.

'What?' I bellow back.

She shouts something else, short and to the point, making a bailing movement as she does so. I think that translated as keep doing what you're doing, but better. It might have contained the word fuck.

I bend back to my task, arms already burning with fatigue, not a whole lot of extra effort available to me. It's not as though I've been saving energy for when it got really bad. Very glad of the life vest she had to make no effort to get me to put on before we set off. If we sink in the next ten minutes though, I'm still not making it. Can't swim for biscuits.

Another howl of the wind, another crash of the waves. Somewhere on my chest, I feel the dampness of the day, as my coat finally joins my boots in conceding defeat.

The tumult continues, the horror does not abate, the sound of the small motor is drowned, the house on the shore edges closer, inch by desperate inch.

* * *

They could easily have seen us a mile off, crossing the loch, at any point in the past twenty minutes. I don't care. If there's the slightest chance they don't know I'm here, I have to cling to it.

We've pulled the boat up onto the side of the loch – Judi Dench knew the best spot within easy walking distance of Ellis's house – and now I'm sitting on a rock, getting myself together, watching her make sure the boat is firmly attached to the land, and won't be sucked back out onto the water.

Given that I'm sure, and I mean, really, really sure, I don't give a fuck about living, dying and anything in between, it seems odd I should be so scared of a life-threatening situation. But my panic out on the waves seems to transcend that. A more primal fear than fear of death. Death I can rationalise and take. That, though? That was just fucking terrifying.

'What's the plan?' says Judi Dench.

She looks along to the side of the house, a couple of hundred yards away. There are no lights on, no obvious sign of anyone being home.

'I need to go along there,' I say. 'You need to stay here.'

I get a quick turn, and a sharp look.

'You want me to stand out in the cold, while you go into the warm house? Well, it's a choice, I suppose.'

'We don't know what's going on in there.' Our voices are raised above the wind, though it is not as ferocious as it was out on the loch.

'I'm not buying your fear, Sergeant. I can't conceive of these murders being carried out by committee. This is a one-man or one-woman job, and it's not going to be some deranged, bizarre killer out of fiction. I do not fear for myself in there, and I'm certainly not standing around out here.'

I don't know what to say. I don't want her in there, but I can hardly order her to do anything, and I'm not going to do what they would've done in a fifties movie – give her a slug to the jaw to take her out of the game while I go about my man-business. And so I look at her, and no words formulate in my head.

'Jesus, Sergeant, you'd better make your mind up how you want to handle this, because I need to get out of this damned storm. If Mr Ellis isn't in, I think I might have to put a window in, and break into the kitchen to make myself a cup of tea.' A short pause, I still don't speak, then she says, 'Come on, we're moving.'

She turns and starts picking her way quickly along the shoreline towards the house. Fuck it, no option. Just have to crack on and, in my usual way, muddle the fuck by when I get there.

We trudge across stones and in between bushes, stepping

198

over small rocks. A classic loch shoreline, white with snow, and already a little less slippery than it might have been an hour ago. Now it is just wet, and while my boots are soaked through, they're at least up to the task of keeping a decent grip. Still, I'm liable to have trench foot by the end of the day.

Judi Dench and I march together in silence, unusual confederates, the wind at our backs, the gusting sleet noisy against my hood. Nothing to be said. The house approaches through the storm, step by step, and I've already shut my mind down to it. I'll know what to do once I get in there.

'You know what this is about yet?' asks the doctor, shouting with the wind.

The words are whisked away down the loch, though I manage to catch them before they disappear.

'I think so,' I yell back.

This isn't the place for a conversation. Nor, in fact, given the subject matter, would anywhere be such a place. I've no idea if I'm on the right track, and it's way too early to share.

I get a short glance from her, she's looking to see if I'm likely to say anything else, then she accepts my silence, and trudges on towards the house.

There's no fence or wall – Ellis owns great swathes of land over here, so there's no need – and then we're standing by the side of the house. All it does is keep us from view of the downstairs windows, but we are still getting the wind full bore.

'Front or back?' she says.

I look both ways. Cannot see either door from here.

She edges a little closer to me, turns her head and shouts in my ear, 'You want to ring the bell or break in?'

Sooner or later one has to make a decision in life.

I've come this far, spent much of the last couple of days breaking into things I oughtn't to be breaking in to. What's one more? Time to grab the bull by the balls.

I take my overused lockpick from my pocket and let her see it, she smiles, and then I make my way round to the back of the house.

Stop for a second by the kitchen window, with a view up the loch. If there has been anyone in there in the past ten minutes, they will have most definitely seen us coming. A big kitchen, a long table behind, but no lights on, no sign here of anyone waiting for us.

Head to the back door, start to fumble with the tool with my wet gloves on, and get nowhere. Gloves off, hands damp and cold, white finger already evident – that's going to sting after I've been inside for ten minutes – then I struggle with the tool in the lock.

Soon enough, numb fingers be damned, the door opens with a rush of wind at our backs, then we're hurriedly inside and closing the door behind us, listening trepidatiously for the slamming of a door with the gust of wind.

Fortunately the kitchen door is closed, and we enter straight into the large kitchen, stopping for a moment in the warm silence.

The regulation big-assed kitchen that literally every fucker has these days.

'Well, here's where we go our separate ways, Sergeant,' says Judi Dench. 'I'm going to make myself a cup of tea, and leave you to your business. If there's anything I should be aware of, perhaps you could let me know.'

She smiles, she doesn't wait for me to do anything, then walks to the far side of the kitchen lifts the kettle, sticks it beneath the tap and gets on with the business of warming herself up.

Quick nod to myself, and now, having stumbled this far with no aforethought and no real clue as to what I was going to do when I got here, it's time to face the music. If there is any playing.

36

I stand still, halfway down the stairs. Listening.

Nothing.

Have been through the house, room to room.

Downstairs, the sitting room and the library, both rich in books and over-priced elegance, monuments to another world. The office, functional and devoid of frippery, furnished from IKEA. A room that might have been described as a music room, with a drum kit – a classic midlife crisis buy if ever there was one – a baby grand piano, a couple of acoustic guitars on elegant stands. A box room, filled with the detritus of life.

Upstairs, the bedrooms I looked through earlier, still nothing of note, nothing to be discovered or uncovered.

And here I am, standing on the stairs, listening for signs of life, and wondering where that life could be if it exists. There are no outbuildings, other than an old shed. Craven's boat, as well as both of Ellis's boats, are tied up at the jetty. Hard to imagine they've walked off into the storm together.

They're still here. Those two, and God knows who else. Constable Mara? Karen Wright? A demonic legion of lodge members, doing some sort of weird cult thing?

Whoever's here, there must be a basement or an attic. A hidden room, perhaps, but I've thought through the dimensions of the house, and I don't see it. Not one of any size, at any rate.

Upstairs there was a door in the ceiling of the hallway. It was locked, and I didn't bother trying to pick that lock. There was no sense of anything happening up there, not a single sound from a floorboard. If all else fails, then I'll need to give it a go, but for now, as I stand on the stairs, listening all around, I've already committed myself to finding a way down into a basement that I don't know actually exists.

The only sound is the storm and this house, with its modern windows and doors, even limits that to a distant nothingness.

I walk slowly down the stairs, and then once again start going room to room, looking for a sign to a hidden door. So many bookshelves, and if they are on an internal wall, I stand staring, aware I'm searching for that corny thing out of a movie. The book that tilts back, opening a door.

The options are endless, and so, self-consciously, even though I'm on my own, I don't touch any of the books. I don't do anything. I stand and study the shelves, I see nothing but books, and then I move on. One room to the next, until I'm back in the kitchen, closing the door behind me.

Instantly, those two doors on the wall to my right hit me over the head with their obviousness.

Dr Judi Dench is sitting at the table. She has her cup of tea, and is doing that thing no one does anymore. Staring into space. Not looking at her phone, not reading anything, not calling anyone. Her coat is over the back of a chair, she looks red in the cheeks.

'The cupboard is bare?' she asks.

'So far.'

'You think this is the kind of place that'll have secret rooms? I mean, if we're being honest, nobody would be surprised. Have you tried tugging books on shelves?'

I don't answer. I'm looking at those two doors. It's the side of the house facing down the glen, but there are no windows. Windows to the left, and in front of me, looking up the loch and to the hills behind, but nothing here. She follows my gaze to the doors, and then we look at each other.

'Hmm,' she says, 'not bad. That is a little odd.' We turn to look at the doors again, then she adds, 'My bet is the one on the left is the pantry, the one on the right... well, who knows what that is?'

Already thinking about the size of the house, and how this kitchen wall here seems further in than the others on that side. And with it a certain confirmation: I get the buzz. I can feel it, for the first time since I got in here. Fuck me, pretty much for the first time since Mara dragged me into this thing.

I go to the door on the left, and open it quietly. The pantry. Stacked shelves, a large, top-opening freezer. The perfect storage space when you live detached like this, when contact with the outside world might be easily disrupted.

Maybe there's a secret door or whatever behind a shelf, or a trapdoor beneath the linoleum, but I can check that in a minute if the other door gives us nothing.

Close the pantry, try the other door handle. Locked. Here

we go again. If we were to take surreptitious entry out of this investigation, I'd still be on doorsteps asking people if they'd seen Alice anywhere.

I get to work, the lock clicks silently round, and I open the door. A quick glance in, and there it is. A flight of stairs. I toss a look over my shoulder.

'Thunderbirds are go.'

'Good luck, Sergeant,' she says, tipping her mug, a wry smile on her face.

'Can I ask you to get the fuck out of Dodge? I mean, seriously, if this turns out to be more than just a basement… God knows how it plays out. If something happens to me, then it could happen to you. If you leave, there's someone to talk to the police tomorrow.'

She doesn't bother shaking her head, but the answer is written on her face. A last look, then I turn away, phone out of my pocket, torch on, and start walking down the steps.

Steep stairs, a closed door at the bottom. I don't bother thinking about what might be down here. There are too many options, from the fantastic, the outlandish and the warped, to the mundane and spider-infested ordinariness, a hundred others in between.

Bottom of the stairs, hesitate for a moment. Music playing inside. Slow, sombre, choral. Mozart's Requiem. I listen for a moment. I don't know why I know this is Mozart's Requiem. Maybe I watched *Amadeus* when I was fifteen.

Requiem. Fuck, that's not a good sign.

Fingers to the door handle, turn and push, the door opens and I'm stepping into the lion's den.

Everyone turns to look at me.

'Jesus,' mutters Ellis, from his position on the bed, 'You are fucking kidding me.'

37

I don't immediately respond. This is the kind of weird, fucked-up shit that needs to be taken in, processed, placed into some sort of context.

The room is low-lit, warmly and classically decorated in rich reds and browns and yellows. Similar erotic art on the walls as they have in the lodge hall. Again, similar furnishing, with a couple of long, heavy wooden cabinets, various artifacts on top. A couple of doors off.

In the centre of the room, however, there is no table. It's a bed. Maroon, silk sheets, four poster, though without the top or the side drapes, just the posts. Ellis is on the bed, naked, lying back. Glistening and erect. Holy shit, he's big. Fuck me.

To the side is Craven, iPhone in hand, filming. And on the bed with Ellis, pleasuring him, are Mara and Karen Wright. They too are both naked, and glistening. What a scene.

This here, this is obviously exactly what Mozart was thinking. Sure, he called it his Requiem, but really he meant sex ritual. Mozart's Sex Ritual.

I hold Mara's gaze for a few moments, and she looks a little dreamily back. And in that, I feel a strange flush of relief. She's here, and Karen Wright is here, because they'll have been given the same drug I was given the night I dreamt about Alice. If it really was a dream. They are not here of their own volition, and however they got here, they're now drugged into compliance.

The set-up, the video, the blackmail.

They are kneeling either side of Ellis, interrupted in the act of fellatio. Mara still has her left hand resting on Ellis's massive cock.

'Fuck me,' I finally say, assessment made, then I take my jacket off, approach Mara, and offer it to her.

'We're busy,' says Ellis.

'Cunt,' says Craven, from the other side of his phone. He hasn't stopped filming.

The two women look at me silently. Neither looks

particularly unhappy with their position, but they are clearly spaced. Very, very spaced. If it wasn't for the fact that Mara is in the middle of a murder investigation, and Karen Wright in the penultimate day of a film shoot she's rushing to get done, I might think I'd just walked into a consensual orgy situation. But I can't believe either of them actually wants to be here.

'Put this on,' I say to Mara.

She looks a little confused, as though there's some internal battle being fought, gives Ellis a quick glance as he mutters, 'Fuck's sake,' then finally removes her fingers from his erection. Then she uncomfortably holds her arms out for me to put the jacket around her, as though aware it will be unpleasant given whatever sex oil they've covered her with.

I zip up the front of the jacket, because I really don't think she would have done, then I whisk off my jumper.

Karen Wright has been watching in a state of confusion, the swirl of emotions evident in her eyes. Doing something she feels driven to do, and she'll be desperate to do, and yet knowing it's wrong, knowing she doesn't want to be here, knowing she's being used. Exploited. Framed.

She stares at the jumper.

'Lift your arms.'

She seems further confused for a moment, then finally raises her arms above her head. As I lean forward to slide the jumper over her head and arms, I notice Ellis give Craven a small nod, then the phone is lowered and slipped into his pocket, while Ellis pulls himself up the bed, swings his legs to the side, sits there for a moment, his back to me, contemplating what exactly he's going to do now, and then he quickly walks to one of the doors, opens it to reveal a small but elegantly designed side room, where he pulls on a pair of trousers and throws on a jumper. He emerges from the room, closes the door, and stands, barefoot and pissed off.

'What the fuck are you doing here?' he says.

We hold the angry gaze for a few moments, then I just go for ballsing the whole thing out.

'I'm taking you all in for questioning, right now. You two clowns are under arrest.'

'Cunt,' barks Craven again.

'On what charge?' says Ellis, contemptuously.

'Abduction,' I say, it being the first thing that comes into my head.

'Oh, fuck off,' snaps Craven. 'They want to be here.'

The women have barely moved, trapped in impotent nothingness, wasted, waiting for decisions to be made on their behalf. I could do with them being on my side, but they've been drugged into submission. Or, at least, drugged into lack of comprehension.

'You have no reason to make an arrest here, Sergeant,' says Ellis, 'and if you go through with this, I can assure you my lawyers will end your career.'

'They're welcome to try, and I doubt I'll care if they succeed. Their clothes are in that room there?'

I don't get an answer.

Fuck it, there's a possibility I've going to have to get into a fight here. Fighting's never been one of my strong points. And yes, let's not get into a discussion on whether I have *any* strong points.

At least one, if not both of these clowns is a murderer, and yet I'm standing here and I'm just pissed off at them.

'There's nothing taking place here that isn't consensual, Sergeant,' says Ellis, his voice measured. 'You have no proof otherwise, because there simply is no proof to be had. Meanwhile you have broken into the lodge hall, and you have broken into my house. There is only one case to be answered, and it is not by anyone here bar you.'

'They're drugged.'

'Because no one voluntarily takes drugs and has sex.'

'They're both working, it's the middle of –'

'I gave them the opportunity this afternoon,' says Ellis. 'They were not going to get the opportunity this evening, or tomorrow. They chose to take it.'

'I don't believe you. This crap you're doing here, how long is it supposed to last?'

Ellis laughs lightly, the head shaking.

'What d'you think, Sergeant?' he says. 'It's sex. It lasts a certain length of time, and then it's over. You and the constable will know all about that.'

I catch the furrow in Mara's brow.

'Ms Wright is making a film called *Endless Crazy Love*,' I say.

'You are boring us, Sergeant,' says Ellis.

'The initials there, ECL, are the important part of it.'

I give him a second, but Ellis has nothing glib to say to that.

206

'Ms Wright was on your wall. She'd had something to do with the lodge. The three victims and Alice, and Elaine here, were all on that wall. They all had the same connection to the lodge. Now Ms Wright wanted specifically to make her movie here, in this village. She was coming here because she was going to use the film to expose you.'

'Fuck me,' he manages, but he's got the look about him. He's listening to uncomfortable truths.

'The movie she's making might not be porn, but it's erotic. Whatever's going on with the lodge, it's sex-related. All that lodge crap, dating back a gazillion years, there's always sex.'

'You've been watching too many movies.'

'What the fuck is this?'

He doesn't answer.

'She came here to expose you. Why she didn't just write a book or go to the Guardian, I don't know, but she's a filmmaker, and this is what she was doing. And the reason all these people are dead is because they were talking to her, they were getting involved, playing their part. And it starts with Alice turning up on the movie set and saying, see that shit you're exposing, it's still going on, and I'm the proof. And now Alice is gone, and three other women are dead, and you two fuckers are coming to the station.'

He smiles, that disturbing *I know so much more than you* smile that the accused will often employ.

'And what exactly is it that all these women are exposing? That they're having sex? The scandal!'

'You're using them. You're exploiting young women, and then using some sort of pull on them to keep them quiet.'

'Interesting,' says Ellis.

Fuck. This feels like the bit in a Bond movie, early on, when Bond thinks he's got the villain cornered, and the villain happily explains how his multinational business empire is indeed manufacturing coat hangers and not poison gas nuclear weapons, and Bond realises he doesn't yet have enough to put him behind bars, not before the shooting and car chases start.

'I will concede that Constable Mara is a little,' and Ellis signifies stoned out of her face with an airy hand movement at the side of his head, 'but you've spent the last few days in her company. Did she strike you as being cowed by the lodge? Did she seem scared? Did she in any way accept that the lodge might be behind these sad events?' A pause, and then, 'I don't think she did.'

Jesus. This is nuts. Standing here having this conversation, Ellis and Craven the other side of the bed from me, and these two women, stoned and half-naked, in between.

'Eroto-comatose lucidity,' I toss into the room. Last attempt, for now, at knocking him off guard. Letting him know I've worked it out. Me, Hutton, the great detective.

'What?' he says warily.

Fuck it, I need to get those clothes. If there's a fight, there's a fight. I walk around them, and open the door to the storage room Ellis used earlier. Neither he nor Craven try to stop me.

'It's your classic, weird, occult lodge type of thing,' I say, as I survey the small side room. 'Using women for this fantastical sex ritual you've got going on. This ECL that Wright was going to expose you for. The Lodge has been doing it for generations.'

I can feel them staring coldly at my back, but there is no sense of movement.

The ladies' clothes, folded neatly over the back of a chair, are evident, but I'm taking a moment to survey the rest of the room.

Elegant shelves, containing weird lodge paraphernalia. Orbs and plaques and braids and there's a sceptre. And a dagger. Well, look the fuck at that.

I kick the door over a little behind me, far enough that they won't see me lift the dagger, although it's absurd and very obvious subterfuge if they're interested in looking for it. Slip the knife into the back of my trousers, like I'm in a fucking movie or something – chances of stabbing myself in the arse, high – then I grab their clothes, kick the door open again, and walk back out.

I hate it when things I have to do in the course of an investigation are like something from a movie. It's never good when you get into a movie situation.

Mozart plays on, and here's another one. Another movie plot development. Something else to add to the mind-fuck of an afternoon.

Everyone is where they were, no one has a weapon in hand, nothing has changed, except now, there's another person in the room.

'Sgt Hutton,' says Alice Schäfer. 'So nice to see you again.'

38

'The fuck did you come from?' I say harshly.

I have no idea what's happening. But really, the missing woman has turned up? Big fucking whoop. Sure, if Gillian Cooper and Margaret Wills walk in here now, then fair enough, I've been played like a kipper. But we're now in a triple murder investigation, and Alice's arrival changes nothing.

'I walked down the stairs. I came to join the fun, and it seems you're here. Why are you here, Sgt Hutton?'

She's wearing a light summer dress, and fair enough, it is at least warm enough in here for that. She lifts her arm, runs her hand seductively through her hair.

'Nothing? Well, *I'm* here to enjoy Mr Ellis's particular talents. Have you seen them?' She laughs. 'I'm not sure why you're being a killjoy, Sergeant, unless you're looking to join the fun.'

I stand with the clothes, contemplating my next move. How much of a fight are these people actually going to put up?

'You and I need to talk, Alice, but we can do that later. At the station. These two clowns are coming with me, they're under arrest.'

'You said you were arresting us for abduction,' says Ellis, his voice deadpan. 'Now here's Alice, free and happy and here of her own accord. Neither Elaine nor Karen is complaining. Who abducted whom, exactly?'

I don't bother with the answer, and now I hand the women their clothes.

'Put these on, we need to leave.'

Karen Wright still seems confused, but she takes the clothes from my hands, then Mara does the same, taking a deep breath as she does so, struggling to emerge from the fug, but at least, possibly, beginning to make the first move. Wright looks for a moment like she doesn't know what she's supposed to do with the clothes, then Mara awkwardly starts getting dressed, and, with the prompt, Wright follows.

There's nothing else to be done now. I need to press on, and I need to get these people back to the station. I need the rain to come, I need Mara to sober up, I need the Feds to arrive from Fort William. I need all of that shit, and I need to hope I'm not making a total idiot of myself.

'Who do you think you are, detective?' says Alice Schäfer. 'This is what it is. It's a group of men and women having sex. It happens. Right now, all around the world, people are having sex.' She pauses, takes a moment to enjoy having my attention. 'So, I had a big fight with Alec on Monday, and I left home. He never said? That's Alec I guess. Doesn't say much.'

'He mentioned calling you a disgusting slut.'

'That? That wasn't a fight. That was Alec being nice. On Monday, we had a *fight*.'

She smiles, like that has all sorts of layers I'm supposed to understand.

Regardless, it has a ring of truth to it. It would explain several things. Alec fought with his daughter, then never told anyone. When Alice disappears, the mum panics and calls the cops. Alec, in turn, panics and doesn't want to admit he fought with her, if for no other reason than he doesn't want his wife to know. He then mentions the lodge to me, perhaps simply as a distraction. Go and look at those guys, maybe they've got something to do with it.

'Not so sure you can trust my mum much either,' she continues. 'But guess what? I'm twenty-two, I'm allowed to leave home. And now I'm here, about to fuck some people. I'm going to fuck Mr Ellis, and I'll fuck Elaine and I'm going to fuck the movie director, and one day, twenty years from now, I'll be sitting watching the tele, and a film will come on and up'll pop her name, and I'll have a wee smile to myself, and I'll say to whoever's sitting next to me, 'Fucked her!' And what of it, Sergeant? You're going to stop us? Who the fuck are you? What kind of police state d'you think we're living in?'

'Wait,' I say, another thought arriving much too slowly on the back of that one. 'Where *did* you just come from?'

Alice Schäfer laughs curiously.

'What does that mean? I don't know, what d'you th –'

'Now! I mean, now. Where did you just come from?'

She smiles, amused, and gestures behind her.

'Down the stairs cowboy, where'd you think?'

I'm about to blurt out about the doctor, and she sees it in

my face, but just in case Judi Dench saw her coming and made herself scarce, I say nothing. I glance at Mara, who gives me little but stupefaction in return, and then I dash back up the stairs to the kitchen.

Someone's been burying that knife in women, and the longer I spent down there with those two men, the less I thought it might be one of them.

Fuck, fuck, fuck, beneath my breath, and then into the kitchen at a run.

Stop in my tracks.

What the actual fuck?

You know that shitty line people say about sport, *such-and-such a cunt is playing chess, every other cunt is playing checkers*? That one. It must be American. *Such-and-such a cunt is playing chess, every other cunt is playing draughts* doesn't have the same ring to it. Whoever said or wrote that first, couldn't have found a better example of it than me right now. And unfortunately, I'm the cunt playing draughts.

'Sgt Hutton,' says Dr Judi Dench.

She smiles. She's changed. Sure, she still looks like Judi Dench, but there's a look in her eyes that wasn't there before. One that transforms who she is.

The cup of tea is still before her, but now she's also holding a knife perpendicular to the table, the end of the blade in the wood, turning it slowly on the end of her fingers. And just like that the killer presents herself.

'Judi fucking Dench,' I say.

'Excuse me?'

I walk further into the room, and then stand across the other side of the table. She wants to be completely cool, but I can see the tensing of her muscles. Ready to react should I make a move.

Footsteps to my right, and I glance back to the door to the basement. Ellis and Alice Schäfer have followed me. Ellis looks cold and unamused. Alice looks like she's having the best day of her life, a huge smile on her face. She leans against the door frame, and takes in the show. Ellis more warily waits to see how this will play out.

'Is the knife a confession?' I ask.

'Why would I confess to anything?'

She lifts the knife and uses it to indicate the door to the rest of the house.

'You'll find that door locked. You'll find the back doors

locked. And yes, you have your lovely little lockpick that you've used all around town, but I think we all know you're not going to have time to use it.'

I look at the doors, I look back at the others in the room. Which way will they turn? Interesting that Ellis, who can very possibly see the knife tucked into the back of my trousers from where he is, says nothing.

'Running isn't an option,' says Judi Dench. 'You have two choices. On the one hand we have a quid pro quo. You may recall, or not, that you had sex with Alice the other night.'

I don't look at Alice, but I know that smile just got a lot bigger.

'You and Alice did some pretty nasty things to each other. Happily for you, because perhaps you can't recall everything that happened, there's footage. Very good quality footage. So, here's the quid and the pro and the quo. You can walk out the door, you can go back to Mr Craven's nice little croft, and you can continue your holiday. And we won't release the footage of you and Alice. Or, you know, you can die here today, and to celebrate your life, we'll release the footage, and everyone you work with and everyone you know will get to see you have sex with someone more than thirty years younger. Indeed, Alice, when having sex, has a very nice way of looking really rather young. Don't you Alice?'

Alice giggles. I wonder if Alice might be a psychopath...

I glance at her, I look at the impassive Ellis, then back to Judi Dench.

Nope, I don't think Alice is a psychopath. I don't think any of these people are. They're a stupid old club with stupid old traditions, one at least of which is exploitative, and they can all get to fuck. And I think Dr MacDonald here might have been lying about having distanced herself from the lodge of her fathers.

'You'll have to do better than that,' I say.

'Really?'

Judi Dench looks amused.

'You're under arrest for the murders of Gillian Cooper, Margaret Wills and Abigail Connolly. You don't have to say anything, but it may harm your defence if you don't mention when questioned something which you later rely on in court. Anything you do say may be given in evidence.'

I get the eye roll. She lifts the knife now, so that it's held blade up, ready to use, though she remains seated.

'Bold,' she says. 'I'm sure your family and your work colleagues will be delighted to see you in action.'

'Look on the fucking Internet. Someone took footage of me having sex, it ended up on my police file, and surprise sur-fucking-prise, it found its way online. Onto some porn channel. Any fucker who wants to see me having sex, it's all there. So, very nice of you to set me up to have sex with Alice, but you needn't have bothered.'

I hold the look, then turn to the others. Alice looks a little disappointed now that her part in proceedings has been diminished. From Alice to Ellis, then back to Alice.

Definitely no psychopaths here. In fact, I think there's only one killer, and she's sitting right there with that knife.

'I've had enough of this bullshit,' I say, then pointing to Judi Dench and Ellis in turn say, 'You're under arrest, you're under arrest. You,' I continue, turning to Alice, 'I have no idea about, but it looks like you had sex with me without my consent, so fuck it, you're also under arrest. You,' I say, now pointing back at Ellis, 'get back down there, make sure those two women are dressed and get them up here.' A pause, then in the face of the inevitable inaction, 'Right now.'

'Jesus,' says Judi Dench, 'check the big balls on fucking Brett here. Sadly, you don't seem to be watching the same movie as the rest of us. You're outnumbered four to one. Maybe even six to one, as those two ladies downstairs have only got one thing on their mind and going home ain't it.'

'Your game's up, Judi Dench,' and she gives me the what-the-fuck look again. 'It doesn't actually matter whether you all come with me now or not. If I leave here alive, then at some point in the next twenty-four hours, the police in Fort William learn everything. So the only way for this to end favourably for you, is for you to use that knife.'

'Now he understands!'

'Except, that's not four to one, is it?'

There's a wariness about her, though she's yet to get to her feet.

'Alice might be willing to have sex with literally anyone, but she's not a killer. Mr Ellis here may have his obscure, ancient sex rite, but he's not a killer. Ditto for the irascible Craven. Which makes it one against one, rather than four or six.'

'Good point,' she says. 'And how many people have *you*

killed in your lifetime, Sergeant?'

Let's not go there, but that question is another demonstration of how little this woman knows about my life.

'I don't think there's any doubt about which one us has the balls to thrust this knife,' she says with a peculiar, laughing snarl. 'Plus, I'm the one who actually has the knife.'

'Well, there's that,' I say. 'But tomorrow, however you look at it, there are going to be fifty police officers here, and there's going to be press, and everyone is going to be all over this story. You really think you're keeping this quiet?'

'Yes, Sergeant, I do. You'll be dead, and perhaps, in death, somehow blamed for the murders. Perhaps Gillian and Margaret and Abigail found out about your part in the rape and disappearance of young Alice here. Perhaps Alice might then be found, and she'll be able to testify.'

She leaves that there, the threat of my good name being discredited – *ha ha ha*, to quote Gnarls – and Alice smiles on from the doorway.

'I'm going to need you to get your boat ready,' I say to Ellis. 'We're all going back across. How many are we safely getting on that vessel in this weather?'

His silence is accompanied by the obvious loud tut from the table.

'Goodness, detective, you really don't get it, do you?'

'Dr Dench, perha –'

'What the fuck is with Dench? Really?'

'Perhaps the easiest thing for me to do here would be to lie and say I'd go along with it. Then, when tomorrow comes, I could turn you all over to the cops when they show up, and your stupid video of me and Alice be damned. I don't give a fuck about that video. The levels to which I don't give a fuck are infinite.' I pause, enjoying the contempt being directed my way. And as I talk, she raises herself from the table. 'So, why don't I just do that? Suits my ends. I don't have to get into a stupid fight with you, and the only bad thing that comes out of it is this video of me and Alice, about which, as I've said, I don't care.'

She's standing by the table. Broad-shouldered, now that I look at her. Powerful arms. A rugby player, possibly, in her younger days. This should go well.

'But instead you're choosing to do the right thing,' she says. 'Well, look at you. So pious and righteous for someone willing to fuck an underage girl.'

Oh, piss off, you lying fuckmuppet.

Time to get on with this. Unfortunately, being pious and righteous, and also there being witnesses, I kind of need to wait until she makes the first move. I turn back to the basement door.

'Mr Ellis, we're leaving. How many people on your boat?'

Still nothing. I think I'm going to need to remove Dr Judi Dench from the board before I can get this guy onside. Or, as onside as I'm ever likely to get him.

'Alice, please go downstairs, make sure the women are dressed properly, and get them back up here.'

She laughs.

'Why, I don't believe I will,' she says, with a strange, mock southern US accent.

'And you,' I say, turning back to the doc.

She makes a quick step forward, knife raised, face impassive. She thrusts, a wide, swinging movement, and I nimbly duck to the side. Nimble, my arse. She catches me on the left arm, a stinging, bloody cut, and a *fuck!* unavoidably curses from my lips.

Shit. Should've been better prepared.

I back away. Putting all three of them in front of me, in case one of the others comes to her aid. Neither of them will think she needs it though.

I need her to swing again, I need to be ready to respond. Fuck it, maybe I just need to let her get a hit, and make sure mine is more decisive.

Fucking moronic that it comes to this.

We stand, poised, for another few seconds, Dr Judi Dench having brought the knife to the fist fight.

'Fucker,' she mutters, the giveaway of the next lunge, then she's coming at me, another quick movement, the knife switched in her hand, raised, brought down in a thumping stab, catching me in the shoulder as I bend away from her. At the same time my hand is reaching behind, the lodge dagger is in my grip, and sweeping up in a great arc, stabbing into her side.

Sharp enough to let me drag the knife through her flesh, then it exits, blood flying. My shoulder screams, I get a great rush of her breath, warm with tea, over me, then she's falling onto her knees, the knife clattering from her fingers onto the floor.

She's on her hands and knees, head down. I bend, lift her knife so that I'm now double-armed, and take a step back. My instinct is to bury the knife in the back of her head. Make sure she doesn't get up. But I guess that's not who we are. The good guys, right? We don't stab people in the back of the head.

Quick glance at the others. No one's moving. Alice isn't smiling anymore.

Waiting for the movement from the floor, the sudden collecting of will and the burst of action, but there's nothing. The slumped figure is struggling for breath, wheezing with the effort, blood pooling on the floor. A loud gasp, and then she falls forward, her face smacks down hard, a great, unnatural heave of her body, a final expulsion of hot breath, and then she's prone on the floor, her face squashed in a puddle of blood.

Silence.

I'm staring down at her from a couple of feet away, just out of reach should she suddenly throw out an arm. But she's dead. I know she's dead. I can feel it. And this ain't some two-bit horror movie, where the should-be dead serial killer is coming back.

Fuck it. I step on her fingers. No reaction. Lean over her, fingers to her neck.

Nothing.

I straighten up, look across the kitchen.

'Mr Ellis. How many people can your boat take in this weather?'

Ellis grits his teeth. But he's going to answer. His is a cabal of weird fuckers doing weird sex shit, and at the same time thinking themselves to be of high moral standing. It's bizarre and from some other century, but they're not killers. There was only one killer.

I lift my arm to hurry him up, and feel the sharp stab of pain in my shoulder, shooting down my arm to join the pain from the first cut.

'Fuck!' Grunt, grimace. 'How many, Mr Ellis? Now!'

'We're good. All of us. But Craven can take his own fucking boat.'

'Get the women dressed, and get them up here. You as well.'

The fun has gone out of it for Alice. She almost looks bored now. She turns away, then Ellis is following her down the stairs into the basement.

I look around for a dishtowel, find one hanging over the oven, fold it and thrust it painfully under my shirt, onto the shoulder wound, cursing as I go. Get it in position, no idea how effective it is, start thinking about which one of the fools I can ask to take a closer look at it, decide none of them, start looking around for something else to stick against the other wound.

'Fuck it,' quietly escapes my lips.

39

There's a hard rain falling. If the temperature was to drop overnight, there would be a killer of an ice-covering tomorrow, but the temperature is due to rise, venturing towards mild by lunchtime.

Have spoken to Fort William, and agreed that we're cool for them to come in the morning. The killer, as far as we know, is dead. There's little to be gained from the police turning up mob-handed and interviewing people at nine o'clock on a Sunday evening. And it's still pretty fucking treacherous out there, just treacherous in a different way.

I'm giving Mara the space, as we sit here at the station. She's sobered up, coming out the other side of her drug-induced nymphomania, hungover, humiliated, head throbbing, and, as Gerard Butler would say, thirsty as fuck.

There not being enough space at the station, I took the combatants to the lodge hall. Ellis hated it, of course, but he was in no real position to argue. He was also not so impressed we left the corpse of Dr Judi Dench lying on his kitchen floor in a sea of blood, covered by a sheet, but she's evidence, and I told him she was staying there until the authorities come in the morning.

I interviewed them one by one, with Ellis initially reluctantly feeding Mara and Wright coffee and water. The ugly loch crossing, the boat tossing in the driving sleet, the cold waves splashing, was a good start to bringing them out of their psychosis.

There were no surprises. For around a hundred years, the lodge had practiced this weird sex ritual, eroto-comatose lucidity, where the recipient of the act would be kept in a state of near orgasm for hour after hour. Apparently, this frenzied state brings them closer to God, as depicted in that weird-ass painting with St Augustine. Yep, sounds like a load of pish, right?

In order to practice their weird sex act, they need women. The women come and go, but they are bound, most of them at any rate, in shame. Some are groomed, some are invited, some are drugged, some are coerced. Some, like Alice Schäfer, are enthusiastic participants. The prosecution is not going to get much, if any, help from Alice.

Karen Wright and Abigail Connolly were making their movie to expose this absurd, exploitative tradition, which some previous grandmaster had decided to start memorialising with his photographic wall of fame. Arguments started on set. Some of those arguments got ugly. Alice had a massive fight with her stepfather, and decided to take herself out of the game. She's been living with Ellis the entire time.

Driven on by the presence of the movie crew, Gillian Cooper and Margaret Wills both intended outing the shit out of the lodge. Tempers flared, things were said. Enter, stage left, Dr Judi Dench.

'The grandmaster,' said Ellis, 'despite the title, is not in charge. The Master Knight of Jerusalem is in charge. For the last thirty years, Dr MacDonald has been the Master Knight of Jerusalem. Like her father was before her, and his father before him.'

It's hard not to laugh at these people. Though on the other hand, they rule the earth, so who's laughing at whom?

It was all part of Ellis's retreat from confrontation with the authorities. He did not murder anyone. There have only been four women involved in the lodge's eroto-comatose lucidity ritual in his time, but they all came in willingly – according to him – and the only one on hand in the village – Alice – was happy to attest to that. 'I'll do it again,' she said, 'and you can't stop me.'

I have no intention of trying.

Nevertheless, there is the matter of Karen Wright and Constable Mara, and Ellis's plan to incriminate them, video them, and blackmail them. Mr Ellis will not be walking away untouched.

'You ready to talk yet?'

Mara lifts her head. She looks terrible: pale face, dark circles around her eyes. She's vomited a lot. Eventually the coffee and tea has started staying down, but the colour has not returned to her cheeks. The horror has not left her.

'I'm sorry,' she says.

'You don't need to say that.'

In the station office, Mara at her position, me at the other desk. Blinds drawn on the dark evening, rain against the windows. The other players all despatched to their respective homes or accommodation, told to await the arrival of the investigating crew tomorrow morning.

'Oh, I do.'

She holds my gaze for a moment, then lowers her eyes. Forehead into the palm of her hand, elbow on the desk.

'I'm such a moron.'

'Well, yeah, OK,' I say, with my familiar glibness. Trying to bring a little light to the conversation. 'I'll give you that. For starters, you slept with me. Not something any rational person does.'

She almost smiles, but it doesn't quite form on her lips.

'You going to talk me through it?' I ask.

'You haven't worked it all out?'

'Sure, but this is how it goes. You tell me stuff, and I see how it fits into the narrative I'm constructing.'

She's nodding by the time I've finished.

'I deserve no more. So, yes, I was one of a long line of young women. I was groomed by... this was seventeen years ago... by a guy who worked at the ecology centre. Did my mum know? I guess maybe she did. It wasn't like I discussed it with her, but looking back, I always knew she understood what was going on. Just something else I didn't want to think about. And so it happened to me, just as it happened to Karen and all those others.' A long pause, perhaps just getting her head straight, struggling to think. If they gave her the same drug that they gave me the other night, I needed a lot of sleep, and my brain was still addled in the morning. 'We are all wilfully blind, telling ourselves that we all say yes, even when we've discovered what's going to happen. But, of course, they feed you the drug. Partly to just completely mess with your head, and partly to increase your lust. You know about the ritual, right?'

'I've read some stuff, they talked about it, though a bit reluctantly. Well, Alice wasn't reluctant. Alice was all in.'

'Quite the girl.'

'Oh, aye.'

'So, I was one of them. One of the girls. And afterwards, I... I think I hated myself. I never knew. I could never tell. I just wanted to not think about it. I just got out of here, like so many others. Then, after uni, you know I don't think I joined the police thinking I'd come back here and get these people, I was still too conflicted for that, but I ended up here all the same, and it was certainly at the back of my mind.'

Another pause. Nothing for me to do but listen.

I got my arm and shoulder treated and strapped by the qualified first aid guy on the movie set. Took some codeine and paracetamol. For the moment, it doesn't hurt too badly, but the pain will be back. 'I strapped Matt Damon's ankle once,' said the first aid guy. I expect he tells everyone that. And sure, why wouldn't you?

'Then I get here and no one's talking about it, of course. I wasn't sure it was still going on, to be honest. A lot of the women who I think had been exploited had moved away, those of us that were left or had come back, like I say, no one was talking.'

'Until Karen and Abigail decided they'd come back here and explode the joint. Using subversive vampire art. What can you say, but good on them.'

She nods, that at least making sense in her still-confused world.

'So, why didn't you just say?' I ask. 'You could've told me this three days ago.'

She dips her head a little further, she closes her eyes for a moment.

'I'm genuinely sorry, Tom, I really am. I was... wilful blindness goes a long way. This thing with the lodge, it was a thing that happened. I couldn't imagine there being a connection. I really couldn't. And, sitting here now, knowing what we now know... it's like a dream.' Jesus. And then, after another long pause, 'And mum's dead.'

'You seriously didn't think it was related?' I say, not allowing her to stop the train of the conversation at the station of her grief. 'Someone goes missing, women start getting murdered, and you didn't think it could have anything to do with the weird sex cult?'

She holds my gaze, she looks apologetic, she eventually shakes her head and lowers her eyes. Looks like she's going to say something, and then doesn't, replying simply with a slow movement of her shoulders.

'And you never knew your mum was this uber-chief at the lodge?'

'Oh my God, no! I mean, really, no! All that long history of my family, all that shit, I had no idea. And that's... that's why I kept your phone when the lad from the movie brought it over. I didn't know how I was going to get into it, but I wanted to see… I wanted to see if mum was on that board. You know, if she was one of the older photographs. I guess I'd always had that thought at the back of my mind. I wanted to see, I wanted to speak to her about it. And I went to see her, and… well, I guess my mother put something in that cup of tea she offered me.'

'And you woke up in Ellis's house.'

'On the boat, but the effect was the same.'

I've got my phone back, and I've had a look. Her mum was never going to be on the wall. I don't bother saying.

She lets out a long, pained sigh, hand to her forehead.

'I'm so stupid. So stupid. I honestly never thought. There are so many MacDonalds. There've always been so many MacDonalds. Who knew? Did anyone know?'

'Ellis claims he was the only one.'

'And did he say what she did? What mum did? What was her part in a secret society of men? I mean, it's just kind of weird, isn't it?'

'*That's* weird? I suppose it is, though I don't think it's the stand-out weird thing here. Turns out the lodge isn't so stand alone as they all make out. They're linked to other lodges, though not, you know, the Masons. It's some other ancient thing. He wouldn't say. He called Judi Dench the conduit to the higher authority.'

She's laughing, shaking her head at the same time.

'You've got to stop calling my mum Judi Dench.'

'That was literally the last time.'

Another small smile, then it goes, and the tiredness sweeps back across her face.

'Alice went home to stay with her mum tonight?'

'Said she was going back to Ellis's place. He seemed non-committal on that, like it was something out of his control. Sounds like Alice and Alec had one of those saying-things-that-can't-be-unsaid arguments. Think maybe her mum is going to have to choose between them.'

'Damn,' she says, although not in a way that implies she actually cares.

There's little more to be said about Alice for the moment. I expect the Feds will have plenty to say to her tomorrow when they arrive. Sadly, of course, they are going to spend many, many hours interviewing me, not least because I killed the suspected murderer. The next few days are going to be a shitshow. Hopefully, however, not as much of a shitshow as the last few.

'Come on,' I say, 'I'll walk you home. We're going to have a lot of talking to do tomorrow. You should get some sleep.'

I also mean, I should get some sleep.

I get a look from her, a look that says the idea has just flitted through her head I'm walking her home with intent, and I can see her recognise as soon as the thought forms that that's not what's going to happen. She nods, lifts the cup at her right hand, puts it to her lips and drains the remnants of cold tea, then pushes her chair back and gets to her feet.

'You don't need to walk me –'

'You know, it's been a long, shit day, and hopefully there'll be no more awfulness, but I'm going to see you home, and I may well put you to bed, then I'm going back to my place, I'm going to pour myself a couple of stiff-as-fuck drinks and go to bed. Then tomorrow... to be honest, I'm going to speak to the guys from Fort William as much as they need, and then I'm going back to my cottage, and I'll get out of your hair. You can have your job back.'

We share a look, and I wonder if that sounds like I just said I was having nothing more to do with her, because that wasn't really what I meant, but it's been too long a day, and we're too tired, for either of us to really care what I did mean.

And so, without another word, we shut up shop. Cups washed, paperwork put away, beleaguered waterproofs back on, lights out, door locked, and we're walking through the storm.

Epilogue

I thought maybe I'd give Mara a call once the dust had settled. Give it a few days, let her get on top of all the shit that was going to come her way. Let her come to terms, insomuch as was possible, with her grief. As it was, the feds arrived and completely took over the investigation. The guy in charge was a total asshole, but what the Hell, none of my concern. Mara and I were more or less treated as witnesses, little more than that. Every single thing we'd done as part of the investigation was rubbished. I, being the senior officer and the detective, came in for the brunt of the criticism. I managed to stop myself saying, well, fuck you, dickhead, but it was close on a couple of occasions. Prick said he'd be sending a report back to my chief. For such times was the word *whatever* invented.

Two weeks later, and here I am, halfway up a mountain, looking back down the glen to the village in the far distance. Fourth or fifth time I've been along here. Weather hasn't been too bad the past week, and I've been managing to get out more. Not drinking any less, but fuck that. Fuck sobriety.

When did I think I would call Mara? Or when would I walk casually into the station? I don't know, but at no time since our part in the investigation ended have I wanted to. I saw her around town just once, and she was with Alan. We spoke briefly. I was a model professional. Alan would never have known what went on between us. Unless she told him.

Maybe she thinks I lost interest in her because of the way the thing played out, because of what I learned about her. But it wasn't that. There was a brief avalanche of life – of crime and death and sex and snow – cascading down upon us for a few days, and then it was over. And just as the murders and that extraordinary blizzard were of their time, so was the sex.

As for the movie, I have no idea. There seemed to be things going on with them for a few more days, beyond their initial end date, though I don't know if they were just clearing up. Maybe they were frantically finishing off the film. I'll look for it some time, maybe in a year, available for 99p on Apple.

I have my tuna sandwich, small bag of Kettle chips, and a flask of wine. All a man needs halfway up a mountain. I've previously been up to the top, so am not driven to get that far today. Just going for a long walk in the hills, more horizontal than vertical, and I'll be home before evening comes, in front of the TV for the Champions League.

Nothing changes.

Spoke to Kallas yesterday. FaceTime. Her husband was out with the kids at a thing. She was home alone on a Monday evening. For two people who can find conversation so difficult, and who can also, when the mood takes them, go weeks without saying *anything*, we found an awful lot to talk about.

God it was lovely. Yep, that's the word. Lovely. That conversation would likely still be going on now, if it wasn't for the fact that inevitably, finally, she saw the lights of the car pull into the driveway, and she had to cut the conversation off with a snap of the fingers.

See you next week.
Yeah.
Goodbye.
Have a nice evening.

And that was that.

Things were said in that hour and forty minutes, however. She now knows about me and CI Hawkins, for example. She took that in her stride, like she'd known all along. And she knows all the details of Mara and me. Again, it was entirely predictable, from her perspective.

'I too had sex at the weekend,' she said at one point, 'although it was with Anders, and not at all remarkable.'

I smiled.

I drain the cup of wine, put the small flask to my mouth in the hope of the dregs being more substantial than I know they are, then put the lid on, flask back in the small backpack, clear up the rest of the afternoon snack detritus, and get to my feet.

Look over my shoulder, survey the land, contemplate whether to head back down the glen, then decide that I'm not ready just yet, and set off on a different path, towards another distant ridge where a herd of deer are standing around, wondering which area of the Highland landscape to go and fuck over next.

By Douglas Lindsay

The Barber, Barney Thomson

The Long Midnight of Barney Thomson
The Cutting Edge of Barney Thomson
A Prayer For Barney Thomson
The King Was In His Counting House
The Last Fish Supper
The Haunting of Barney Thomson
The Final Cut
Aye, Barney
Curse Of The Clown

The Barbershop 7 (Novels 1-7)

Other Barney Thomson

The Face of Death
The End of Days
Barney Thomson: Zombie Slayer
The Curse of Barney Thomson & Other Stories
Scenes From The Barbershop Floor Vol 1
Scenes From The Barbershop Floor Vol 2

DS Hutton

The Unburied Dead
A Plague Of Crows
The Blood That Stains Your Hands
See That My Grave Is Kept Clean
In My Time Of Dying
Implements Of The Model Maker
Let Me Die In My Footsteps

DCI Jericho

We Are The Hanged Man
We Are Death

———

227

DI Westphall

Song of the Dead
Boy In the Well
The Art of Dying

Pereira & Bain

Cold Cuts
The Judas Flower

Stand Alone Novels

Lost in Juarez
Being For The Benefit Of Mr Kite!
A Room With No Natural Light
Ballad In Blue
These Are The Stories We Tell

Other

Santa's Christmas Eve Blues
Cold September

Printed in Great Britain
by Amazon

87597263R00140